HOUSES
OF
IVORY

HOUSES
OF
IVORY

stories by **Hart Wegner**

All rights reserved under International and Pan-American Copyright Conventions. Published in the United States by Soho Press, Inc., 1 Union Square, New York, NY 10003.

The following stories were previously published, some in slightly different form, in MSS: "The Stoning of Stanislava" (Fall/Winter 1981); "A Death in a Quiet Town" (Fall/Winter 1982); "Cyankali" (Summer 1983); "Miner's Tattoo" (Fall 1984); and "The Counter of Lvov" (Summer 1986).

Library of Congress Cataloging-in-Publication Data
Wegner, Hart.
    Houses of Ivory.

    Contents: Cyankali—The Huzul Flute—The stoning of Stanislava—[etc.]
    1. Title.
PS3573.E367H6   1988   813'.54   87-28530
ISBN 0-939149-13-3
Manufactured in the United States of America

FIRST EDITION

For Oskar and Hildegard Wegner

CONTENTS

*And I will smite the winter
house with the summer house;
and the houses of ivory shall
perish, and the great houses
shall have an end, saith the Lord.*

Amos 3:15

I
The
Summer
House

Cyankali _____

Years later my father still referred to our maid of that year as Pela-the-beautiful-who-let-in-the-thieves. Although servants didn't last long in our household, Pela was remembered and her name was often spoken at our dinner table. Sometimes Father's cry of "Pela" introduced a tirade on the ingratitude of his employees at work; on other days he spoke of her gently and wistfully, like an evocation of Our Lady of Vladimir, the Virgin of Tenderness.

My twin sister and I were already in school then— the first year of the *Nazaretanki*—and most of the time Pela took us, holding each of us firmly by the hand. Except on our first day of school it wasn't Pela who walked with us to the wrought-iron gate of the Sisters of the Holy Family of Nazareth, but Mother herself. At

3

her side, next to my sister, walked Pan Yaceniuk, a Greek-Catholic priest—a Ukrainian—who belied the popular image of Orthodox priests as devout believers, who were medieval, strange and maybe even mad. He was a slight, conservatively dressed man with an intense pale face and gold-rimmed glasses.

I don't know why we walked in such solemn procession nor why we couldn't have gone to school by ourselves; after all, our windows faced the schoolyard and if, during recess, Mother wanted to watch, she could look straight down from our apartment and see us at play. Maybe she walked with us because the first day of school was a dramatic moment and she thrived on such occasions. Pan Yaceniuk accompanied us that day not solely out of his deep friendship for Mother, but also because it was his own son's first day. Orestes Yaceniuk, smaller than we were, had to walk to yet another private school, because only girls were enrolled at the *Nazaretanki*. From then on Orestes played with us—but only in the limited and guarded way other children were allowed to play with us.

One day Yaceniuk called on Mother for one of their frequent walks and Orestes came along. We grabbed his hands and pulled him along the steep Kurkova Ulica, our brown shoes slapping down hard and our hair flying in the wind. We knew that we couldn't stop until the street leveled off and so we screamed as we ran, fearing all the time that we would fall as shouts of "Ora! Ora!" faded behind us.

We waited breathless at the bottom of the hill, until the adults caught up with us; they took our hands firmly and didn't release us until we reached the park. Mother and Yaceniuk sat down on a secluded bench, their legs and arms angled toward each other, both deathly pale. Not knowing what to do with our unaccustomed freedom we watched them for a while, with a thunderstorm threatening over the Zamek Park.

When they paid no attention to us we began to chase each other, but it was too hot to play catch, instead, we sailed little bark boats on the murky water of the pond. The park was like one of those painted postcards Mother had collected in a large black album: the leaves had always fallen and covered the walks or had drifted onto the dark water, and in the background were Greek temple ruins overgrown by ivy. More weeds grew in the real park, even through the red clay of the abandoned tennis courts.

We had thrown rocks at our boats, scattering the flotilla and now we grew impatient with Mother and Yaceniuk. It had been hours since we had come to the park. I convinced Orestes and my sister that we should listen to their conversation and so we crept up to the bench and played quietly right behind it.

That day I found out about Yaceniuk's life, and what I didn't discover from the conversation on the bench I found out by helping polish the silver or stack the plates in our kitchen. Of course, the servants didn't confide in me, but the cook talked to the maid and I listened.

Yaceniuk's marriage was bad, but he couldn't be divorced for reasons not mentioned. He had married for money and had overlooked the fact that she was hunchbacked. She was not a hunched dwarf like those I saw scrabbling through the narrow streets of Lvov, nor was she a tall woman like her sister whose tailored suits and mannish hats impressed us. Mme. Yaceniuk's voice was sharp and it made us sit on the edges of our chairs, even if she wasn't admonishing us. I can still hear her hoarse voice echoing through the apartment calling her son "Ora! Ora!" and Orestes came, quietly and obediently. Their house was close by, across the street from the Ukrainian church and right next door to the Franciscans, but Mme. Yaceniuk so terrified us that we didn't like to go with Mother to visit.

I'm not sure that Mme. Yaceniuk trusted her husband with my mother and in later years I often thought it possible that she only maintained relations with the Zielinskis because of a certain social advantage. When I was younger I had believed that cats were the wives of dogs and that in the country cows were the mates of horses, but then I still believed that Poles lived in cities and that all country people were Ukrainians, unless they worked in a city household as maids or cooks.

Yaceniuk didn't care for his wife, but he had loved deeply once and continued to worship his lost love as long as he lived. She had been a fellow enthusiast, who, before she turned twenty, shot herself on an island in a park lake. It wasn't the same park where we had listened to Yaceniuk's secrets, but another painted postcard park where I had been from time to time: overgrown and almost wild, melancholy with browns and gold as the branches grew bare. On a wooded island in this park she paced back and forth all afternoon, smoking nervously while her family observed her from the hilly shore where they sat at a picnic. It was a formal picnic with linen table cloths spread on the grass and wicker hampers spilling over with wine, paté, breads and cheeses. They didn't worry when they saw her in such melodramatic distress, because that was part of her nature. Once before she had tried suicide, by attempting to strangle herself with a necktie—whose, I don't know—but this time she succeeded with a single revolver bullet. Every detail of that afternoon had been retold many times over the years and all relatives agreed that her motive had been unrequited love, not for the priest Yaceniuk, but for Trojanovski, a gentleman farmer. This speculation in no way altered

6

Yaceniuk's feeling for his true love. Although it was almost certain that she wasn't in love with him when she
killed herself, he still preserved a lock of her hair, cut
off when, in a capricious moment, she had declared
the possibility of her love for the intense priest. This
precious lock of hair nestled in a small satin-lined
jewel box Yaceniuk kept safe in a drawer of his desk.
Why didn't he marry Hela? I don't know. Maybe she
was as poor as he, although I doubt it, since she came
from my mother's side of the family. I know that he still
adored the memory of Hela on that day in the park,
when we listened to him under overcast skies heavy
with rain.

What I heard and will never forget was that his
wife, the hunchback, found the shrine to his lost love
in his desk and in a fit of pique substituted cow hair for
it. If it hadn't really happened I wouldn't believe it—
cow hair and human hair being so different from each
other—but it happened this way. He went to his desk
drawer, took out the jewel box, kissed it and wept over
the hair. Then his wife and her sister burst into the
study and laughed in the doorway, shouting, "Fool,
fool," at the pale, mortified man.

Our walks with the priest stopped soon after, and
not even accidentally did we see our friend Orestes. I
felt guilty for having eavesdropped on their conversation and so I didn't ask Mother what had happened to
the Yaceniuks. We went back to school and soon the
winds from the east piled snow high in the streets.

During the early part of winter another story occupied my mother and her friends, discussed only in
whispers but quite clearly overheard by us from our
hiding place in the Makart drapes between the dining
room and the salon. Apparently a woman named
Zaremba or Zarembina killed someone with an axe. It
was either her husband or a rival of hers—it may have

7

been her own daughter—all I remember is that it was about love.

Shortly after Christmas my mother was on her way to the Franciscans when she decided we should accompany her as far as the church door; from there Pela could pull us back home on our new sled. It was already dark and we huddled in identical coats, knit caps and shawls on the sled, listening to the crunch of the steel runners on the frozen snow. Mother stopped at the corner, for she had recognized under the gaslight the sister of the hunchbacked woman. Since there wasn't any place where we could be sent, we stayed on our sled next to a wall of snow that loomed up to Pela's shoulder, and there we waited in the half shadows, protected from the wind. I sat behind my sister and with my face on her shoulder I looked over at the two women in the blue light of the gas lantern.

At first Mme. Yaceniuk's sister whispered, her breath clouding my mother's cheek, then she spoke louder and we could hear every word. What she told had by then become a scandal, but Mother either didn't know yet or, to hear the other woman's version, pretended not to know. Yaceniuk had taken the wife of a railroad man as mistress and he visited her apartment whenever her husband went out on a train run. My mother asked what she was like and the answer shrilled in bursts of breath: "Blond, bleached blond." I felt good, because my own hair was dark brown, but I pulled my woolen cap farther down and snuggled up to my sister. "Blond, bleached blond," she repeated angrily as if she were the voice of the Last Judgment.

Once while the priest was at that woman's house her husband came home; his train had been blocked by snow, and he could not leave. When the priest heard the key in the door he leaped from the first floor window, while she, leaning across the same window-

8

sill, shouted after the running man: "Thief! Thief! Hold that thief!" Mme. Yaceniuk's sister explained—as if she were the only person qualified to discuss the sordid details of this case—"She shouted to put her husband off, because he had seen a man jump into the street from her bedroom."

Passersby under the woman's window heard her frantic cries and in turn shouted, "Thief, thief, stop the thief," and their shouts overtook the running priest. A policeman patrolling the tenement area intercepted the fleeing man and, since Yaceniuk was dressed like any other man, the policeman couldn't know that he was a priest. Yaceniuk, too scared to think of anything else, pulled a silver-plated *terzerol* from his coat pocket and shot the policeman, who died in the snowy street. The priest ran home and hid. Why he carried a pistol I don't know; many people did in those days. The newspaper attributed the crime to a fleeing burglar and, since the priest had remained unrecognized that night, he was not in any way connected to the shooting.

Three days later Pan Yaceniuk swallowed poison.

I hugged my sister to keep warm and peered over her shoulder into my mother's face, but she didn't speak. Instead I saw a cloud of breath float toward her face and for the first time in my life I heard the word *cyankali*. Then it was chopped into smaller, slower puffs and I heard it again, very clearly this time, "*cy-an-ka-li*." By the way the two figures talked under the gaslight, I could tell that the word must mean something grave and I shuddered. The cyanide didn't kill him immediately—as a matter of fact, I don't even know if it really was cyanide, as she claimed, or another poison—but it fused the lining of his stomach. That is what she told my mother that night.

Yaceniuk's dying took more than two weeks and

his death was not a quiet one. Those who lay sick in the hospital of St. Pantaleimon the Healer heard his voice reverberate harshly through the winding corridors as he screamed out his soul in fear of hell's fire and damnation. The nuns shuddered in the shadows of the dying-room as they listened to sin after sin from his blistered lips: the priest lying in the bed of the adulterous wife; Yaceniuk, pistol in hand, bent over the bleeding policeman, and finally, the priest sitting at his desk, taking poison.

When my sister and I had our breakfast milk in the kitchen we overheard the servants' whispers from the pantry and when Mother's friends visited in the afternoon and they murmured over tea, we always heard the word *cyankali.*

One day we were to have our bath and Pela had fired up the stove and filled the tub. We undressed and ran through the steamy bathroom evading her grasp. My sister hid behind Pela who had entered into our game of catch. Peering out from behind her apron she grinned at me and whispered *cyankali.* For once I laughed, I, who used to shake with fear at the mention of this word, but in the wraiths of steam and assured by Pela's presence, I laughed and grabbed my stomach, rubbed it and doubled over, moaning and chanting *cy-an-ka-li-cy-an-ka-li.*

My sister darted out from behind Pela's apron and mimicked my agony. It was as if I danced in front of a clouded mirror as our sweating bodies writhed and we shouted and sang *cy-an-ka-li-cy-an-ka-li.* Our curls were plastered to our round heads and we screamed while we clutched our bellies. Pela stood up—I couldn't see her face through the steam—and when she reached down to pull us apart and to wrench our hands from our bellies, I heard her sob. I couldn't understand why she cried, but once we were in the bathtub, facing each other, we were quiet. I looked at my sister's mouth and saw it twitch; I whispered "*cy*," and then I slapped my hand over my mouth to stifle a giggle and to stop the word that made Pela cry.

During the same winter Mother gave a formal dinner and she told us to stay in the children's room, but we escaped—first to the kitchen where we watched the sweating cook prepare a feast which we weren't allowed to share, and then to the wine-red velour drapes framing the entrance to the dining room. We snuggled together in the folds of the same drape and the velvet muffled the joyful sounds of dinner.

We took turns spying on our enemy, the dentist Dr. Kasprzycki, who, as I found out many years later, looked like Rainer Maria Rilke. On Wednesday evenings Mother went to his literary circles and before and after these visits to his house she often suffered from migraine. When he came to our apartment he brought us expensive toys which were lavishly wrapped, but we hated him so much for his attentions to Mother that we refused to play with the toys he gave us. Now we watched him as he ate, observing the progress of his silver fork toward his soft brown mustache. We embraced each other in our secret hiding place and my sister nudged me whenever *he* smiled at Mother.

The diners had finished dessert and Dr. Kasprzycki rose, bowed to Mother and left. I gloated, but in a moment he walked back into the room, carrying a heavily wrapped flat package.

"I want all of you to see this, before Albin takes the gentlemen to sample his cognac." He smiled at Mother and my sister nudged me. "Zofia, this is for you . . . but let me open it first." He propped the package against the back of his chair and pulled a silver pocket knife from his vest. The knife flashed in his hand as he cut

11

the seams of the burlap wrap. The flash of his knife reminded me of the dentist chair and the instruments he
used and I remembered that I bit him once when he
tortured me.

"Here, Zofia, this is for you," and he held up a
large wooden slab, lacquered so heavily that it glistened. "Can you see what it is? The light is . . . ," and
he adjusted the angle of the picture in the crook of his
arm. "Here . . . ," and we heard the ahs and ohs from
the table and I even managed to have a glimpse of the
picture. It was an icon. I whispered this to my sister
and we both giggled because we knew that Mother
didn't care for saints—because there were so many of
them and all seemed to be of equal standing—only for
the *matka boska*, for Mary, the Mother of God.

"I present you, my dearest *patrona*, with a picture of your sacred namesake." He bowed to my
blushing mother.

"You mean *zimna Zofia*, brrr . . . ," my uncle Maniu
shouted laughingly from the other end of the table.

"*Die Eisheilige?*" His wife, my aunt Lola—whom
we didn't like for her miserliness—interrupted her
husband. But she was right, Mother's name day falls
along with the saints Pankratius, Servatius and
Bonifatius on the proverbially coldest days of late
spring. When the three severe lords swoop in, so does
Sophia, destroying with biting night frosts the young
blossoms of fruit trees. But even then I could tell that
my aunt meant something else than just a reference to
the calendar saint of a cold day in May.

"I know how some of you feel about religion," he
looked straight at Pan Golabiowski, the chief of police
of Lvov, who sat erect in his dining room chair, "and
certainly you know what *I* think of religion . . . that . . .
that . . . poetry for the unpoetic . . ."

"Tadeusz, please," my father interrupted wearily,

12

"we know that your rhetoric is dear to you, but have mercy on some unpoetic souls who sit parched before you. . . ."

"No, Albin, you absolutely have to wait, because what I hold here is precious . . . artless folk art, so to speak. I found it on a bicycle tour in the darkest Ukraine . . ."

"Found it? Found it?" Pan Golabiowski chuckled jovially. "The question to me as a professional is, my dear doctor: *where* did you steal it? All of us here," and he looked around the festive table without moving his back at all, "we know how paranoid the Soviets are about their religious treasures. They don't believe and yet they don't want to let them go." From where we stood his massive face was framed by empty wine bottles. "You probably got it from some church converted into a stable in the middle of a mudhole village . . . while no one was looking. Hah, found it, hah!" He pushed his empty glass to the middle of the table and Pela, who was standing behind him, took this for a signal to fill up his glass. She poured—and only then did I see that her face was purple with anger—and she continued to pour, even after the *Römer*, which my parents used as wine glasses, had been filled and the pale wine spilled out over the table cloth.

Dr. Kasprzycki paid no attention to either the chief of police or Pela; instead he waved his right arm imperiously and the others fell silent as he bent over the icon.

"Let me show you . . . just look at this," he pointed to a spot near the top of the burnished panel. "There! There's a God. The little man, who looks like a sugarloaf wrapped in blue paper, that's God. He's holding things in His hands, but I can't decipher what they are." His chagrined voice changed almost immediately to one of pure delight. "Look! Don't you love those naive curly clouds? They look crocheted." He laughed at his own observation. "And here . . . look over here on the left . . . David is playing his golden harp and on the right is King Solomon, who, if I remember correctly from my oh-so-distant bible class, loved many strange women."

My mother blushed again and a woman giggled from the other end of the table.

"Let me see this man," Uncle Maniu yelled.

Dr. Kasprzycki turned solemnly with the icon in his arm—like Moses might have with the Commandments—so that the dinner party could view the crowned figure standing on a small square of red carpet.

"And now, for the pièce de résistance—this is Zofia." He pointed with a thin elegant finger at the focus of the picture and then I didn't see anymore because my sister pushed me away so that *she* could see her mother's image.

"But she's red," my sister hissed angrily in my ear. "Red, I tell you." Then I heard Dr. Kasprzycki's voice again.

"She's supposed to be Christ, or Christ is painted to look like Zofia and she's dressed in a dalmatic, like a bishop . . ."

"Red?" I whispered. "Let me see!" But my sister didn't move. "Why should she be red?" I tried to push my sister away, but she wouldn't budge.

"I tell you, red as a brick . . ." My sister whispered back.

"What? Her dress?" I asked.

"That, too, but her whole face." I didn't believe it because my sister often lied. "What does it mean?" she wondered.

"Let me see, I want to see too." I gave my sister such a push that we lost our balance and spilled from the warm safety of the drape into the bright dining room, just as Dr. Kasprzycki read aloud the inscription from the bottom of the icon.

"Thine arrows are sharp in the heart of the king's enemies; whereby the people fall under thee . . ."

We scrambled up from the floor and stood hand in hand in the glistening light of the crystal chandelier while everyone stared at us. I happened to be standing close to the icon and I saw that the woman in its center had a sword across her lap and a face as red as fire. Then Mother pulled us closer to the table. I don't know why she introduced us to her guests; maybe in our nightgowns we reminded her of the Lenbach painting in our salon, showing one of the artist's daughters in a sleeveless frock with hair untidily curling to her shoulders. What I most remember about her were her eyes, luminous in a child's face. Maybe my mother couldn't think of a simpler way of getting us out of the dining room. Then we were still a novelty in Mother's circle: the twins, identically dressed, indistinguishable from one another, except, and she didn't mention that to the other ladies over tea, she loved one of us more.

I was afraid that someone from the table would ask us to dance, sing or, worst of all, recite a patriotic ballad. In embarrassment I hugged my sister. I can't explain what happened next nor do I know who started it. We embraced each other extravagantly like little adults who hadn't seen each other for many years, and then we began to rub our bellies against each other and smack kisses on each other's face. Silence fell over the dinner table while we continued to grind our bodies against each other. My aunt composed herself first and firmly said, "pfui," while Mother, disgust on her face, pulled us apart. Even separated, we didn't give up our dance and tried to twist away from Mother's hands. Father stood up from the head of the table and asked sternly: "Where have you seen something as shameful as that?"

Giddied by all the attention I answered his rhetorical question. "Mother does it. With Dr. Kasprzycki."

I don't know why I lied nor what had inspired our lascivious movements, but I remember how Mother yanked me away to our room, then slammed me down on my bed and, in exasperation, beat me wherever she could find my body. I tried to dodge my mother's flailing arms and covered myself as best I could, but she hit me in the face, the back of my head, my shoulders, my back and legs. I cried while my sister cowered silently in the far corner of the room by our toy chest. I pulled a pillow over my head and warded off some of her blows. Then my mother spun around and hit my sister, but only a few times and not very hard. When she heard my sobbing, she looked over her shoulder as if she remembered me and took the few steps back to my bed. Mother was breathing harder and her face had flushed; when she turned to hit me she saw Pela in the open door, taller than I had ever seen her before. With her dark eyes Pela looked straight at Mother. She didn't hit me again and said gruffly to Pela: "Look after them," and left the room. Pela sat down on the edge of my bed—on each cheekbone a bright red spot—and pulled me to her. I cried for a long time cuddled against her linen blouse with the blue garlands embroidered across her breasts, smelling of the lavender twigs that lay in all of our wardrobes.

Pela stayed on and Mother didn't treat her any worse than the others; at times I even noticed a certain friendliness on Mother's part which was gravely accepted by Pela, with a small smile at the corners of her usually downturned lips.

At Easter Pela painted intricately designed and

colored eggs for our family and presented Mother formally with a basket of such *pisanki*. Maybe this was one of the reasons I was permitted to go with Pela on the late summer pilgrimage. I couldn't believe that Mother actually let me go—for once without my sister—and then with Pela who wasn't even Roman-Catholic like us, but Greek-Catholic like the other Ukrainians.

On the morning of our departure we stood ready to leave, the white peasant bundle between us in which we had tied all of our carefully folded necessities. Pela had refused the loan of one of the family's leather suitcases as not right for a pilgrimage. Father took one look at us and ordered a cab to take us to the railroad station because he didn't want to be seen in the streets of Lvov carrying a peasant girl's bundle, while she followed in her Ukrainian-village finery clutching a large birchwood cross.

On the train I gripped Pela's hand and held it happily for the whole journey. This was quite different from my travels with my mother. I usually became sick by the time we arrived at the railroad station and when we boarded the train I vomited. Once a lady passenger inquired worriedly if my mother was taking me to Warsaw to consult a specialist while I sat waxen-faced with bulging eyes and looked deathly ill.

The closer we came to our destination the more people with crosses climbed on the train. One cross was so big that a man sweating in his black Sunday suit, could barely carry its stem on his shoulders while his wife and daughter each held ends of the cross-bar. The conductor ordered them away from our door and dejectedly they loaded the cross on a handcart. A railroad worker ran with his handcart to the baggage car so that the cross wouldn't miss the train to the Feast of the Transfiguration of Christ.

17

In our crowded compartment I had a seat by the window and directly across from me sat an old woman, whose forehead was so wrinkled that she scared me. She had a small cross tucked under her arm and she never laid it down, except when she pulled out bread and sausage and cut slices for us, too. Then she picked up her cross again, but I wasn't afraid anymore.

We passed through field after field in harvest, with men, up to their chests in grain, swinging their scythes while women in white scarves hunched over the sheaves. When we passed they straightened up and waved, resting for just a moment before bending back down. I swung my handkerchief in answer, but Pela didn't wave.

"They're cutting early this year."

"They're talking about war. They want to have the harvest in their barns before the men are drafted." The woman with the cross under her arm was as sad as Pela. I nodded gravely although they didn't speak to me and I didn't really care about a war. The pictures I had seen in one of Father's books on the Polish cavalry had been filled with bright flags and sabers flashing in the sunlight so that I couldn't understand why the woman with the cross under her arm cried.

Pela carried her cross all the way up the mountain, while I shouldered our bundle, my arm hooked under the carefully tied knot. She kept her eyes on the dusty path in front of her, the embroidered scarf pulled down to her dark eyebrows. Soon sweat beaded out under the scarf's edge and she moaned as we climbed the steep forest road, never resting as we were swept along by the stream of crosses. Women in front of us and way behind us sang, but I couldn't understand any of the words.

When we finally took our last stumbling steps to the top of the mountain, I saw the shrine, a small church crowded by trees and crosses. Plain wooden crosses were everywhere, some withered and some shiny new; some already leant into each other with age, while many of them had writing on them or strips of cloth tied to the cross bar. None of the crosses carried the body of Christ. Before some of the larger crosses women knelt or lay supine with their arms outstretched, while next to them other women chatted around food baskets as if they were on a picnic. Groups of newcomers were met by priests who herded them in various directions to the mountain top. A young priest singled Pela out and helped us with the planting of our cross. Pela had been here before and she knew what to do; she wound a crisply pressed white linen cloth around the base of the cross and fastened it with string while the priest dug the hole. We watched the linen-swathed wood disappear into the dark earth and then we stamped down the soil around the base so that the cross would stand forever.

"What might your name be?" The young priest asked Pela, but he looked at me as I stomped down the rich sticky dirt, my shoes being the only ones small enough to fit into the narrow hole next to the cross.

"Pela." She, too, watched the progress of my brown shoes in the hole.

"Pelagia of Antioch. Pelagia . . ."

I stopped stamping. "No, not Pelagia. Pela. Pel-la is her name." I was adamant to correct what I took to be a mispronunciation and I was angry at his intrusion on our pilgrimage. But he didn't seem to hear me.

"Pelagia the Beautiful?"

How did he know that father called her "*die Schöne*?" So I said once more, "Pela," resigned to the fact that adults didn't listen when children spoke.

"Pelagia, who danced before the bishop."

Pela sighed and pulled two envelopes from our

19

bundle and carefully tied them to the cross-bar, winding her long cloth-strip many times around the pale wood.

The young priest smiled often at Pela. He left briefly only to return with a small wooden bucket. He dipped a frond into it and sprayed our cross with holy water.

"From the river Jordan," he assured Pela.

She knelt to pray before her own cross and I, too, knelt on the soft forest soil, so different from the cold stone floor and the hard prayer benches of the Franciscan church where Mother took me. I folded my hands like Pela, but since I didn't understand the murmurs I knelt silently by her side.

Soon it was dark—though far away the sky was still a brighter blue and other hills were purple ridges—and we settled down among the hundreds of crosses crowding the mountain top. Pela leaned against a withered cross, which looked as if it had grown right here with the old twisted trees, and she peeled hard-boiled eggs for us, burying the shells at the foot of the cross. Not far from us we saw women breaking apart old crosses that had fallen down, and they started a fire.

"Why did you tie those envelopes to the cross?" I asked.

She was silent and the fire reddened her face. The women, huddled around the watch fire, had pulled their blankets over their heads and I could hear their singing, low and muffled.

"You saw the names written on some crosses and cloth tied to others? These are problems people have," she said, staring at the fire. "Everything that's on this mountain, the church and the other buildings, was built because of problems. Many years ago—many, many years ago—a cholera fell on the land and everybody died." She pulled her shawl up to the back of her head. "Swelled up and died. One peasant had a dream that the disease would end, if people could find this mountain. A priest led those who were able to walk over the mountains and sometimes through dusty passes, and they walked for many days until they came at last through the swamps and the same pine forest we walked through today. The priest prayed with those pilgrims—they prayed for days—and they didn't die."

"Never?"

"No," she laughed, "they died eventually, but they didn't die of the cholera."

"Cho-le-ra. Cholera," I mused, "did it glue their stomachs together . . . like . . . Pan Yaceniuk at St. Pantaleimon's?"

She looked silently at the fire. Some of the women had fallen asleep, their heads buried in the laps on those still awake, leaning against the crosses, singing softly.

"Pantaleimon . . . *he* truly suffered before he was killed."

"Who was he?" She must not have heard my other question.

"A good man who helped to heal people." Pela's voice was sorrowful. "They took ropes and tied him to an olive tree and then nailed his hands to his head . . . but with all that suffering and pain he still prayed for those wicked soldiers . . ."

I shuddered and she reached over to stroke my hair.

"And Christ heard him and he spoke from the clouds." She might have added this to quiet me down, but I could see those curly dark clouds, as in Mother's painting.

"What did he say?"

21

"Merciful, the voice called him the merciful one. That's what the voice said."

I hoped that now came the part of the story where someone helped the poor man and took him to the hospital. But they hadn't helped Pan Yaceniuk at the hospital either.

"Did the soldiers stop when they heard the voice?"

"No. They took their long swords and cut off his head." Her voice was hard and she spoke quickly.

"No, no, they shouldn't have . . ." I whispered in agitation, but she didn't stop and she didn't comfort me.

"And when they had cut off his head and the soldiers were laughing and standing around waiting for the blood to spurt out, there was no blood but a stream of milk came from his neck. Warm white milk."

I was quiet and I didn't know what to think and Pela was quiet too, staring at the fire again.

"They'll sing all night. There will always be someone awake, singing." Then she remembered my question. "I guess with the cholera it was like it was with Pan Yaceniuk. Our priest didn't really tell us, just that they swelled up . . . like the plague, the Black Plague." She laughed. "We had a cow once that swelled up and my father had to punch a hole into her stomach. I guess she ate too much wet grass . . ."

"Did she die?"

"No, she didn't die." She laughed again. "She was up and feeding the next day. When I was as old as you are now, that's when our village priest told us about . . ."

"What was in those envelopes you tied to the cross?" I hadn't forgotten my question over her story. Pela didn't answer. She bent over our bundle and pulled out a small plaid blanket, which Mother draped across her lap on railroad trips. Pela wrapped me in that plaid blanket while she stayed at the cross pulling her woolen scarf tighter across her shoulders.

"Like those people who walked here, scared of dying, these people bring crosses and with each cross . . . comes a sorrow . . . and they write their sorrows on their crosses."

"What did *you* write?"

"One envelope isn't from me." She stopped and sighed at my persistence. "It's *my* cross. I paid for it. Had it made at the casket shop . . . No, the cross is mine, but one of the envelopes is . . . from your mother."

"What worry could she have?" She ruled our world and I couldn't imagine her asking for anyone's help, God's or a maid's.

"The envelope she handed me wasn't for herself. Maybe she's afraid. Strong people are . . . sometimes."

"You know what's in her envelope?"

She didn't answer but instead looked at the peasant women who had stretched their naked legs toward the fire. Some had white work scarves pulled over their nodding heads, others brightly colored prints, which glowed in the fire's light. One of them had a white cross and a white Christ figure pinned to a gaudy bandana.

I had fallen asleep and when I suddenly woke up I knew somebody else was there. Pela still stared into the fire, which threw wavering shadows of crosses into the night, but I had heard the faint voices amid the popping and hissing of the fire. Pela-pelapela. His voice was soft and sweet, but I understood much of what it said ". . . The bishop loved her when she danced in Antioch," he whispered.

I didn't dare turn to look. Pela must have asked a question, because I heard that voice again.

"Nonnus," it said. "Bishop Nonnus. She was beautiful when she danced. The bishop loved her and he said that we could learn from her."

Pela laughed.

"No. Don't laugh." He spoke with an even softer voice. I squeezed my eyes shut, to concentrate on what I heard. "He said that she worked harder on her beauty and her dancing than the bishops did on their sermons and on the care of their flocks. So all of us should learn from Pelagia the Beautiful."

Pela laughed shyly and whispered.

"What became of her?" The young priest repeated the question thoughtfully and I was scared that Pelagia had died a martyr's death—roasted, pierced by arrows or mauled by ugly beasts which nuzzled her naked body before devouring her. In the silence that followed the question I thought of all the grisly horrors I had heard from the lives of the saints.

"She stopped dancing and went to live in the wilderness. Naturally, she had to become a man to do that." He laughed.

"You're making fun of me just because I'm a country girl." Pela sounded insulted.

"No. I'm serious. She took the name Pelagius and lived as a man in the wilderness."

But there are wild animals in the wilderness, I thought and fell asleep. When I woke up later that night I saw Pela laying wood on the fire, carefully placing each stick so that sparks wouldn't fly on the women sleeping under their crosses. From somewhere in the darkness I heard singing. Pela crawled under my blanket and drew me to her body. I didn't dare breathe, but she wasn't fooled.

"You should sleep. Tomorrow will be such a long day for you. Many things will happen and you want to be awake, don't you?"

"Yes, Pela." I snuggled still closer to her and with

the obstinacy of the tired girl I was, I asked her: "What kind of a problem is in that envelope?"

"It's too big for one to carry, so it's tied to the cross and God or an angel will help carry it."

"What can't Mother carry? She's strong."

"It's not for herself." She hesitated. "I don't know if you can understand this . . . the envelope was tied to the cross for a friend . . . who can't do it anymore." Her whispers had turned to sobs. If I hadn't been so young I would have guessed the unfortunate's name. She told it to me, not reluctant anymore, as if our intimacy in that night permitted such confidence. "Your mother told me herself. You have to believe me that I never looked into the envelope." I believed her. "She told me herself that she wrote Pan Yaceniuk's name down on that paper. He lived such a sorrowful life and she asked me to pray for him."

I was silent and thought of Orestes and how we had played in the park where we had found out so much about his father's life. Poor Orestes, poor Pan Yaceniuk. Maybe I could tie an envelope to the cross. Pela didn't sleep either. I whispered again to her.

"What was in the other envelope?"

She twisted away from me, but still stayed under the blanket.

"The other envelope?" Her voice was so low that I could barely understand her words. "Your mother's name." After a long silence she added, "May she find peace."

Pela scared me. She sounded as if she prayed over a dead woman, but my mother was alive. I knew it. She had tucked my handkerchief into my jacket pocket when we left on our journey, the same handkerchief that I had waved with, to the harvesters in the fields. I felt in my pocket and there it was. She's alive.

"May she find peace. Peace. Peace." And she held me tighter and fell asleep.

Although Pela slept, I stayed awake and saw red glowing fires and yellow auras flickering form the votive candles through the night. Poor Yaceniuk, I thought, this candle is for you and this fire is for you.

"Arise! Arise! Arise!" A voice boomed across our camp. A priest chanted among the crosses, stepping carefully over the sleepers. Sleepily I reached for Pela. She was gone.

"Arise! Arise! Arise!" Already the voice chanted farther away. "Arise . . . his raiment was white and glistening."

The fire was dead and the women were tying their blankets back into their bundles. Large black birds wheeled under the low clouds.

Suddenly Pela stood beside me.

"Where were you?" I asked. Maybe she'd been with the young priest.

"I washed at the pump. I should take you over to the pump, but there's too long a line. Instead I brought you a washcloth. Here," and she thrust the rag dipped into ice-cold mountain water into my face and started to scrub. "You're going to be a clean girl when you face the Lord," and she rubbed harder while I screamed as I always did when anyone washed my face. The women at the fire stopped packing and looked disapprovingly at Pela. The priest's voice sounded closer.

"His raiment is white."

"He's coming back. Quick! Stop crying and get ready." She retied the bundle and pulled me along in the direction of the church. "It's going to start. Hurry!" I stumbled along on her hand. "There'll be a crowd at the door and we won't even be able to get in."

We did get into the shrine and Pela was happy. I remember only flashes of the events of that day—not their sequence—because I didn't understand what the priests said nor what they did. They came out through doors behind the altar, walked about, left and reappeared, dressed splendidly in gold and green. A scary one, dressed all in black, scowled fiercely under his cowl embroidered with a cross. Pela tugged at my sleeve.

"This is the metropolitan. The one coming now." I didn't know what she meant but I dutifully looked at the altar. He was a coarse-faced priest, with a broad bulbous nose, whose tiara—a picture of Christ was among its gold ornaments—was pulled down to his bushy eyebrows, just like Pela's scarf. A crucifix and many medallions clanked on his wide gold-covered chest. In his left hand he clutched still another crucifix, while in his right he held an elaborately sculpted candlestick; its two tall candles, bent toward each other, were tied together with a strip of cloth over a crucifix. This I remember well. I asked Pela why none of the priests wore white, but she didn't know. They should be wearing white, I thought; the priest who woke me up had promised.

It rained when we walked back and a rack-wagon, straw still clinging to its ladders, took us along to the railroad station. We huddled together with others under two black umbrellas while the horse trotted easily down the incline.

We were crammed into a stuffy compartment with others who had come down from the holy mountain. Wet shawls and coats were draped from the overhead baggage racks and soon food and drink were passed as if all of us had survived a catastrophe. As the train rattled over the worn tracks Pela hummed happily. I looked up at her face but she didn't look at me and I heard the young priest whispering "Pelagiapelagia, dance for the bishop." I felt jealous

27

just as I did when Mother hugged my sister: more, harder and sweeter than she hugged me. Maybe she, she, who looked like me down to every curl of her hair, was more loved because she was named after our mother, while I was left with the name of a strange Russian czarina.

Although my clothes had dried by the time the train pulled into Lvov, my mother at once suspected neglect and mistook my excitement for a nascent fever. On the station platform, right in front of our train compartment's window, Mother scolded Pela for endangering my health. Pela stood still, carrying our bundle now that she didn't have to worry about the cross anymore, and didn't answer any of Mother's accusations. Behind the rain-streaked window I could see the other passengers who had traveled with us, watching Pela being scolded.

From the day of our return Mother was never friendly to Pela again. I cried often because I wished myself back on the mountain with Pela. I wanted her to hold me and I wished myself to be away from my mother and sister.

While we had been away on our journey, Father had painted, which he did rarely enough, a small winter scene—a straw-thatched cottage hovering in the primrose pink of an early nightfall with a woman trudging through the snow toward its warmly lit windows. Father showed it to us with a smile while Mother commented that the woman was undoubtedly on her way to gossip with a neighbor. It was hung in the children's room—I'm sure that Mother thought it not accomplished enough to share the walls of our salon with her cherished reproductions.

After our return Mother went out of her way to persecute Pela whom I was determined to help. If only *she* could be my mother, but what an idle thought—

Mother ruled and she was as permanent as everything around us: our apartment, our house and the whole city of Lvov. I wanted to convince her that Pela was a good woman and I thought it best to approach my mother when we were very close together. One morning, when she was dressing me for school and she bent over me to pin the sky blue badge of Nazaret to the beret of my school uniform, I felt that the moment was right for my purpose. My mother's breath coolly fanned my cheek and I knew that this was as close as my mother would ever be to me.

"Mother . . ." I hesitated because I had never talked to my mother about anything that important, "Pela took good care of me when we were away. Her name is really Pelagia the Beautiful . . . and she didn't let me get wet on purpose. It just rained on all of us on the wagon." She didn't answer and instead concentrated on my badge.

"Hold still . . . or I'll stick you with the pin."

I stood still to make it easier for her, but I knew that Pela needed more help than I had given her.

"She did what you told her to do."

"Be quiet!" She was already impatient. "Just stand still and I'll be finished in a second."

"She put your envelope on the cross . . . the envelope with Pan Yaceniuk's name in it and she even prayed for him."

Mother stopped moving.

"She prayed for him." I eagerly repeated, using Mother's silence to add as much as I could to help Pela. "I heard her pray, I heard her myself. She did exactly as you had told her to do." I was flushed with excitement, because I had delivered myself of everything that I had wanted to say to Mother. For once she had listened to me. When I looked up at her—expecting praise for Pela and for myself—I saw instead that her face had turned dark red with rage, as red as the drapes where we had hidden on the night of the dinner. I pulled back in fear that she would beat me, just as she had then. As I drew back, she pulled the pin from my beret and she stood there, holding the blue enameled cross between her fingers.

When my sister and I came home from school we found Pela dismissed and heard in the kitchen that she was already on the way to her village. I couldn't believe it until I looked in her room and found it as empty as Mother had threatened it to be. Every trace of Pela was gone, from her room as well as the whole apartment, even the basket of *pisanki* had been taken from the polished mahogany table in the entrance hall. Twice I climbed upstairs to the maid's room to search for her—as if somehow I might have overlooked Pela and her belongings—but her room was bare and filled with sunlight.

That evening, while we, at Mother's insistence, attended mass at the Franciscans, our apartment was burglarized. Nothing much was taken and Father even joked about it. He contended that a band of armed marauders had swung Tarzan-like from the acacia trees onto our balcony—and that just to steal the St. Zophia icon. Mother felt insulted and violated and immediately called Pan Golabiowski, who agreed with Mother that the burglary must have been the work of a disgruntled servant and he promised that his men, with the help of the country constabulary, would track down Pela.

Lying in bed I remembered that I had insulted Pela. Walking along an arcade by the side of our building, I had called her stupid. I couldn't understand why it had offended her. Mother called our help stupid, to their faces and to her friends, when she complained how long it took them to learn the ways of a city household. Pela said that she wouldn't go on with me and protect me from the *dziady* if I didn't apologize. Now that she was gone, who would protect me from the *dziady*, the thieves and beggars scrabbling through the night.

Before I fell asleep I saw Pela again, wandering a country road in the rain. With every step she had to bend into the wind and she didn't seem to see her pursuers: mounted policemen—rain sprayed from their stiff blue tunics—who whipped their horses, their single file strung out behind Pela as far as I could see into the darkness. I wanted to call out to her, as I did at our puppet theater: "Watch out! Kasperl, watch out! The bad witch is behind you!" No, I couldn't call, I couldn't even talk to anyone anymore, not even to Father, because he slept in the same room with Mother and took her side too often. There was no one to talk to now with Pela gone. I began to cry, lying on my side. I looked across the room at my sister's bed. In the light of the gas lamp in the street I could see her outline—she breathed evenly in her sleep—and above her bed the frame of Father's painting. I gazed at the picture. There wasn't enough light to really see, but I had looked at it so many times since Pela and I had come back, that I could fill in the shapes and colors: the scratchy blue of the winter sky, the smoky and yet homely streaks over the house, and the hard crystal blue of the snow. Then I started to cry so hard that I couldn't see at all anymore, but I knew by heart the bend of the woman's back and the purple of her shadow on the snow.

During next day's first class I pondered what I could do for Pela, but it wasn't until we ran down the stone steps to recess that it came to me. In the corner of our schoolyard, right by the side of our house, was a grotto sheltering a small marble statue of Mary holding the Christ child in her arms. I made up my mind to pray, although I had always hated to, except that day on the mountain. None of the other girls played near the grotto and as I walked slowly over to it, I muttered to myself, pretending to rehearse a poem for recital in class. When I came to the grotto I stopped and hastily murmured my thoughts— forgive my wickedness, forgive me for losing Pela her position, forgive me for losing Pela. Here I was so overcome by a sense of my own sinfulness that I began to cry, quite suddenly, as children do, but I continued to speak, knowing that I couldn't stay in contemplation in front of the grotto without being laughed at by the other girls. Please help her, I added, keep her safe, like you kept us safe on the mountain. Keep her safe on the road and away from the police . . . keep her safe. With that I nodded quickly in the direction of the small Mary and the even smaller Christ and I bent my right leg, wishing that I could kneel.

As I stepped back from the grotto and glanced up at the windows of our apartment I saw my mother looking solemnly at me. I knew that she could look right into and through me and that she was aware why I had prayed. Guiltily I ran over to the other girls playing near the gate.

I dreaded going home, sure that my mother would scold me for praying in public like a child from a superstitious poor family, but she didn't say a word to me. And when I walked into the entrance hall I saw that the Easter eggs Pela had decorated for us had been put back on the table by the mirror.

In the years since, Mother never once mentioned that she had seen me at the grotto of the schoolyard of the *Nazaretanki*, not even when we reminisced about our house in the Kurkova Ulica. I noticed also, that whenever Father, in a fit of aggravation, evoked Pela-the-beautiful-who-let-in-the-thieves, Mother never joined him in his recriminations.

The Huzul Flute___

"*Real* bears?" It scared me a little that we were traveling into such a wilderness.

"Real *bears* as big as me." A man leaned forward from the opposite bench of our compartment. "Not just bears but wolves, too. Packs of them roamed through the mountains, right where you are going, attacking the sleighs traveling through the dark winter woods." With bulging eyes he stared at us as we listened open-mouthed.

"The grown-ups," he lowered his voice while tugging at his collar, which was cutting into his double chin, "they sometimes had to throw small children from the sleighs to keep the wolves from eating all of them."

"No," I gasped, "no."

"Please," Mother laughed, "no more."

"Especially girls like you two," he said quickly, before he had to laugh, too. "Maybe they just threw a small dog . . ."

"No! No!" we shouted. To me this seemed even worse because I thought of Nicki at home.

"This is too much," Mother intervened, still laughing. "If you tell any more old wives' tales, they won't stir from the house during our whole vacation."

"But Madame, the stories are true. Most of them happened a long time ago, but there are still bears in the Carpathians, and wolves, too."

The man scared me, but not enough so that I didn't want to see the bears, although I was not too curious about the wolves.

"And the mountain people are still savages," he said, as he pulled his suitcase from the overhead rack and the train rolled to a stop.

I wasn't sure if I could trust what he had told us. Since he was short and squat, he didn't look like a mountain man. As I watched him struggle down to the platform I thought that he might be telling the truth anyway.

"The next time the train stops, we'll be there," Mother said. "Why don't you have some lemonade?" She filled two small cups from the bottle she had brought from home.

Amid the hissing of steam the train was slowing down and it became darker.

"Is this a tunnel?" Zofia asked.

"What happened?" I pointed into the swirling darkness which enfolded our train.

Mother strained at the window, trying to push it up as smoke wafted into our compartment.

"It must be the elevation," she said, meticulously wiping a trace of soot from her hands, and then cough-

35

ing again. My twin sister Zofia and I—as if on command—coughed loudly.

"Stop this!" Mother still rubbed the almost invisible spot with one of her linen handkerchiefs.

We both fell silent.

"It tastes bitter," I grumbled, licking my lips.

"Stop complaining, Ala," Mother snapped, "that is just the sulphur from the smoke."

"I'm cold," Zofia whined.

"It's the damp from the river," Mother said, the way adults in fairy-tales did when they were lying to their children.

"I'm scared." I pulled my doll closer. She had no name. I just called her *lalka*, doll.

Just then the train slowed down so that we could have run alongside of it—if Mother would ever let us do anything so daring—and gradually the grey damp smoke and steam lifted and we rolled into a sunny green valley. We clung to the rim of the window—which she had lowered again as the train reduced its speed—looking out while Mother tried to pull us away so that the wind would not harm our eyes. When the train stopped, Mother stepped down onto the platform—or what would have been called a platform were this like the railroad station back home in Lvov—leaving us two behind. The moment she was gone, we stood on the wooden benches and leaned out of the window. Instead of climbing back up to us, she sent in a small dark man in red pants and a white shirt who was to carry our suitcases to his horsecart.

When the cart pulled up in front of a small farm building, Mother climbed down to find the owner, calling this with one sweep of her arm "our summer home," although it looked like nothing more than a hut to me, no different from those we had seen by the roadside. She had told us that the Huzul family had moved from the hut to their barn, to make room for us, their summer guests.

We still sat obediently in the horsecart when we saw Michalko peering around the corner of the barn. Crouched on the ground he seemed less a human child than a worried dog, until he finally smiled all over his round face when he saw us pointing our fingers at him. He was not our age; he looked to be about two years old. Jumping from the cart we ran over to the barn but his face disappeared around the corner. Then Mother called and we couldn't follow him.

"Look up there," she whispered.

A stork stood on the steepest part of the roof, pointing his long red beak at us in the courtyard below. At the other end of the roof stood the largest nest I had ever seen, built on top of an old cartwheel. A second stork peered over its rim.

"They bring good luck," Mother whispered, "and they come back every year to the same nest, with the same mate."

When we finished unpacking, Mother took us outside. We stood next to each other and watched the setting of the sun behind a range of mountains across the valley from us. Mother enjoyed it very much. When Zofia fidgeted, Mother yanked my sister's arm.

"Why can't you stand still for a single moment?"

"It's so quiet," she complained, squirming in the tight grip of Mother's hand. In the peach-colored afterglow of the sunset the clear notes of a shepherd's flute sounded from a far meadow.

"Is he calling someone?" I asked.

Mother pulled us closer to her. While the unseen shepherd played, night fell.

At dinner time we huddled in darkness around a heavy wooden table. I slid my hands over its worn top, feeling the grain raised by what must have been years

37

of scouring, and the knife scars cutting across the rills. Our kitchen table at home was smooth and the table in the dining room was always covered with a tablecloth. Then I felt the draft of the door opening and a woman entered silently. Her face was averted from us as she placed a kerosene lamp on the table, turning Mother and Zofia into bright blotches in the darkness which began behind their heads and reached out through the windows into the night.

Then from faraway I heard the croaking of a frog and soon—nearer to us—others responded. Just as the quiet during the setting of the sun had worried me, now I was scared by the din of the frogs in the night.

After breakfast Mother took us for a walk down to the river Prut. Hidden in the high grass frogs croaked here and there, sounding like sentries signaling our arrival. We couldn't see them because the grass and other plants whose names I didn't know had grown taller than we were. I would have liked to go and explore but I dreaded happening, among the reeds, upon a hidden pond crowded with frogs half-submerged in a green slime. I walked nervously by Mother's side and listened to the hollow voices of the frogs, grumbling low and satisfied, as if they were burping after last night's big dinner.

We walked so close together that Zofia stumbled over Mother's feet. She must have sensed our fear from the tight sweaty grip of our hands and so she stopped at a stand of trees. We didn't dare to sit down until Mother had searched the grass for frogs. The grass in the shade of the trees was shorter and finally seemed safe. Mother picked up a dry branch, cropped its twigs and gave it to Zofia for our protection. Then she had to look for another stick, just like it, because I wanted my own. While Mother worked on our sticks my sister and I ate sandwiches, which Tusia had prepared at home for our long journey, carefully wrapping each sandwich in large sheets of white paper. When Mother had finished trimming the sticks, she took the butcher paper, smoothed it out and folded soldiers' hats for us.

"To keep you from being sunstruck," she said, placing the tricornered hats on our brows with such care she might have been crowning us. Now we bravely walked ahead of her, our faces hidden in the shadows cast by our soldiers' hats. I walked on the left and my sister on the right of the road down to the river, beating the ground with our sticks to scare away the frogs. The earth was so hard-baked that it sounded hollow under our feet. Every few steps we thrust our sticks into the high grass and gave the stalks a whack, but only a very quick one, before jumping back from the dangerous edge of the grassland.

Looking over at my sister I saw sweat soaking through the butcher paper of her hat. The closer we came to the river, the more humid it became, the moist heat bringing out strongly fragrant smells from the strange plants on both sides of the road. The sun stood high and bright over the tops of the stalks and mosquitoes swarmed around us like veils.

We had to stop so that Mother could wipe her face. Her thoughts seemed to be somewhere else. "My little soldiers," she called us, sounding tired, but we didn't want to stop and rest. We tugged impatiently at her hands, because all we wanted to do was rush down to the river.

I loped ahead of the others, like our dog Nicki at home, the ground bonging under my stick. Then I slashed at the high grass, twisting around so I could grin back at Mother. She could see that I was not afraid anymore. "Watch me," I even called out, while stabbing into the tangled growth. When I looked down—my stick suspended in the dense green—I saw below my outthrust arm the enormous head of a frog staring up at me. The massive head, brown as cork, was turned toward me. Its only sign of life was the lazy blinking of its snake-like eyes.

I didn't move, not daring to anger it, him.

Mother passed by without looking at me. From far away—through the croaking and humming—I heard the drumming of my sister's stick on the baked earth. Tock, tock, tock, she was calling me, but I couldn't run to her because I had turned to stone and instead had to stare at the frog. The stick in my outstretched hand shook softly, as if suspended, above the frog, while sweat trickled down my cheeks. Something forced me to stare at the heavy square head sunk deep into his brown massive body.

I licked at the salt on my lips. Now the King of Frogs holds me captive, because I entered his forbidden kingdom. In the fairy-tale the princess could bring herself to pick up a slimy frog and put him on her table or even in her bed. I shuddered. Should I hit him with my stick? Pray, pray, I thought, but my little rosary was back at the house and I couldn't think of a prayer for a girl threatened by a frog. Maybe I would have to stay here forever and become a small statue by the wayside. I sobbed and didn't worry if the frog heard me or not.

"Ala, Ala!"

I jumped when I heard my mother's voice, not because I wanted to, but because I always jumped when Mother called my name. Without looking back I ran toward Mother, with both hands clutching at my paper hat. She stood in the middle of the road with my sister close by her side. Safe, I sobbed, but during the last stumbling steps I saw our path to the river—as far as I could see—blocked by frogs leaping across the road,

all brown as cork. Mother smiled at me and said that
we wouldn't go to the river today and would try again
another day.

✿   ✿   ✿

I couldn't fall asleep because I wasn't used to the
prickly straw sack that make my skin itch. By my side
Zofia stirred in her sleep, nudging me with her knee.
Mother lay quietly on her back. Against the lighter
darkness of the window, her face was outlined as a
sharp silhouette, as if I had cut her from shiny black
paper, smooth and cold to the touch. When I did a silhouette of Mother at home, I cut her nose smaller than
it was in real life.

As I lay listening to the croaking outside, I
thought, at least in here I am safe. Staring in the dark
at the shape of my hand, I wondered how the princess, if she was a girl like me, could have held the frog
in her hand. Surely, he overflowed her palm, even if
he were a small frog, his legs dangling limply between
her fingers.

The croaking grew more insistent and I pressed
my face into the clammy pillow. I had wanted to bring
my own pillow but Mother told me that we had already
too much luggage. My pillow at home, like all of our
linen, had absorbed the gentle fragrance of the lavender sprigs Tusia and Mother laid in the drawers of our
wardrobes. Buried in my new pillow, I sniffed the
sharp smell of the grasslands where today I had met
the King of Frogs and I knew that even here I wasn't
safe anymore.

✿   ✿   ✿

While Zofia and I were coloring flowers in our
drawing books, Mother walked back and forth in front

41

of the big table. The crisp sheets of a letter crackled between her nervous fingers.

"Tomorrow we will have a guest," she said, slipping the letter back into its mauve envelope.

"Papa?" I asked happily.

"No, Dr. Kasprzycki."

I barely understood his name, because—while speaking—she had turned toward the window, almost as if she expected him this very minute, walking up the path to our cottage.

"I want you to be very nice and polite to him."

We didn't say anything.

"He is driving up from Lvov." She turned around to face us.

I thought that she looked sad.

"In his automobile," she said, pronouncing each syllable of "automobile" distinctly.

"Driving his au-to-mo-bile," Zofia said eagerly, speaking as carefully as Mother.

I bent over my drawing—a flower Mother had picked, because, she said, it grew only here on the slopes of Dora—rubbing my brush impatiently on a block of watercolor because it was not the right shade of blue and I wished that Father also owned an automobile.

✿   ✿   ✿

At night I lay awake listening to the croaking of the frogs outside of the small window.

So Dr. Kasprzycki, our dentist and Mother's special friend, was coming to visit. Back in Lvov on Wednesday nights she attended his literary circle. On those days she had a headache—already in the morning—and she stayed in her darkened bedroom all day. I thought about his fingers probing my mouth

42

and how I had bitten him once. Mother said that he had sensitive hands.

Then I worried about the frogs. The house must be surrounded by them. It sounded to me as if they had advanced since yesterday, laying siege to our house the way I did to my play castle at home. I thought that I could hear the rustling of the grass under their heavy bellies as they crept closer in the darkness.

✿   ✿   ✿

Late next afternoon we heard the bleating of a car horn from far away and both of us ran to the door.

"Stop!" Mother called sharply. "You are *not* going to stand in the dust by the side of the road, like peasant children waiting for the dead czar, still hoping for some sugar cakes."

"Is he really going to bring sugar cakes?" Zofia interrupted.

"We are going to wait in here like ladies," Mother continued, ignoring Zofia's question.

The automobile horn honked, sounding louder this time and more demanding, summoning us to stand in the road with our arms raised high, waiting for sugar cakes.

Instead we had to sit on a wooden bench by the far wall, listening longingly to the sound of the motor laboring up the mountain. We kept glancing at the open window but we had been told to stay seated on the bench. When brakes squeaked Mother rose—but only after she had heard the slam of a car door—pulling us up behind her. Just at that moment, when we were still firmly held by Mother's hands, Dr. Kasprzycki entered, silhouetted against the bright afternoon clouds.

He didn't arrive dressed in touring coat and goggles, as I had imagined he would, but instead wore an

43

elegant grey suit. Standing in the doorway, his head was tilted to one side, resting in the small cradle formed by extending index finger along cheekbone, while his middle finger lay curled back under his chin. He stood still, like a browser fascinated by a store shelf, and looked at us as if we had suddenly wandered into his field of vision. Now, having recognized us as friends, he said in a startled voice: "Oh, there you are."

Zofia and I had been carefully dressed in red skirts and embroidered white blouses with red pom-poms tied around our necks, in the style of Kolomyia, a town down river on the Prut where Mother had lived as a little girl. But now her dress didn't match ours. Hers had sleeves puffing out from a long flowing dress, embroidered in pale green thread with the outlines and in the same shade as the herbs I had seen on our walks in the grasslands of Dora.

"And there you are, Tadeusz," she said solemnly.

Thinking about it later, as I often did over the years, I wondered if it had been *then* that she decided to enter into his theatrical way of speaking and doing things—maybe playfully ironic at first, as the idea of dressing city girls in peasant costumes must have been. Because it was *then* that she dropped my hand from hers so she could reach for her scarf which she drew back slowly. And still *then*, with small shivers, she shook loose her black hair.

I looked proudly at Mother.

"Where are your suitcases?" Zofia asked impatiently.

"My luggage is already in the farm house destined to be my domicile in Dora." He must have sensed

Zofia's disappointment. "One moment," he said and went out to his car.

He had spoken softly just as he did when we had to see him in his office or when he came to dinner at our house. His voice, as well as his whole appearance and behavior, were that of a deeply civilized man. He must have reminded himself that only an error of fate could be responsible for the fact that he was forced to exist in the Lvov of the late thirties instead of living in Paris or Vienna at the turn of the century.

Now I think this way about him, but then—as I stood by Mother's side, listening to the murmuring of his voice—my lips and gums felt again the probing fingers of the dentist. "He has the sensitive hands of an artist," Mother used to say, but when I sat in Dr. Kasprzycki's chair, my tongue tasted soap on his hands and the leather smell of tobacco mingled with the slight bitterness of his small mirror clicking against the enamel of my teeth.

I now know how unusual a man he was. Besides dentistry he had studied medicine and become an innovative surgeon, been published in the field of linguistics, and, in his youth, and in spite of it, he had been admitted to the circle gathered around Ludwig Lazarus Zamenhof, the inventor of the universal language of Esperanto. He was also quite interested in literature and on Wednesday nights he conducted group discussions of literary masterpieces which my mother attended along with other ladies of Lvov's society. He was also an accomplished painter who worked in an expressionistic style. That he appeared in our lives in the shape of "dentist" now seems almost coincidental, as if it happened to be his guise on the day we met.

One of the few pictures I was able to save from the years before the war shows his face, dominated by the arch of a high, well-rounded forehead, whose whiteness has prevailed until now over the gradual dissolution of the outline of all shapes on the yellowing photographic paper. As I look at the picture—curled like a dried leaf in the palm of my hand—I can see his strength flaming from his eyes, piercing and alive despite the murky sepia, like the eyes painted on Greek marble statues.

Now I can see it, but then we disliked him very much.

The car door slammed.

When he came into the room his hands were hidden behind his back.

"The first of my presents is for the twins." He held a book out to us, but neither one of us reached for it, because we didn't like presents that we had to share.

"Here, take it, it's a book of Polish folk dances, here." He thrust the book at us and this time we both reached for it, because we had been taught to be polite.

"And now, dearest Zofia, this far too small offering is for you." Standing close to Mother he pressed a tiny box wrapped in silver foil into her palm. She retreated from the gift in his outstretched hand, but he stepped closer and held his present out to her until she accepted it blushingly.

"And here, for my own two little shepherdesses, original authentic Huzul flutes." He stuck a flute of blond wood into my sister's hand and gave me a brown one.

"I selected different colors so that you could tell them apart," he said apologetically when he saw that I looked unsmilingly at my flute, carved of darker wood than my sister's.

Although we never liked any of the presents Dr. Kasprzycki brought or sent to our home, we now picked up our flutes and out of boredom began to finger the soundholes. First we wheezed and grunted, then we simply blew as hard as we could. After that Mother decided that it would be best if we practiced our music in the healthy mountain air. We happily ran outside, but the other children never came out while we played our flutes.

Finally Mother and Dr. Kasprzycki walked into the courtyard smiling. I was happy to see them but I also felt a little sad that we had missed the unwrapping of Mother's small silver package.

"The storks are admirable birds," Dr. Kasprzycki said, pointing up to the roof, "symbols of prudence, piety and chastity."

We tried to sneak over to the barn where we finally saw the other children.

"No, come back, you should hear this."

Dutifully we stood by the adults.

"They not only stuff frogs down the little throats of their young, but they also feed the old when they can no longer hunt for themselves. Like *you* are supposed to do."

I looked up at the stork which had thin legs and knobby knees just like me.

"And they marry only once," Mother said.

"Why do storks stand on one leg?" I asked, without thinking about Mother, who seemed sad.

"These vigilant birds will guard you while you are living in Dora," he said, sounding like one of our teachers, "like the geese guarded the capitol in ancient Rome. One of them is always on guard and so as not to fall asleep, he stands on one leg, holding a rock in the other. Should he fall asleep, then the stone drops on his other foot, waking him up."

"Oh, you're just telling stories," Zofia said disappointedly. I decided not to believe him either.

"Why don't you take a look for yourself?" he asked my sister.

We tried to sneak up on storks standing in the meadows, but when we came too close, they awkwardly flew off. Just once, when we were hidden by shrubs, did we come close enough to clearly see, though it wasn't a rock he clutched, but a struggling brown frog.

Zofia blew into her flute.

"They seem to like their flutes," Mother said, looking in the direction of Dr. Kasprzycki, "but you are spoiling them as if you were St. Nicholas."

"A simple gift to remind them of their summer vacation of 1939. Your mentioning of St. Nicholas reminds me of a story . . ."

"Oh, good, a story," Zofia exclaimed.

"No, first let's go inside, it's a little chilly," Mother said.

Dr. Kasprzycki sat down in a chair with carved armrests. Outside it was getting dark.

"One day St. Nicholas was traveling and he stopped overnight . . ."

"At the Hotel Krakowski," my sister joked.

"No, not at the Hotel Krakowski, besides the innkeeper was not a gracious hotelier like your father, no, this evil innkeeper kidnapped small children—like the Lindbergh baby was stolen—and then he slaughtered them . . ."

"No, no," we shouted together.

"Oh, yes, like piglets, even serving them to his guests. And if he didn't have any patrons, he put them in big pickle barrels to keep them from spoiling. You know the same way the woman on your street keeps the herring fresh . . ."

"Pan Barach's wife," Zofia said.

"As soon as St. Nicholas opened the door to the

inn he sniffed the evil nature of the innkeeper and he went straight to the cellar. He saw how the dead children swam in the brine, bobbing up here and there . . ."

"Tadeusz!" Mother shook her index finger warningly.

"What happened next? Tell us what happened next," we begged.

He took a cigarette from his silver case.

"Being a saint he did what saints do, he made the sign of the cross over the brine full of bodies . . ."

"And?"

"And? He brought them all back to life."

"Good." Our faces glowed with excitement about such a fine gruesome story and it seemed to me that Mother looked with admiration at Dr. Kasprzycki.

As night was falling some flutes still sounded from the sloping meadows, above the maize fields, where the herds grazed.

"Have you shined your shoes for tomorrow?" Mother asked.

"If we had taken Tusia along she could have shined our shoes for us," complained Zofia.

"Now get your shoe polish kits . . ."

"Why didn't Tusia . . ."

"Zofia!"

"Yes, Mama."

"You know that Tusia has to look after Father. Besides, I am sure that you are able to shine your own shoes." We both knew that Mother was polite and patient with us because Dr. Kasprzycki was sitting in the big wooden chair. Otherwise she would have slapped one or both of us for not obeying immediately.

Sitting in the corner on the board floor we spread brown polish with small brushes on our shoes, messily daubing on too much from the tins we had brought from home, where we never had to polish shoes.

Then we heard steps in front of our door.

"Maciek, Maciek," a drunken voice bawled out. Then it stopped again and in the silence we heard a loud belch.

"Maciek, there he lies . . ." sang the voice as it slowly passed the house. I imagined him staggering into the darkest night, away from the lighted window of our house.

"Maciek, there he lies, dead on a board," he sang mournfully, his voice fading slowly.

"But if you would just play, he would jump up and dance." The singer stopped, then he repeated—now almost inaudibly—the last word, "and dance and dance and dance."

I had dropped my brush and strained to listen.

"Terrible, those drunken peasants. And the worst of it is, that they don't even sing the truly authentic folksongs anymore." He angrily expelled a puff of smoke from his nostrils in the direction the singer had taken.

The last of the flutes had sounded and in the darkness, the frogs croaked louder when I picked up my brush to shine my shoes for tomorrow.

Early in the morning Dr. Kasprzycki was already at our door with a bouquet of wildflowers. He handed it carefully to Mother so that the dew would not spill from the petals. While she put the flowers in our water pitcher, he paced nervously.

"Today I am going to paint a picture of your mother," he announced finally.

"A picture of Mother? Can we watch?" Zofia asked.

"No, no," he held up his hands, "she must by no means be disturbed, otherwise her face changes. That is why I am painting her in the house I rented."

"And you two, you stay right here in this room."
Mother pointed at the floor. "Read Dr. Kasprzycki's
book and do some coloring. Paint the wildflowers."
She slipped a jacket over her dress. Dr. Kasprzycki had
walked out ahead of her, when she turned once more.
"Stay in the living room and you'll be safe."
I ran after her.
"Papa knows how to paint," I said quickly, "why
doesn't *he* do your portrait?"
"Papa . . . oh . . . he only paints landscapes." She
hesitated, looking through the open door at the meadows glistening in the morning sun. "But you know that,
Ala, because his pictures hang in our apartment."
It was true, Father usually painted houses, some
standing in villages, others in orderly, neatly fenced
gardens. Although, I remembered, in one of them a
woman walks across the street to another house. "To
gossip," Mother mocked whenever she saw me looking
at it. But I had to admit, that woman's face was turned
away, maybe Papa couldn't paint faces.
I didn't say anymore to Mother nor she to me.
When the door had closed, we ran to the window
to follow Mother and Dr. Kasprzycki with our eyes.
Blowing our flutes as hard as we could, we watched
them as they walked next to each other without touching. Not even their arms touched by chance as they
strode briskly downhill, like a group of wanderers we
had seen at the outset of a long day's tour.
When they were lost from sight I picked ı ı Dr.
Kasprzycki's book where one of us had drop· d it
after we had been given the flutes. I measurι the
square book idly with my flute and it was exactly one
flute high and one flute wide. On its cardboard cover a
blond man danced with a woman whose hair color I
could not tell because it was covered by a headdress
with fluttery ribbons, but I hoped that she had brown

hair like mine. His long dark blue jacket was shaped like an old-fashioned uniform coat and he had tucked his red pants into black shiny boots. He was stamping his feet and his lips were parted as if he was shouting something to the woman, maybe, "Dance, dance." Written in an arch above the dancers, in block letters in alternating colors, it said "FOR ALA AND ZOFIA." It had been written so artfully in red, green, blue and yellow, that it looked as if it had been published just like that. I even imagined the painter turning out hundreds, maybe even thousands, of books dedicated to Ala and Zofia. To Ala.

Idly I looked at the book. On one side poems were printed and the accompanying music on the page facing it. The girls in all of the drawings seemed to be poor: one guarded geese, another was shoeless, while a blond was herding pigs. When I dropped the book, it fell open to its title page. Next to an ornament of two entwined bellflowers—which may or may not have been drawn by Dr. Kasprzycki—it said in careful handwriting: "To my little daughters."

I jumped up to get my sister.

"To ... my ... little ... daughters," she read aloud as if in school.

"Shhh," I whispered, "do you want anyone to hear this?"

"But we are alone," she said, but she also dropped her voice to a whisper.

"*He* is our father?" she asked.

"No, our father is in the Hotel Krakowski," I said adamantly.

"Dr. Kasprzycki could be *my* father, and our old Father could be *your* father," she said after thinking for a while.

"Be quiet. Mother shouldn't hear about this," I

said, "she would be very angry. Nobody should hear about this. Hide the book."

Then we didn't mention the dedication anymore and after a while we stopped talking to each other. The flies were buzzing around the table where Zofia now read the book, page after page. I pulled a dog-eared calendar from a nail in the wall and thumbed through it. Each month featured a painting relating to the seasons of the year, a sleigh race for January, greening trees for April, and a boy and girl sitting amid flowers in May. The painting for February interested me very much and I sat on the window bench to look at it more closely.

It showed a sleigh drawn by three horses, a shiny black one, flanked by a pale brown one on one side and a white horse on the other. On a luxurious red carpet spread over the bench of the sleigh reclined not the man or woman passenger I had expected but a big brown bear waving his right paw at the peasants. The picture fascinated me, but it also made me shiver, because I wondered if the bear might have devoured the rightful owners of the sleigh. A man and a woman standing in front of their log cabin looked astonished by the unusual sight but not frightened by it, although they could be the very next ones to be eaten. There are bears in the Carpathians, the man in the train had said. The other people in the painting stood too far away for me to tell if they were afraid or not, but I worried although the door was closed and outside of the window the meadows glistened brightly under the afternoon sun.

When we heard Mother at the door, we ran to her, glad that she finally had come home. She paused in the entrance and I saw that she wore a wreath of daisies which encircled her dark hair like a white crown. She smiled, standing framed by the dark wood of the entrance, a smile more shining than in Lvov, but that shining might have been the whiteness of the daisies in her hair. That made me sad, because Mother used to bind wreaths for us when we went for walks, and when we came home, tired from the excursion yet flushed with excitement, we had proudly worn daisy sashes over our dresses.

She still smiled when she sliced bread for us. Zofia and I were already at the kitchen table when she placed a plate with sandwiches between us. Suddenly Zofia grabbed Mother's hand.

"A ring," she yelled, "your are wearing a new ring."

Then I saw it, too, a big ruby ring on my mother's hand.

"Oh, the ring, yes, I wore that for the painting session today," she said, pulling her hand out of Zofia's grasp.

"May I see it again?" I asked.

"I have had it for some time," Mother said as she briefly held her hand in front of my eyes. Then she turned from us, humming softly, "Maciek, there he lies . . ."

That night Dr. Kasprzycki came to dinner. It was late for us and we were giddy with sleepiness. Mother had lit more candles than usual and she was still preparing dinner. Dr. Kasprzycki sat with us at the kitchen table while all around wobbled unsteady shadows cast by the candles.

"Tadeusz, you know so much, why don't you tell them some stories while I finish dinner. About the mountains . . . maybe even the bears." She laughed.

"I can't tell you where they are, but I know a few things about bears . . ."

"Yes, tell us bear stories," Zofia demanded.

"Do you have a teddy bear at home?"

"Yes, we each have one," I answered. "You gave them to us. They have button eyes."

"Please, partake with us of a simple country repast," Mother said as she put the last dish in front of us. "Our guest first."

"Thank you, Zofia." As he took some seasoned tomatoes, my sister asked impatiently, "What about the bears?"

"The bears. I really don't know about the Carpathian bears, but the bears in the Bible . . ."

"You, Tadeusz, of all people, tell stories from the Bible?" Mother laughed.

"My dear Zofia, any educated person has to know the Bible. Besides that, I have a biblical name."

What does Tadeusz mean?" she asked.

"It comes from the Aramaic word for 'breast,' and would mean 'beloved' . . ."

"Why don't you tell about the bears," Mother said quickly.

"Yes, tell," Zofia said.

"A prophet was walking, the way you hike through the mountains." He was now talking directly to my sister. "He was on his way to Beth-El when children ran down the hill and made fun of him."

"What did they do?" Zofia wanted to know.

"What's Beth-El?" I asked.

"Oh, one at a time," he laughed. "Beth-El is a town like any town but its name means 'House of God.' The children of that town made jokes because the prophet had a bald head."

We giggled.

"Did they throw snowballs at him?" Zofia asked.

From a window in our apartment we had watched how some boys threw snowballs at a man walking up the Kurkowa Ulica. They had knocked his hat off. It

rolled down the hill and we had laughed at that, not at
the man who was bald-headed.

"No, they didn't throw snowballs. What they did
do was laugh at him and shout 'Hey, baldy.' You don't
yell, 'baldy,' at a prophet of God. He became very
angry and cursed the children. Suddenly, down from
the mountains, came two bears and devoured all forty-
two of the children."

"Devoured them all?" I could not believe what he
had told us.

"Devoured them all," he said, blowing perfectly
rounded smoke rings at the candle.

Soon the conversation changed and we were sent
to bed.

At first I didn't know why his story should bother
me; it came, after all, from the Bible. Then I thought
that forty-two children were more than all the girls in
my school class at the Sisters of Nazareth. We weren't
even forty-two and strangely enough there were two
other sets of twin girls in the same classroom with us.
If we were to be cursed, then all of us would suddenly
be gone.

I didn't know how fast time was passing as I lay in
the dark. The voices of the grown-ups came through
the door as I heard the croaking of the frogs outside.
Then, much later, I heard *him* singing "Maciek,
Maciek," under our window, or it could have been the
same man who had sung there the other night.

❋   ❋   ❋

Over breakfast Mother told us that she would have
to leave again for a painting session. Today we didn't
play our flutes as we had the day before, but instead
watched silently from the window as she walked
through the meadows shiny with night dew.

Before leaving she had told us repeatedly not to

leave the room and we obeyed at first. We were even more bored than yesterday and began to argue with each other. Then, for a moment, we saw the face of a girl peering into our window. I don't know if we would have stayed inside if this girl had not taunted us, but we ran into the yard.

The dark-haired girl and a swarthy boy, who looked as if he might have been her brother, were older than we, while round-faced, red-haired Michalko was much smaller than any of us. We didn't talk to each other. They simply ran away from us, stopping merely long enough to turn around, giggle and see if we were following them. Soon enough we were playing hide-and-seek by the barn, our faces red and sweaty with excitement. If Mother could see us she would have stopped this immediately, because we were considered frail and in need of rest.

Running behind the barn, I stumbled and fell over Michalko who was sitting by the well. The older boy stopped and yelled at Michalko but I didn't understand what he said. The small boy giggled and it was then that the brother and sister began to kick him. At first they didn't kick him very hard and Michalko laughed as he rolled among their feet. Then they invited us with gestures to come and kick the little boy. We were so excited to be able—for once—to play with children of our own age, that we did as they asked. We had to, I told myself later; if we wanted to play with these children at all we had to play their game. So my sister and I bent over Michalko lying on the ground and poked him with stiff fingers—we even may have slapped him on his buttocks—but we never kicked him the way the others did.

"Come here at once!" That was Mother's voice.

The boy and his sister ran into the dark interior of

the open barn, while we stayed where we were, still bent over Michalko lying between our legs.

"Now!"

We were breathing hard and our hair was sweatily stuck to our heads as we walked by Mother's side to the house, worrying what her punishment might be for disobeying her.

"I told you to play indoors," Mother said pulling us sharply into the house. "Besides, I want you to stay away from these children. They are always sniveling and full of bacteria."

When I told Mother that we had been bored because she had left us alone, she didn't answer and, what was even more surprising, she did not punish us for having left the house against her most explicit orders.

❀   ❀   ❀

Mother told us to play with our dolls when she left us again the next morning. Resentfully, we argued with each other when we heard a bump at the entrance. Zofia opened the door and Michalko laughingly crawled in on all fours. Although his face was dirty, his reddish-blond hair shone in the sunshine slanting through the window. We were so startled that we sat back down at the table while he crawled on the floor to my chair.

Michalko's scurrying on the floor must have reminded us of our dog back home and just as we fed Nicki scraps from the table we began feeding the little boy pieces of left-over bread from breakfast. We wadded it up and threw him small bread balls which he picked up from the floor, thanking us in a surprisingly deep voice. Each time his grimy fingers found a ball of bread on the slivery boards, he raised his head to us and from his small body sounded a deep voice saying, "Blessed be Jesus Christ." What surprised us was not what he said but that these were the first and only words any of the Huzul children had said to us and that of the three it was Michalko—whom we had thought to be slow-witted—who spoke to us.

The game with the bread balls entertained us so much that we made many more and we fed Michalko for a long time. When we finally became bored one of us happened to find a dead fly and kneaded it idly into one of the bread balls. We watched Michalko eat this one, too, and he thanked us again. Now we jumped up and ran over to the window to catch more flies, pushing them with our thumbs deep into the balls of dark bread. Again and again Michalko's deep voice said, "Blessed be Jesus Christ." When he had his fill he crawled to the door, his chubby white legs flashing in the sunlight, with the dirty soles of his bare feet turned toward us.

I so clearly remember the soles of his feet as he crawled to the door—cupped like wrinkled grimy hands asking for God knows what—because it was the last I saw of Michalko. It was a day, or at most two days later, that he died.

We were sitting at the edge of a stand of oak trees—we were making acorn men—when Mother told us, matter-of-factly, the way she told us of many other events that she had heard being talked about in the village. I remember that I stopped playing and that the acorns spilled from my lap. Mother didn't have much to tell, except that he was dead and that we would not attend his funeral because we were to go on an excursion.

I glanced at Zofia and I thought that I could see guilt on her face. Looking at my twin sister was always like looking at myself. And since she looked guilty I had to be guilty, too, because both of us had knelt on the floor, rolling the dark bread balls along the cracks between the dusty floorboards. And after each one he had said, "Blessed be Jesus Christ."

If I were to tell anyone now that Mother left us alone in that house—I had said that I didn't feel well enough for a hiking trip and my sister decided to stay with me—nobody would believe that a woman could be so callous, but it was another time and children were often left alone. Mother did worry about me, but I could tell that she really wanted to go on this excursion into the mountains.

I stared at the squat dark loaf in the middle of the table. Michalko dead? Today I would cut a whole slice for you, I thought, a big clean slice of bread for you alone, if you would just come through that door again. Bashfully he had drawn up his forearm in front of his eyes, hiding his freckled face, and that is how I saw him now.

Zofia had fallen asleep on the bench, moaning from time to time in the afternoon heat. Through the window I heard voices of grown-ups coming to view Michalko's body. How was he laid out? I saw moon-faced Michalko bundled on straw, looking as serious as the dead I had seen staring from their coffins in the chapel of the Franciscans at home in Lvov. Now he can't say anymore "Blessed be Jesus Christ," sounding like an old man. Later, I thought of Michalko's voice again, when I was passing the open doors of an orthodox church at Easter time and heard the priest's basso booming, "Christ has risen."

At the kitchen table I laid my head down on my arms and I grieved as best as I could. It was then that I heard it for the first time, the indistinct sounds coming from below the floor. Cocking my head I listened to the wheezing and scratching and a faraway whistling somewhere under the floor. I got up and pressed my ear against the floor. Now it sounded like small feet running, at first nearby, then fading into the distance. Listening breathlessly to what sounded now more like sighing, I knew that Michalko had come back to torment me.

Nearby a flute cried out; in the barn they were playing for Michalko. I raised my head so quickly from the floor that I had to crawl back to the kitchen table. Leaning my head against the table leg I murmured, play, play louder, make the *leniuch* rise up, the lazy boy. Reaching for my flute I put it to my lips but I couldn't blow into it. I don't know how to play, I told myself, besides it's nothing but a child's toy. Make him dance, I wanted to call out to the musician, but I kept quiet, because then they would have known that I was in here.

Putting the flute in my lap, I sat on the floor listening to the music which had become so loud it was as if the musician stood at my door. Play, play, I said, Maciek got up, so can you. Gradually I quieted down, but while it slowly grew dark in the room I kept my eyes on the door.

Because she had slept so long, Zofia was sullen when Mother came at last, while I cried with relief. When she asked me why, I wouldn't say anything while my sister was in the room and so it wasn't until next morning that I was able to describe for her what I had heard under the floor. I didn't tell her of my fear that it might be Michalko because then I would have had to confess about the bread balls.

Mother promised that she would do something about the strange noises.

✿   ✿   ✿

It may have been three or four days after Michalko's funeral that Mother took us to a fairly distant country inn. Our walk back was so leisurely that it seemed as if she purposely delayed our return to Dora. The door to our house was ajar, but Mother wasn't surprised, not even when we found a Huzul man in our kitchen. I recognized him as the driver who had brought us from the railroad station. He stood by the open trap door to the cellar and pointed silently to a wooden box at his feet with five or six wiggling pink bodies. We knelt down for a closer look. Mother told us that the man had killed rats in the cellar—surely the source of the sounds that had scared me on the day of Michalko's funeral—but he had saved the young ones for us, so that we could look at them before they were taken away. While he waited for us to finish, we begged Mother for permission to keep the litter.

"No," she said, looking into the box.

"We can't let him take them away," pleaded Zofia.

"They are rats."

"Yes," I argued, "but they are babies."

"No."

"Can't we keep them at least till tomorrow?" I sobbed.

"No."

"Please, Mama," we both begged and by now Zofia was crying, too.

"Just till tomorrow," she finally agreed with a sigh as if we had broken her heart.

We were happy to have saved them, but we still had to be careful. Zofia took the bread knife from the kitchen table and gouged holes into a piece of cardboard we could use as a lid. Although they were too young to climb the walls of the box, they were still rats.

I don't know whose idea it was, but we decided that tomorrow, we would not hand over the box. Although we weren't sure how we were going to do it, we were determined to save the little rats.

Mother should have noticed how agitated we

were all evening, but she seemed to be thinking of something else. When she asked us—earlier than usual—if we weren't tired from the long walk, we agreed quickly, even yawning so that she would believe us.

"I don't know why, but I sleep much better in Dora," Mother said, "it must be the pure mountain air." She yawned, too.

When I woke up it was already late at night. Putting my hand over Zofia's mouth I shook her awake. Neither one of us dared to glance in the direction of Mother's bed, hoping that, if we didn't look at her, she wouldn't see us. The night was not cold and we tiptoed out of the room in our flannel nightshirts. In the kitchen we pulled on the heavy hiking boots Father had bought us for this vacation. From Mother's handbag I pulled a flat flashlight she carried so that she could find her way to a candle when we came home after dark. In the meantime Zofia put on the soldier's hat Mother had folded for her and found her stick. I pulled a scarf over my head and tied it under my chin, so bats wouldn't fly in my hair when I walked through the darkness.

Since their box was too heavy to carry, I lifted each one of the small warm bodies and placed them carefully in the bottom of a canvas shoulder bag. They tickled my palm with their wriggling and I had to giggle.

"Shh," Zofia said thrusting her stick at unseen enemies in the dark of the kitchen lit only by the weak beam of the flashlight.

"Will you help me instead?" I whispered. "We have to take water for them."

She stopped hitting the air long enough to pry the lid from a shoe polish tin, pouring water from the big jug on our washstand.

Then we walked into the night, Zofia first, carrying her stick and the flashlight, which cut a bright path at our feet. The only direction we really knew was along the road to the river. When we had wondered yesterday where we would take the little rats, we decided that, first of all, they needed food and drink. For food we wanted them to live in a *kukuruz* field, where the maize kernels would drop from the stalks right into their nest. Water we would have to bring every day as long as we were in Dora, hoping that, by the time we went home, they would have grown big enough to find their own water.

Somewhere in the dark frogs croaked. My teeth rattled as if I had fever. The one *kukuruz* field which we remembered from our walk was not too far from our house. We hoped to be able to find it before we stumbled into the grassland where the frogs lived. Zofia wanted to leave them by the side of the road, but I said no, they have to be in the field so they can have food. Besides, dogs might roam from the houses in Dora and eat them if we left the little rats by the side of the road. Zofia didn't say anything after that as I followed the reassuring swoosh of her stick lashing at the night. I had to walk very slowly so as not to spill the water from the shallow lid of the shoe polish can.

Soon we saw broken cornstalks in the fading beam of the flashlight and we knew that we were close to the field. We turned from the road and walked into the field, the stalks tugging with every step at the sleeves of my nightgown.

"Let's not go on," I whispered, "they'll find enough food right here."

Zofia prodded the cracked ground with her stick.

"It's too hard for them to sleep here," I worried.

"We'll make a nest," Zofia said, plucking grass from a sparse patch.

"That isn't soft enough." I set the bag and the

water dish down. Then I tugged at the collar of my night shirt, tearing the pompoms off the drawstring. Zofia put flashlight and stick on the ground and then also plucked off her pompoms, placing the four woolen balls on top of the handful of grass. One by one I lifted the tiny bodies from the safety of their bag.

"Let me touch them, too," Zofia said, as she took a step toward the nest, overturning the lid of the shoe polish can.

"You fool," I shouted, pushing her away from the nest. "What are they going to drink?"

Zofia pointed the flashlight at the lid and turned it upright. Seeing the empty tin angered me so that I pushed her again. For once she didn't fight back but kept the flashlight beam on the dry water dish.

I knelt down to pick up the empty dish, but when my knees felt the spilt water seeping through the flannel of my nightshirt, I began to cry.

Zofia didn't speak. I tried to think of a place where we could find water in the darkness, but all that came to mind were the faraway river and the frog pond, which had to be somewhere in the tall grass.

"We'll have to get water at the frog pond . . . near here." I tried to sound reassuring.

"But how will we find *them* again?" The beam of light described a circle around the nest. "We didn't even bring bread crumbs to mark the trail." She, too, was sniffling.

Already, after a few steps on the main road, we saw frogs. They were not jumping, but sat in the middle of the road like pieces of wood that had fallen from a cart.

"I want to go home," Zofia sobbed. We hugged each other.

"Yes," I said, but I knew that we had to go on. If the frogs wouldn't let us pass on the road, then we would have to go back into the tall grass where I had met the King of Frogs.

We staggered, fell, cried and walked on, but finally couldn't push anymore through the matted thicket of grass, weeds and reed and stumbled back toward the road. I don't know how long we walked, but when we reached the road, we simply stood still among the frogs, because we couldn't walk on. Zofia didn't dare to shine the flashlight anywhere else except directly in front of our feet for fear of angering the frogs.

Then we heard the noise of a motor from behind the oak grove and saw flashes of light through the thicket. We wanted to hide, but were too scared and tired to go back into the tall grass. So we stayed where we were—in the middle of the road—shivering in torn dirty nightshirts, Zofia still wearing her paper hat. The headlights became big and blinded us when the car stopped a few feet from us. For one more terrible moment I thought that someone would kill us or kidnap us, the way gypsies did with children. Then Dr. Kasprzycki rushed over to us, followed by Mother. And then we were hugged and we hugged back and were scolded and cried over at the same time.

At home we were washed with a sponge dipped in cold water and toweled dry until our skin shone reddish in the mellow light of the candles. Finally we stood next to each other, dressed in clean white nightshirts.

"Like little angels," Dr. Kasprzycki said, close to tears.

Then Mother hugged us once more and both of us buried our noses like little animals in the soft folds of her woolen dress.

✿   ✿   ✿

Even after a short night of sleep we were so anxious to go back to the *kukuruz* field that it was easy to convince Mother to take us. Thunderclouds were moving across the mountains and the sun was burning hotly as we walked down the river road in mid-morning. We searched to the left of the road and again I carried water, this time in a carefully stoppered lemonade bottle. The sun herself signaled to us, glinting whitely from the shoe polish can. We soon found the nest in the scraggly field of mountain corn, but it was as empty as the lid. We searched that corner of the field as best we could. Mother said that they had crawled away in search of food. I don't know if we believed her, but I poured water into the lid, so it would be there when they came scrabbling back to their nest.

Mother was more friendly than usual, but very quiet as we walked home a different way. At a roadside shrine she insisted that we wait outside while she disappeared into the dark interior. Instead of resting on a bench in the shade of a tree—as she had told us to do—we chased each other around the chapel.

Out of breath, I leaned against the chapel wall, next to one of its few slit-like windows. Pressing my face against the glass, I peered into the gloomy interior. After my eyes became used to the dark, I suddenly became aware that my mother's hands were directly on the other side of the window. Shining white against the dark wood of the pew, they didn't lie still—as when she prayed—but struggled with each other. Twisted around her right hand was her mother-of-pearl rosary, which—encased in a tiny pewter box shaped like a Bible—she always carried in her handbag, while from the other hand sparkled brightly her ruby ring. Touched by the sunlight, its red rays flashed through the gloom of the chapel as her hands moved back and forth as if she were washing them without water.

Suddenly her hands were withdrawn from my

sight, maybe she had seen my shadow in the window. When she came out she was pulling on her gloves and I could see that she had been crying.

❉   ❉   ❉

Finally we were to see the river Prut.

When Dr. Kasprzycki arrived in his car we watched how he folded down the canvas top and then invited Mother, with a bow and a smile, to share the front seat. Mother didn't smile back. She told us to climb into the back seat which we shared with our dolls. A warm breeze fluffed up our hair as we drove slowly through meadows rising toward the mountains. We didn't really need the comforter tucked around our bare legs. Then the car slowed down even more and finally had to stop, because we were hemmed in by a herd of bleating sheep crowding across the road. Kneeling on the backseat we reached down to stroke them, but since we worried that they might bite, we prodded their woolly backs with quick stabs of our fingers. We couldn't see a herdsman anywhere, only a dog, who charged with hoarse barks at lingering stragglers. A sour smell hung heavily over the flock and Mother—with quick irritated movements—dashed cologne on her handkerchief. "Where is the lazy shepherd?" she asked. "He should be hurrying his flock across the road."

"There," Dr. Kasprzycki stood up and pointed in the direction of the music, "there is your shepherd, lying, no doubt, beside a shepherdess in the shadow of an oak." He smiled down at Mother, who seemed to be looking for the shepherd on the other side of the road.

"He's enjoying a *Schäferstündchen* with her." He looked wistfully at the high meadow. "As Mephistopheles says in *Faust*, the hour of the shepherd." Still standing behind the steering wheel, he stretched out his arm over the windshield—as if blessing the sheep whose backs rose and fell in dirty-grey waves before the radiator—and then he said, pronouncing each syllable with great care, "et in Arcadia ego."

Mother silently looked in the other direction, while Zofia and I—bolder now—stroked the long nose of the sheep lingering by the fender of the car.

"The hour of the shepherd," Dr. Kasprzycki said once more—now almost in a whisper—as he sat down, closer to Mother than before. "Since we can't find the herdsman, dear Zofia, I am reminded of an old saying, a lazy shepherd needs a good dog." He chuckled while speaking to Mother and his voice was so soft that he must have meant what he said only for her.

Mother slid closer to the door and then turned toward him.

"You surely know all the sayings, the old and the new," she murmured. Then neither of them said anything and we heard the flute trill again.

"I wish Father were here," I said into the silence. Even now I don't know why I said it just then, when we were so drowsily content in the back seat on a warm summer's afternoon in the country.

Dr. Kasprzycki turned slowly to look at me with such sadness in his brown eyes, that I blushed, sensing that I had said something inappropriate. In a flash I remembered the dedication "to my little daughters." Although I still didn't know what to think of that, I definitely didn't want to feel sorry for him.

I felt terribly awkward because he kept looking at me and Mother was of no help because she didn't say anything but—with her eyes shielded by her hand—followed the progress of the flock, which was just now reaching the dark patch of shade under the oak trees. Dr. Kasprzycki turned his head very slowly, looking straight ahead at the empty road. In the silence I heard the flute calling from the shadows by the trees—sounding now low and hollow as when Zofia had blown into the empty lemonade bottle—and it made me shiver.

Dr. Kasprzycki started the motor and then he turned the car around in the narrow road, instead of taking us down to the river as promised. With the noise of the engine and the wind blowing harder than before into the backseat, I couldn't hear the flute anymore.

After he let us off in Dora, Mother said that tomorrow we would go on a short trip to Jaremcze, just the three of us. She didn't explain why Dr. Kasprzycki had not been invited, although I wasn't surprised. After he had silently turned around and not gone to the river with us, everything had seemed so final, that I was sure we would never see him again.

❀   ❀   ❀

As the train bringing us back from Jaremcze rolled into the station, we knew already before it came to its rattling and shaking stop, that something was oddly different. Mother was pulling down the window of our compartment—so that she could immediately spot our driver—when she said that the air was so much fresher, while I was sure that it smelled of sulphur as if many matches had been struck at once.

"Look, it's snowed," Zofia shouted, "the ground is all white."

"Hail," Mother said, "it's hail."

The driver held his whip high in salutation, but he didn't help Mother climb into the cart. I tried to see if it was the same man who had brought us to Dora, but he stared straight ahead, the rim on his round black hat turned up all around, looking like the hat of a girl's school uniform.

The flowers in front of the houses were smashed, the gardens covered by broken roof tiles. Through jagged windows I saw inside the houses where men were shoveling hail, tossing it over their shoulders as if it were grain on the threshing floor. The fields that had stood tall in stalk, now lay beaten flat, not to be harvested that year, Mother said. The trees stood bare by the side of the road as if it were already winter. Hail drifts covered the road, its gritty white surface broken only here and there by the brown humps of dead frogs. The grassland where the frogs had lived was now a stubbly white plain. All was silent except for the crunching of the wheels.

When we drove into our yard, Mother exclaimed, "Thank God, our roof survived."

I looked up and saw one of our storks standing stiff-legged in its nest, over the body of its mate, whose long neck dangled snake-like over the rim.

"Now we don't have to be afraid from day to day that the war will break out," said the driver bitterly. "Everything we have is already destroyed." He swung his whip angrily at his horse.

It was then that Mother told us that we would travel home tomorrow.

While Mother was packing I happened to pick up the book of folk dances Dr. Kasprzycki had given us. I saw immediately that one of the corners of the cardboard covers had been broken off. Sliding my fingers over the rough edge of the break, I though that someone must have thrown that book very hard. When I opened it, the title page flopped in my hand because a large section had been cut out. Where it once had said, "To my little daughters," there was nothing, not even paper, but on the facing page a picture had been painted, as if to compensate for the mutilation. It showed two kneeling girls—I could see that it was

71

Zofia and I, although the painting was not very large—
their hands raised in the gesture of prayer. We knelt
before a man looking like a bishop, carrying not only
the crooked staff, but also a bag, so that it could only be
St. Nicholas bringing presents to good girls. Scrutinizing the face of St. Nicholas—brought to life by a few
strokes of a watercolor brush—I imagined that the
face looked like Dr. Kasprzycki. It was difficult to tell
in the meager light of the room, but it seemed that the
painter had given more attention to the mitre—
daubing scarlet meticulously into the cleft between
the two golden peaks of the hat—while neglecting, for
a reason of his own, the face of the bishop. Dr.
Kasprzycki did not have a beard, while the beard of
the bishop inexplicably had been painted turquoise,
but by then I already knew that Nicholases—like Father presenting Christmas gifts to us—wore false
beards. I decided not to tell Zofia about the painting;
she would find out soon enough.

That night I lay awake for a long time.

So much had happened, like that terrible hail,
that I couldn't make sense out of anything anymore.
One of the storks, whom I had loved from afar, hung
dead from its nest. They brought good luck, were supposed to bring babies, and they ate frogs. Now the
stork was dead and the frogs were dead—killed by the
same hail—and I was sure that the baby rats were also
dead. I imagined their pink bodies lying under a hail
drift, like Michalko in his grave.

I listened drowsily to the sounds from the kitchen
and wondered what Mother was doing. Was she walking around, stopping in front of the calendar from another year where all the holidays were wrong, the one
I had liked so much? But since there was no electric
light, how could she see the same small things that I
had noticed, like the wreath of smudged fingerprints

on the glossy black border surrounding the cheerfully colored pictures? I thought of "February" and the troika drawing the sleigh. Back home Pela had pulled us on a sled, and Zofia and I had hugged each other so that we wouldn't tumble into the snow.

But now it wasn't Pela trudging through the snow, not *her* back in one of Mother's old overcoats, that was bent over the rope pulling us, but the broad backs of horses, pale, black and white, steaming in the wintery air. People stared at us from their houses, stared at the bear sitting in the front seat of the sleigh, whipping the horses with a chain dangling from his paw. We sat in the back seat, but it wasn't Zofia holding me, it was Michalko who clutched my arm. Then the bear reached back and flung Michalko to the wolves jostling the sleigh. Looking for Michalko among the grey bodies, I couldn't find him. Instead it was I who lay in the snow, looking up into the black muzzles of the wolves, their moist breath fanning my face. I tried to scream but no sound came from my throat.

※　※　※

Of the journey home I remember distinctly the acrid smell of steam and smoke driven low by the rain, that made me sick to my stomach, and the boredom in our damp compartment, where we were the only passengers. I didn't look forward to home, although—as I thought then—I didn't want to stay in the mountains. When Zofia and I became whiny, Mother alternately tried to cheer us up or calm us down, by offering us something from her handbag, cough drops, painted post cards, even dabbing eau de cologne on our wrists. When none of this helped, she began peeling an apple, remembering in the last second that she was wearing traveling gloves. It was a fawn-colored pair that I loved to touch when they lay in our hall in front of the mirror.

73

When she handed me an apple wedge on one of her folded handkerchiefs, I saw that her ringfinger was naked. I glanced up into her face, but she was staring absentmindedly through the rainy window and I didn't dare to ask why she was not wearing her ruby ring now.

When the train stopped Mother complained about its slowness, until the door was pulled open and a woman climbed in, dressed as if she, too, lived in the city. Zofia was standing on the bench by the window and Mother tugged at the hem of her dress to get her to sit down.

"Zofia, please," Mother said, her voice sounding sweeter than it had before the woman came into our compartment.

"Such pretty twins," the other woman said, having sat down as far away from us as possible.

"But you have to watch them all the time." Mother smiled at the new passenger while still trying to pull down Zofia.

"Yes, I am sure, especially with twins."

"Fortunately, I can spend most of the time with them and, of course, in Lvov I have help. But when you can't watch them . . . Zofia, do sit down! Now!"

Zofia did and the woman smiled patiently at Mother.

"We are returning from our summer vacation in the Carpathians."

"Did you see any bears?" The woman interrupted laughingly, as if this was a joke all children were told about the mountains.

We didn't laugh.

"They used to say that a child who rides on the back of a bear wouldn't ever get whooping cough," the woman said.

"There are no bears and wolves," I said sullenly.

"Have *you* ever seen a bear?" challenged Zofia.

"Besides, we already had our whooping coughs."

The woman didn't know what to say.

"As *I* was saying," Mother spoke firmly, "you have to watch them constantly. Naturally, it is easier if you have a maid, but what I began to tell you, one of the children drowned, a boy from the family who rented its house to us . . ."

"Michalko drowned?" I interrupted.

"There were so many children running about," Mother was talking to the woman, shrugging her shoulders as if she had been asked a difficult but unimportant question. "Michalko, yes, that could have been his name."

"A small child," I jumped up, "just this high," and held my hand up to show Mother how tall I thought Michalko had been.

"Ala, do sit down." She gently pushed me back onto the bench. "They had so many children, you know, poor people. I just have these two and if it weren't for the fact that they were twins, I would have only had one."

"Michalko *drowned*?" I couldn't believe what Mother was saying. She had to be mistaken. She sometimes did say things that weren't true.

"They shouldn't let small children near a river," the woman said.

"Oh, no, he didn't drown in the Prut, but in a small pond, hidden in the tall grass . . ."

"Did we, the three of us, ever walk there?" I interrupted again.

"We may have, maybe on the day when we were surrounded by the horrid frogs."

He drowned. So we didn't poison him after all, didn't kill him with our bread balls. But it's too easy, I thought, it sounds simple the way she tells it, but if it is so natural, why did he have to die, why couldn't he just as naturally go on living?

"Yes, I think we walked there," Mother said, "I now remember looking over the tops of the tall grass and seeing a pond. It looked like one of the romantic overgrown ponds you see on picture postcards of old parks . . . People heard him shout . . ."

"Why didn't they save him then?" I jumped up again.

"Ala, don't interrupt me and do sit down," she pushed me back, harder this time. "You know how these mountain people are," Mother spoke to the woman, who nodded at Mother. "They were making hay when this child shouted, but a storm was coming up and they tried to bring the hay under roof before it got wet . . ."

"So they could have pulled him out?" I asked quietly, hoping not to anger her, because then she wouldn't tell us anything and she was the only one here who knew the story.

"Oh, they must have thought that it was just the crazy boy screaming again, the way he did without rhyme or reason." She looked through the rainy window as if the answer lay out there. "It isn't as if I know what happened. All I know is what the woman told me in whose house we lived. And you know that they don't tell city people anything at all."

Could they have saved him? No, I thought, they couldn't have saved him, because the King of Frogs wanted him dead. Maybe any child would have satisfied him, maybe even one of us. Or maybe it would have been enough if we had brought the baby rats to the King of Frogs to make him feel better, the way we gave little presents to Mother when she was angry. No, they couldn't have saved him, he had to die.

"He used to come to our door, begging for table

scraps," Zofia said to the lady in the corner. When I heard her say that, I began to cry.

"As you heard, my girls knew the boy who drowned," Mother said in an apologetic voice, then she turned to me to comfort me, squeezing my shoulder.

"Your girls, they seem terribly overstimulated," the woman said in a tone of voice as if she were commiserating with Mother.

"Actually, they have a well-developed imagination," Mother said. Then she bent closer to the woman and said—in a voice that was supposed to exclude us, but we heard what she said,—"They were tested and were found to have the highest I.Q. in school."

The woman didn't know what that meant and Mother promised to tell her—in detail, I was sure—but first she would give us something to eat, to occupy us and to calm me. She unwrapped a parcel of food—prepared late last night on the kitchen table in Dora—and handed each one of us a sandwich, serving it ceremoniously on white handkerchiefs. Then she turned back to the woman and began to tell her about the young nun who had come to the *Nazaretanki* school and had instructed psychological testing.

Without looking down at the dark slices of bread in my lap, I absentmindedly plucked at the hard crust and began rolling bread balls between my fingers. They felt harder and smaller than those we had made for Michalko. Holding them between my fingertips, they felt more like the beads of my rosary, packed in my small suitcase, along with Lalka and my flute. We hadn't really learned how to say the rosary. I knew there were fifteen Pater Nosters and Glorias, but there seemed to be too many of the Aves to remember their number.

Holding each bead of bread briefly between index finger and thumb, I silently said the name of a

person and tried to conjure up a picture of the one I remembered. Bead after bead passed through my fingers and since I had made only a few, some passed
through more than once, each time with a different
name.

I saw Mother in the darkness of the chapel, alone,
with the rosary twisted around her hands and faraway I
saw Father—whom I loved—looking on, pale and silent. Michalko laughed, his mouth wide open and
round, his red hair glowing in the sunlight of the
kitchen window. The brother and sister who had
played with us scurried once more into the dark barn.
Tadeusz Kasprzycki looked sad as he held out his hand
with his gift for me, the Huzul flute, while the pink
bodies scrabbled on my hip. We lost you and we tried
so hard to save you. And the frog, brown as cork, what
did he want from me? Didn't he know that I was just a
twin and twin girls are never princesses?

Zofia and I, may we, too, be saved.

The warmth of the compartment and the drone of
Mother's whispering voice tired me and I leaned back
into the corner. Zofia was sketching with her finger in
the condensation on the window pane. Drowsily I
watched her drawing dark lines in the whitish mois-
ture beading on the glass, lines whose meaning I could
not tell.

The Stoning
Of Stanislava————————

It was during the mid-summer of 1939 that
Stanislava walked into Lvov and caused much talk by
preaching in the marketplace.

❁   ❁   ❁

Tusia pinned a Virgin Mary card to the wall by the
stove when Zofia Zielinski came into the room.

"Look what she gave me," she said, turning with
pride to her mistress. "She walked all the way from
Jerusalem to Lvov."

"Who?" Mme. Zielinski sounded irritated.

"Stanislava. They say she walked all the way . . ."

"Yes, so you told me already," Mme. Zielinski interrupted her, thinking, "Oh, that nun."

Sitting down at the kitchen table she remembered

what Mme. Golabiowski—whose husband, as chief of police, should know—had told her about this imposter. Some police officials, suspicious of her frequent border crossings into the Soviet Ukraine, thought her to be a spy. They had no proof; it was certain only that Stanislava Stempién was not a nun, did not belong to any religious order and was—as the rhetorical Col. Golabiowski called her—"A counterfeit voice in the desert."

"You really should hear her talk," Tusia said, wiping a corner of the kitchen table which was already clean, "like an angel. She talks of walking up to the Mount of Olives and all around Palestine." When Mme. Zielinski still wasn't drawn into the conversation, Tusia tried flattery. "I don't know where all those places are, but you, you know where everything is. You even speak French." And still Mme. Zielinski didn't speak to her maid, but in less than an hour a beaming Tusia followed her mistress to the market. Why Tusia persisted—when she easily could have gone by herself to hear the nun, and what finally convinced Mme. Zielinski to listen to her—when she could have stayed in the cool apartment awaiting the return of her husband and her twin girls, neither could recall when they later thought about this memorable day.

It was all the more surprising because Zofia Zielinski's servants all came from the Ukraine and she had developed a proper contempt for Ukrainians in general. To go with her Ukrainian girl to this spectacle of an itinerant nun was certainly not customary in her household.

It wasn't far to the market—just down the steep Swietego Antoniego—but Mme. Zielinski dabbed a cologne-dipped handkerchief at her temples and stayed in the cool shade of the old houses to protect the pallor of her skin. Tusia, though, walked in the sun,

swinging her market basket and whistling in anticipa-
tion of the nun. She wore her best blouse with the blue
embroidery and had wound her red scarf tightly
around her head, wearing it so low that her dark eyebrows ran into the furled edge of the scarf.

When they reached the bottom of the street, they
saw a crowd at the far corner. Stanislava's voice rose
high and piercing over the heads of the people. The
two women couldn't understand anything the nun
said; her words were distorted by the hoarse chants of
the fish peddlers and poultry hawkers. Tusia pushed
on resolutely and Mme. Zielinski slipped through behind her to the front of the crowd. The people around
them had tried to find shade, some by covering their
heads with newspapers folded rakishly to look like na-
poleonic hats, others by standing in the shade of the
market stalls.

When Mme. Zielinski finally saw Stanislava, she
was disappointed. She had expected someone more
dramatic to justify her walk in the heat. The nun's
dusty habit and pale face blended into the dust in
which she stood. Looking down, Mme. Zielinski saw
that the nun was not quite alone in the open circle left
by the respectful crowd. Lolek, the market boy, a
waterheaded child of five, crawled among the wilted
cabbage leaves and dead-eyed fishheads nodding his
monstrous head to the shrill voice of the nun.

The front of her cape, sheathed with dried mud,
was dominated by a crudely stitched red cross. But the
most extraordinary thing about her was a picture of
Christ she carried on a golden chain around her neck.
It was a picture one might find at a personal altar or in a
chapel, but certainly not carried around by anyone.
The portrait glowed a dusky red beneath heavy glass.
It was framed in warm, elaborately crafted gold. The
picture covered Stanislava's whole breast and while

she spoke, it heaved and glinted in the sun. She spoke constantly, sometimes loud and wailing like a flagellant during the Black Plague, at other times mumbling like the shriveled old woman she was. To Mme. Zielinski the nun seemed near exhaustion. Sweat ran through the furrows of her face, dripping on the icon of Christ swinging on her chest.

". . . and every eye shall see Him and you also that pierced Him and all kindreds of the earth! Amen."

She didn't pause after Amen but quoted and mingled her quotations with curses at the unbelievers, threatening with eternal doom those who took her message lightly.

"Tusia, we should go. If someone sees me here, they'll think I've lost my mind. I'll be compromised standing around with teamsters and servants. I should never listen to your stories from the market." Tusia said nothing, but looked intently at the nun.

". . . for we wrestle not against the flesh and blood, but against something bigger and more evil; kings and presidents . . ."

She was interrupted by the market master who waved his arms from the fringes of the crowd.

"Hey, you have to stop! I need this space."

He pushed his way through the newspaper-covered crowd to Stanislava, keeping his veined hands on the official leather pouch slung low across his belly.

Stanislava looked at him and continued talking while the crowd jostled the market master into a corner. He stayed there, wedged against a wooden fence and had to listen.

The nun told of St. John the Divine, and as she spoke, her words came faster and faster, tumbling from her thin-lipped mouth.

". . . and their dead bodies shall lie in the street of

the great city called Sodom and Egypt where the Lord was crucified. And they—of—the people—"

She stood open-mouthed and silent, choking as she tried to force words through her dry throat. Then she listened with her head tilted to one side, standing quietly erect in her dusty court, then she swayed and fell forward into the dust. Everyone heard the clatter of the picture on the ground. A woman screamed when the nun fell, but no one moved to help. All looked at the spot where Stanislava had stood, but only the men and women in the front rows could see the body.

Lolek shrieked and hobbled over to her, his head rolling from one shoulder to the other. He stroked her stringy grey hair. Spittle dribbled from his face onto her dusty back. A hand suddenly reached out and pulled him by the collar of his dirty shirt back to the edge of the crowd.

The woman wedged against Mme. Zielinski forced Lolek's head against her knees while his body struggled against this restraint. He wanted to be back with *her*, but the woman's arm across his throat kept him in place. Suddenly Mme. Zielinski felt Lolek's hand clutching her hem as he tugged furiously at her dress. She glanced at Tusia, but she, like everyone else, was fascinated by the still figure in the dust. So Zofia Zielinski slipped her hand over his and she soon felt him calm down.

Tusia whispered to her: "Why doesn't someone help her?"

But no one moved and Tusia stayed in the front row clutching her basket.

At last the nun lifted her head and the people in the front row twisted their necks to look into her face. Her arms stiffened under her body and she pushed herself up, but her legs were still stretched out like stilts.

A woman yelled from the crowd:

"Help her! For the love of Christ . . ."

She didn't finish and the last word was muffled as if a hand had been clamped over her mouth.

Stanislava pulled her knees up under her body and as she knelt, she began preaching. She rose, swaying, and at the same time brushed the portrait with her sleeve. The eyes in her dusty face looked dull as if they too had turned to dust and her tongue choked the words.

"You will die! All of you will die in the fire from the sky that will burn you, body and soul. All of you will die!"

She stabbed her skinny finger at a man in a white butcher's cap who stood in front of her. He tried to shrink back, but the crowd was firm.

"You—before this year is over—yes, you, your corpse will lie in the street. Your relatives will wail over your body. You'll lie there with your white cap pulled over your dead eyes."

The man turned to smile at the people behind him, but no one else smiled.

Now she pointed at a fat woman twisting her apron in her pudgy hands.

"And you, you'll be raped while your children stand and watch. And you," pointing at another man in a blacksmith's apron, "you'll have your arms hacked off. You'll run through the empty streets with your bleeding stumps, but your friends will lock their doors when you scream for help."

Mme. Zielinski listened the way Tusia had listened to the old woman with the wailing voice, transfixed, fascinated by the horror.

"And you," Stanislava said, her fingers playing

over the faces in the crowd, "you'll have your tongue nailed to the table! And you, you'll try to crawl without your feet through the marketplace. You'll drag your entrails behind you. Clutching the headless bodies of your children to your breasts will be in vain." She kept pointing at others and waving her hands back and forth, so that none and all felt spoken to.

"You'll clutch your head where your ears once were. Cut off. Gone. The Swedes and the Tartars and the Huns and the plague and the fire. Your eyes gouged and your ribs crushed and you still won't pray, no, you hardhearted breed, you won't even pray in the presence of the Lord. But you will curse your fathers and your mothers for giving you birth. You'll be mangled and maimed. The marrow of your bones will rot, and you, you'll—"

Mme. Zielinski couldn't understand the rest, for now the crowd was pressing silently past her toward the nun, the people's anger rising. Feet shuffled closer and Stanislava was absorbed by the crowd. The people surged into the street and Mme. Zielinski, stretching her neck this way and that, lost sight of the nun.

Lolek played quietly nearby with a dead sparrow, unmoved by the shouting in the street, spreading the bird's wings and pulling him through the air in make-believe flight.

Tusia and Mme. Zielinski watched the boy in distaste, then turned and followed the crowd down the Zolkiev road. Cherry trees lined the streets and soon they reached the mob pushing the nun along the country road. Mme. Zielinski and her maid took a path behind the trees on the side of a field of yellow oats, the stalks rubbing against each other in dry whispers. The women heard Stanislava wheezing as she walked, the icon thumping against her chest.

At a roadside chapel Stanislava paused, breathing

hoarsely, her hunched shoulders rising and falling beneath her dusty cape.

A man in the middle of the group threw the first stone at the nun's back. It wasn't a big stone, smaller than a child's fist, but it nearly toppled Stanislava when it hit her with a hollow thump. Rocks, thrown halfheartedly, fell to the ground. One missed the nun so far that it thudded against the trunk of a cherry tree on the far side of the road. Stanislava turned slowly until she faced the people, staring straight at them. She frightened the smaller boys, who sneaked to the back to hide behind the men. The air grew still and the sun glistened on the golden frame of the softly smiling Christ. Another rock, aimed straight at the nun, hit the icon squarely, spraying slivers of glass through the sunlight.

Stanislava was silent and no one in the crowd moved.

The nun looked at the broken glass glittering in the dust at her feet and slowly pulled the chain over her head. She held the mutilated picture in her hands. Then she straightened up, looking taller than she had at the marketplace, and, swinging the picture by its chain over her head, flung it into the crowd. It hit the chest of a man in the front row and he stumbled back. She scooped the broken glass with her bare hands, cutting her fingers, and threw the fragments after the picture. Confused, the people raised up their arms to shield themselves from the jagged flying glass. They huddled and turned their backs to the attack, glancing over at Mme. Zielinski and Tusia.

The nun picked up rocks thrown at her and pelted the crowd randomly. She even advanced a few steps to hit them harder.

The people became frightened and turned toward town. Stanislava stood in the middle of the road and threw stones with her bloody fingers, even after her tormentors had run too far away to be hit. Her black robe flapped in a gust of wind like the wings of an angry crow.

Tusia was red-faced with excitement and she knelt in the middle of the gravel path, with her mouth open, but Mme. Zielinski pulled her up. She, too, was happy to see Stanislava escape, and kept Tusia's hand in hers as both watched the nun from the path. Stanislava bent down and picked up the picture, looked at it from all sides and ceremoniously hung it back around her neck. Even from this distance, Mme. Zielinski saw the red smudges Stanislava's hands left on the image of Christ. Then Stanislava walked in the same direction in which the mob had pushed her, appearing very small and dark between the parallel rows of cherry trees.

Suddenly, Mme. Zielinski slipped her hand from Tusia's and opened her purse. She pulled out some of the larger bills and pressed them into Tusia's fingers.

"Quick, tell her . . . it's for the glass. Run!"

Tusia ran after Stanislava while Mme. Zielinski walked into the shady entrance of the small chapel. She knelt down on the worn prayer bench, but could think of nothing to say. She kept her head bowed for a few moments, then rose and walked quickly back into the bright sun before Tusia could see where she had been.

"I gave her the money, Madame. She didn't say anything, nothing at all."

Mme. Zielinski thought how disappointing that must have been for Tusia. She had probably expected another picture from Stanislava, like the one the nun had given her before. I'll buy her some when we get back, Mme. Zielinski thought, at the Franciscan Church maybe. With golden flowers and a flaming heart.

"Yes, Tusia, she's just a fraud, I only gave her the money because she's a. . ."

But Mme. Zielinski stopped in the middle of her excuse and took Tusia's arm and held it till they reached the outskirts of town, then she dropped it and walked again as close as she could to the houses.

Back at the marketplace the stalls were being pulled down with the muffled clump of stretched and shaken canvas, and the clatter of scaffolding dropped into wooden horse carts. The two women passed a poulterer near the fountain who was still trading. Mme. Zielinski stopped and pressed against the rough boards of the table to look closely at the pigeons crowding and cooing in the dirty cage. Her mind was still on the bloodied nun as she gazed into the amber eyes of the pigeons. Why she did it, she was unable to tell, but in the midst of this remembrance she thought of supper. Almost as in a dream she pointed to one of the pigeons and the hawker unlatched the lattice door and thrust his arm into the flutter, grabbing a bird by its wing.

"Is that one right, Madame?"

Mme. Zielinski nodded and the poulterer latched the cage door. Pressing the pigeon with his left hand against his leather apron he slipped two fingers of his right hand under the bird's head and jerked and twisted it off.

He dropped the severed head on the ground where it fell between his boots. Yellow lids lowered slowly over the pigeon's dead eyes. A multitude of heads lay in the dust like a red and grey carpet. The poulterer swung the plump body by its legs to drain all the blood from its neck, and in swinging the bird, spattered blood on his leather apron, the table, and on the heads nestled between his boots.

Tusia waited uncomplainingly, while Mme. Zielinski impatiently offered the poulterer a bill, suddenly sickened by the sight of the slaughter, the heat, and her encounter with the false prophetess.

"But you want me to drain it, don't you? It'll only take a minute. Were you here when they chased the nun out? She was bad for business, all that talk about sinning and dying."

Mme. Zielinski threw the bill on the table which was sticky with feathers and blood.

"Right. I'm usually gone at this time . . . and the heat, too." He saw how upset Mme. Zielinski had become and he offered her his bench, lifting off stacks of wrapping paper. She sat down and hid her face in her hands. When he saw that she was not looking, the poulterer picked up the carcass and swung it once more and another spurt of blood rained down on the head between his boots and on all the other severed heads that covered the ground like red plumed fruit.

The poulterer pulled a sheet of coarse grey paper from a stack on the table weighed down by a granite cobblestone. Blood soaked through the single sheet and he pulled another from the stack. Again blood soaked through the porous paper. But he threw it just like that into Tusia's basket and she followed Mme. Zielinski, who had already gone, unable to watch any longer.

They walked back together up the steep Swietego Antoniego—bending forward with each step—Tusia at the curb and Mme. Zielinski close to the old houses, the shadows of their high gables throwing the street into gloom.

That night both women dreamed: Tusia, in the narrow servant's room under the roof hot with the heat of the day, and Mme. Zielinski lying next to her husband who slept as quietly as if he were not sharing her bed at all.

Tusia dreamed of horses laboring up the steep

street in front of the house. She was alone in the kitchen looking down into the Swietego Antoniego watching the horses straining to pull their heavy loads up the street. They slipped on the cobblestones and their drivers cursed and whipped them. Each one of the horses had to be saved, Tusia told herself, and she pulled them on invisible ropes up the slippery street. She was faint from fatigue and yet she would not stop pulling the horses, thinking that she had overlooked one somewhere.

Zofia Zielinski lay twisted and still in her bed with her head on her arms, in an attitude she would have found unbecoming had she been awake. Her face was contorted as if she were straining to hear and see everything very accurately.

She dreamed she saw a column march across the marketplace, advancing steadily on the far corner of the square, where Stanislava had stood. She could not quite see what kind of column it was. Then she saw that everyone had bags over their heads, simple brown burlap bags like the ones that held winter potatoes. The marketplace was as always; Zofia recognized the market master with his leather pouch and some of the hawkers, now curiously silent. Lolek, the market boy, stared at the marchers with his dead eyes, sitting still on the poulterer's bloody and feathery table, his head cocked as if listening. Then Mme. Zielinski saw that Lolek smiled as the marchers crunched over everything in their path.

During the following weeks, Mme. Zielinski and Tusia spoke now and then about the nun. Mme. Zielinski nodded to all this—but they never mentioned their dreams nor did they speak about the nun's prophecies.

✿   ✿   ✿

In September, the Russians marched into Lvov and it became unusual for people to show interest in the lives of others. There was no fighting when they marched into town. Everyone had been told to hide in basements and so the Zielinskis waited, and when they finally decided to see what was happening, the Russians were there. There was some looting at the beginning, but it was mostly done by locals, while Russian soldiers looked on and smiled at such greed.

One young Russian soldier became a permanent guard in front of the Zielinski house for no apparent reason. Every morning he marched up the street with his old rifle and his field pack and stood guard between an acacia tree and a gas street lamp. He talked to Tusia and told her how he longed for his girl back home and each day he became more morose.

One morning he shot himself.

Mr. Zielinski laid the soldier's field pack on his shattered face and spread sawdust on the blood. It stayed there for a long time, because it did not rain and the pedestrians walked carefully around the stain.

Shortly thereafter Tusia announced that she was leaving their service to return to her village, because her mother needed her on the farm. She said good-bye in the living room and Mme. Zielinski walked her to the door leading into the street. Impulsively Mme. Zielinski embraced Tusia and both women started to cry, holding each other for a long time. Shaking hands for the last time, Mme. Zielinski felt a piece of paper pressed into her palm and she knew immediately that it was Tusia's treasure, the flaming heart of Stanislava. Tusia stopped crying and her face was bright under the rim of her good red scarf as she walked briskly to the milk cart, whose driver was to take her back to her village. Zofia Zielinski waved until the cart had reached the bottom of the hill.

❊   ❊   ❊

The fate of Mme. Zielinski and her family, Tusia and the nun, was overshadowed by the fate of the whole town and by the war itself. A series of occupations, liberations, purges, and more liberations destroyed much of Lvov and scattered those who survived.

Stanislava may have wandered a few more times along the dusty roads of this part of Galicia; the Zielinskis fled to relatives in Warsaw. Finally Zofia Zielinski could live in the capital, but under German occupation it was not what she had dreamed it would be. In her village Tusia may have survived the war, but nobody knows.

The Counter
Of Lvov

When I walked into her room at the nursing
home—I can find my way blindfolded: ten steps
through the lobby, turn right, then seventeen steps,
turn left—an aide I had never seen before was already
stuffing my mother's clothing into a plastic bag. At the
bottom of the bag I saw her bright red woolen robe
through the pale green plastic, then the dusty pink
and pale blue Biedermeier panels of her flannel nightshirt, the tiny hedge-roses pressed against the plastic
and the big black block letters of her name and her
room number marked inside the collar, showing
through: ZIELINSKI 316.

"I am her daughter."

The aide nodded and kept on putting a pink comforter into the bag—less forcefully than before—and

on top she placed the corduroy and velour toss pillows she had always had propped up at the head of her bed.

I had to turn away and I looked instead at the dressing table, built in between her narrow closet and the door to the toilet. She had never been able to use the table since she had already been paralyzed when she was brought here, on one side anyway, and the dressing table had been used for her television. It now flickered on a game show, the images of a spinning wheel following each other silently up the screen. When I had come to visit I always wanted to see the television on and I had often argued with the head nurse and had left notes for the morning shift: "Leave Mrs. Zielinski's television on. It's good for her." She sometimes had laughed when she happened to look at it when I was with her.

The bag was full and the aide had propped it against the foot end of the hospital bed, and I saw the numbers again through the plastic. I had seen them whenever I hugged her just before going home because—marked by a felt tip pen—they had bled through the flannel and her head hung down when I hugged her. After her stroke I had brought soup, every night, for six years and ten days, two thousand two hundred and one jars of noodles—with chicken or beef—each spoonful fed to a mouth at times expectantly and trustingly open like a child's, while on other evenings I had to gently force apart her dry lips, ever so gently with the tip of the soup spoon, the lips I had kissed when I had been a child, her child. Her lips . . . I brought a lipstick for her and made up her lips but she pulled them in and sucked on them. . .

"What do you want me to do with this?" She stood in front of the nightstand, indecisive, her hands buried in her apron pocket, "And the Christmas tree?" She pointed, accusingly—or so I thought—at the small nightstand crowded with pictures, an entire Alpine village, its lighted windows blinking through clouds of angel hair, a music box—playing "For Elizabeth" when its lid was lifted—with an angel holding a trumpet on top, and the Christmas tree.

For her first Christmas at the nursing home, I had brought a live fir tree—not a big one, just right for the top of her nightstand—but the administrator pasted a note to her mirror, pointing out the fire hazard. The year after I brought an artificial tree and decorated it with so much red, green, blue and silver, glass balls, chains and straw ornaments from back home, and lights, that I could hardly see that it was not a real tree. To the anger of the administrator and the disapproving glances of the aides I left the tree up until late in January—just as we had done back home in Lvov— and when I saw him I thought, what does he know about Chaldea and the feast of the Three Wise Men?

On some nights I stayed in the chair by my mother's bed long after she had fallen asleep and the night nurse had turned out the bright ceiling light. Leaning back, I watched the softly tinted shapes cast over the walls and the ceiling and when the tree lights blinked on and off it looked as if my mother smiled, but I knew that she was asleep because her heavy breathing evenly filled the room. That light gave a blush to her cheeks and made her carefully curled hair glisten on the pillow. I had seen to it that once a week the hairdresser who came to the nursing home would do her hair so she would still feel like a woman and not look like some of the patients hanging in their restrainers like mangy old birds dozing. Or like Mrs. Teleshkin with her chopped off grey strands hanging over her ears.

One Christmas season when I came to visit I heard my mother's agitated voice already from the corridor.

I ran the last few steps and when I reached the door I saw my mother stabbing her good hand at a tiny old woman, Mrs. Teleshkin, who was plucking the figures of the nativity scene from the nightstand. I pulled her away from Mother's bed and pushed her to the door. "Your room is down the hall," I said turning her to the right, but she muttered angrily and didn't want to go. Another time I found her at night out in the parking lot, dressed only in her short hospital nightgown—open in the back—clutching a sweater and a blouse, wrapped in a newspaper, to her chest. When I came upon her she was only a few steps from the cars rushing by on Maryland Parkway. I pulled her gently back inside the glass doors of the nursing home and told her again where her room was, but she cursed me in Russian—spitting with anger—"You scabby carcass, you."

When I didn't talk to Mrs. Teleshkin the next time I saw her after I had saved her, she called out to me from the door of her room and asked me why I hadn't said, "Good evening," or anything else to her. "You cursed me, called me a rotten carcass," I said as I continued to my mother's room and she cried after me, "No, no, no." I found out that she had lived in Warsaw just like we had for a while and I thought how nice it would be if these two old women could talk to each other, but by then it was too late for both. Sometimes she roamed the corridor bright with fluorescent light, walking without a smile between the rows of wheelchairs along the walls, mixing Polish and Russian in her curses, but most often she just peered at me from the door to her room.

"The tree?" The aide looked at me over her shoulder—a sturdy, short-legged Filipina, like many who worked in the nursing home—and then she pointed at the door: "The other rooms. I must do the other rooms."

"I'll take care of the rest myself, thank you." She was so impatient to get on with her work. She'll learn and quit like the others. They gave them too many patients, too many rooms to do, or maybe they couldn't take the dying that went on all the time.

She stayed in front of the tree. Maybe she wanted a tip or the nursing home had a policy that only the staff could pack so that nothing would be stolen.

"I'll call you when I'm finished packing. I'll call you before I leave."

"That's fine, ma'am," and in a few moments I heard her rummaging in the closet of the adjoining room. She will learn and work slowly and not even look up, just like the others who last.

Kneeling on the mattress I reached up to empty the shelf over her bed. There wasn't much on it, mostly overflow from the nightstand now that the tree was up. They didn't like it when the relatives surrounded the patients with personal possessions, and thought of it—as one administrator told me—as a sign of guilt. The blue Polish-English dictionary was up there— hers since she had come to America in the late 1950s—and a brass stand in the shape of a tree from whose branches hung—like apples—pictures of her grandchildren and their children in round gilt frames, and the small mahogany box which always had been by her side, ever since Lvov.

Yes, Lvov. And where was I, her *wyliczajko*? Sitting in America, counting my mother's possessions spread out over a plastic-covered mattress smelling of disinfectant. I should count everything and make a list from the television (one Sony Trinitron, used) to the picture on the wall (one picture, cut from magazine,

97

shows house by lake at night with a light shining from a window, frame inexpensive, value: possibly none).

It was really my mother's fault. Maybe if she hadn't called me *wyliczajko*, the counter or listmaker, my life would have been different, but to be just, she hadn't actually invented this name for me—someone else had done that—but she had used it for so many years whenever she wanted me, that still today I hear her voice calling me as she had on a busy street, in an empty apartment, or in a railroad station fearing that she might have lost me: "*Wyliczajko! Wyliczajko!*" I am not sure of the correct spelling—I rarely speak the language of my childhood—and when I tried to find it in my mother's blue dictionary no such word was listed. Leafing through the dictionary I tried to pronounce likely words carefully, but they didn't sound right, because my mother's voice was missing and missing was the shake of her head when she called me in exasperation, wondering aloud how she could have given birth to a girl such as me.

In the late 1930s, when we still lived in Lvov, relatives from my father's side—Danube Swabians of German descent—had driven up in their horsecart for market day and were having coffee and cake in our kitchen. They tried to pronounce my name and failed, one after the other, and in embarrassment they lowered their heads and silently dunked pieces of almond cake into their coffee cups.

"Those Swabians," my mother scolded after they had left, "they have lived here at least since Maria Theresia was empress, and they should be able by now to rattle off *wyliczajkowyliczajko-wyliczajkowyliczajko*," she stopped to catch her breath, "backwards and forwards, at that."

But they really couldn't, as hard as they tried. When the word had been translated by my father, his sister exclaimed happily: "*O, der Aufzähler!*" But my uncle doubted the gender of the article: "Are you sure, Albin? Shouldn't it be *die Aufzählerin*? She's a girl, our Ala," and he lifted me on his knee, although I thought that I was already too big for this. But my aunt, of a more literal mind than my uncle, said: "No, this one here is the little listmaker *Männle*," and she added the Swabian diminutive to "man." She smiled at me and I felt proud, because for once I was a whole single person and I didn't have to share the honor with my twin sister Zofia.

As to being the listmaker and chronicler—it is true—I counted everything that mattered and later even things that wouldn't matter to anyone else. Almost as far back as I can look, I see myself bent over paper, writing, making lists as diligently as if it had been assigned to me—and in a very personal way it had become my assigned task to record—with my inkstained middle finger where the penholder was tightly pressed against a knobby protruberance that had formed there from the pressure. Now, since my mother's death, I must keep the lists more diligently than ever, who else would but me? And who is left who remembers the people and what happened to them?

I have carried the stories out of the past so long— from the time when I began to record the people and things in my life and the events which befell them— that I have to keep writing like a chronicler whose life and work have become so intertwined with each other that he would die if he ceased to write. Some occurrences appear so chimeric—even to me who lived them—that they sound like *märchen* where children, ghosts of the dead and headless horsemen inhabit the same fearful night. Even if at times those people seem grotesque, their overwrought emotions just as incomprehensible now—and in this country—as their stoic acceptance of bizarre fates, they did live and in a very real city, called variously Lvov, Lwów, Lwiw or Lemberg by its inhabitants, depending on their language. It was an enlightened city where I was born, not a Galician village where one would expect superstition and blind faith, mystic rabbis and miracle-working messiahs. The city had an opera house, several theaters and its university was founded in 1661 by King Jan Kazimierz—who had been a cardinal in France before becoming the Polish king—and a technical institute was added later; even a college of veterinary science. Just as Jan Kazimierz had ties to religion, the city of Lvov was a city of churches of many different faiths. It was the home of an orthodox bishop; the cornerstone of my hometown's cathedral was laid in 1480. But as my mother—being of Armenian ancestry—pointed out proudly, the Armenian cathedral was even older and could be traced back to 1370. The first synagogue was established in 1582 and by the time I was born more than one fourth of all the inhabitants of Lvov were Jewish, crowding the streets so that at times it seemed as if there were more Jews than others.

Our family was not Jewish, but Jews came to our house, like Pan Barach, from his store down the street to prepare fish in our kitchen. And another came, who was to change our lives forever.

How did it all begin?

One day a man rang our doorbell.

My twin sister and I were home alone with the maid. She was stacking dishes and we watched her across the big kitchen as she reached up to slide a stack of dinner plates into the cupboard, when the doorbell rang. It was a mechanical bell which you had to twist. I remember that sharp metallic twang echoing shrilly off the kitchen tiles and the white walls, and then—as if it had been caused by the twang piercing the quiet evening—a plate fell and shattered on the floor tiles. The maid stood still, her arms outstretched and her empty hands open as if she still held the plate and then she suddenly ran to answer the door. My sister and I stayed in the kitchen and listened by the door to the corridor.

A man's voice asked for my mother, not by name, but he asked if the *pani domu*, the lady of the house, might be in. And only then, after a silence, did he ask for the gentleman of the house. The maid—it might have been Tusia or Pela, no, it was 1939 so it must have been Tusia—told him lengthily that the master and mistress were at the theater and it would be hours before they were expected back. We barely could hear his voice although the maid had left the kitchen door open—he may have been whispering—but we understood enough to know that he was going to wait for them down in the street. After Tusia had closed the heavy door and bolted it securely, we pulled her over to a chair and questioned her about the stranger.

"Who was he?" I asked.

"He didn't say, Ala."

"Maybe he's from a foreign country?" my sister wanted to know.

"That may be so. He could be a foreigner, but one thing I know he is, he is definitely a Jew." She was crouching on the floor sweeping up the pieces of the broken plate.

"A Jew?" my sister asked, sounding disappointed.

Tusia straightened up and went back to her task of putting the dinner plates into the cupboard.

A Jew, I thought, just like Pan Barach, who delivered groceries to us from his store on the other side of the street and down the hill by the next corner. He was a boisterous man and when he came in with his load of groceries he laughingly slapped the fish on the kitchen counter and when he spoke to you he smelled of garlic.

Jew or not, we ran into the living room and pulled the drapes away from the window. Maybe, I thought, he might be an American or an anarchist, words I had heard in the conversations of my parents that had intrigued me. Looking down into the dark Swietego Antoniego we saw the stranger under the gaslight, facing down the street in the direction from which our parents were to return. He didn't lean against the wall as Pan Barach did after he had swept in front of his store and he didn't gaze up into the acacia tree, but stood like a sentinel in the middle of the sidewalk.

Somehow he scared us.

Tusia pulled us away from the window grabbing us by the collars of our dresses—elaborate collars, I remember, which came down in ruffles to the ends of our short sleeves—and the collar choked me as she dragged me away from the window.

"He might see you," she whispered, as if he could hear what we were saying to each other on the second floor. I nodded and thought that Tusia had saved my life, had saved me from *him*—although I wasn't sure just why if he was just a Jew like Pan Barach—and I promised that I would never go near that window again.

When the drapes had swung back we felt safe once again in the salon. Tusia asked us to sit with her in that room, a rare treat for us, because we were only allowed to be in the salon on special occasions. It was strange that Mother didn't want us in there, because we knew that we were born in this same room. Why we weren't born in the bedroom we were never told, but I had always loved the wallpaper in the salon— exotically pale ferns on a dark orange background—

and I imagined that it was the first thing my eyes ever saw.

Excitedly we waited for our parents. To keep us quiet Tusia brought out the two pairs of headsets we had for our radio and she let us sit in the big carved chairs by the round table under the Huzul wall hanging with its geometric peasant designs woven into the carpet. The chairs seemed enormous to us then; the tops of our heads did not even reach the walnut carvings forming the upper part of the chairbacks. Nestled into the moss-green back cushions I listened to the crackling voices in my headset as if they were secret messages from the mysterious man in the street. I was so intent on what I heard—keeping my eyes pressed shut—that my leg would twitch involuntarily when the sleek fringes of the silk tablecloth tickled my bare knees.

Tusia sat between Zofia and me, where Mother usually sat, and from time to time she idly reached for an emerald green ball hanging from a cord right by her chair and she pushed the button hidden in it, the button Mother used to call Tusia. We heard the ringing in the empty kitchen and we looked at each other and laughed. When we became bored listening to the voices in our headsets Tusia brought us each an issue of *Teatr*, a magazine Mother subscribed to, and we solemnly leafed through pretending to read the articles. And we waited. When I looked across the table—past the pewter statue of a hunting dog leaping over a tree stump—I could see my sister's face flaming red with excitement and the bangs of her pageboy plastered to her forehead shiny with sweat, as if she had a fever.

When we finally heard my parents at the door we ran into the corridor pushing each other to be the first to tell about the stranger. They couldn't have been home more than a minute when the doorbell rang again. It rang just once, sharp and twanging, but no one answered it as we all stood silently in the muted light of the stained glass lantern of the corridor. Then he knocked softly and I imagined white hands with velvet and lace at the cuffs. My mother walked to the door and opened it wide while my father stayed with us, to protect us from the stranger, I imagined.

My mother invited him into the anteroom, after having looked at him carefully. We walked after Mother and I remember sniffing her perfume as I followed her and when I looked over my shoulder to see where Father was, I saw him hanging up his hat at the wardrobe and slowly walking into his study, as if everything was safe in our house and the stranger was not talking to our mother in the salon. We walked close to Mother, like pages flanking a queen in our book of *märchen*. He stood before us without velvet and lace and instead wore a *kaftan* like the others in the street. Everything about him was clean; this must have been why Mother let him enter. Although he appeared humble—like someone about to be knighted in our dog-eared book—he stood with dignity in the middle of the large open space of parquet floor surrounded by overstuffed furniture which we loved dearly but were rarely allowed to sit in.

"Who are you?" Mother asked him sternly, standing straight in her black silk dress and then and there I vowed that I would be just like her, elegant and brave, staring down the stranger.

"Itzek Najhudel is my name," he answered calmly and quietly, not with pride, but yet as if my mother should have heard of him.

"What do you want?"

"Penance."

"Who sent you?"

"God."

The questions and answers had come quickly as if these two were in a play and knew exactly what to do and what to say, because someone had written it for them. They looked each other straight into the eyes. My mother stood tall and there was no slump to her shoulders—indeed, there never was as long as she lived—and he stood in front of her without fear—not the way Zofia and I did when she scolded us—looking at her evenly with deep dark eyes.

When my mother heard the word "God," she stopped questioning him and instead asked him to sit down, pointing to *my* chair, where *I* had sat waiting for Father and Mother to come home. He hesitated, then nodded almost as if consenting regally and sat down, pulling the chair away from the table. We were forgotten by Mother and *him* as if we had never been born and hadn't entered the salon by our mother's side. The word *penance* became a secret password for them like *bohopki* for us which our father sang while bouncing us on his knees. What did *bohopki* mean and what *penance*?

So it took only one word spoken under the Huzul hanging in the salon to invite Itzek Najhudel into our lives.

It wasn't really true when he told Mother "God" had sent him because he had found her through Philomena, a devout spinster, who, from her earnings as money lender—and with the help of her older sister—had sent through seminary her nephew who now—to her joy—had become a priest. Philomena had met Mother at the Church of the Carmelites and she had been so impressed by Mother's faith and devotion that she had mentioned Mme. Zielinski to Pan Najhudel.

Mother didn't come in to say goodnight and instead Tusia tucked us in and hurriedly turned out the light, no doubt to talk to the maid from downstairs who—like Tusia—had her room on the top floor of the apartment building. We had pretended to sleep when Tusia left—our heavy breathing would never have fooled Mother—but now we talked about the stranger in our house. Across the dark room we now taunted and scared each other with the black man who was going to sneak in and grab us. Our giggles turned to fear and we ran in our nightshirts out into the dark corridor. We held each other's hands as we crept through the blackness of the windowless corridor to our parent's bedroom door. It was closed—as it always was at night—and we pushed our noses flat against the waxed floor and our ears to the crack of light under the door. Being so close to our parents made us feel safe. My sister's hair was pressed against the top of my own head as we lay curled up by the door.

The bed creaked.

"Who is this man?" My father spoke.

"Itzek Najhudel."

"Itzek Najhudel?" My father laughed. "I've heard of a Mendel Neigreschl, a poet from right here in Galicia, but no Najhudel. What does he want from us?" My father's voice sounded farther away than my mother's. Maybe he was the one who made the bed creak and my mother still sat in front of her mirror.

"Penance."

"Penance?"

"Penance."

"If he wants penance, let him go to a priest."

"Please, Albin, this is a serious religious problem."

"You mean, because he's a Jew?"

"Of course."

"Jews don't do penance."

My mother didn't answer.

"Why come to us?"

"Philomena sent him. She knows me from the Carmelites."

There was silence and then—from the direction of the make-up table—came the sounds of drawers being pushed shut.

"Philomena Magocsy should stick to money-lending. . . "

"Albin, you know about her nephew, the priest, now she's even more religious."

"What is this Jew going to do here?"

"Penance. I told you."

"Penance for what?" Now my father's voice sounded louder and more insistent.

My mother didn't answer immediately. When she spoke I heard her voice from another part of the bedroom.

"Pan Najhudel, in his own way, is a very religious man . . . and in his deep sorrow he has turned to us. His son—his only son—has fallen in love with a gentile girl. He is mortified, because the girl is Catholic," and after a pause, "like us."

My father didn't answer, so my mother continued.

"Don't you feel pity for a father with such a burden?"

I didn't hear my father say anything, but he may have nodded, because my mother spoke again.

"I knew that you would understand this, Albin, however strange his request seems. He will be with us from tomorrow on."

My father didn't speak and when next I heard my mother's voice, it was very loud.

"It's been a long day, but I just want to look in on the twins."

We jumped up and were at least standing and not lying on the floor like dogs when the light from the opened door fell on us.

"What are you doing here?" my mother said sharply. "Didn't Tusia put you to bed?"

"Oh," my sister was the first to speak, "the ghosts . . . we were scared of the ghosts," and she grabbed my mother's hand. I looked into the bright room and at my father lying on his side of the big bed, raised on his elbow. He was smiling.

"Zofia, let them come in, it's been an exciting day for them too."

We ran past Mother, who stood in the doorway, and jumped from her side into the middle of the bed. Lying next to Father I looked up into the mellow light of the lamp hanging over us, glass panes glowing with villages in the snow, skaters on wintery ponds, and hunters amid rows and rows of pines.

I snuggled in between my father and my sister and when Mother turned out the light, I shouted: "Now dare and come to haunt me all you little ghosties," and we all laughed in the dark.

❋   ❋   ❋

He had come on a Friday night and so the next day being Saturday we only had to go to school for half a day. At breakfast we laughed in the kitchen with Tusia and felt as if we were on a holiday. But from time to time we glanced over at the dark brown door leading to the corridor, where *he* had entered last night. Finally Zofia grabbed a piece of chalk from the counter and ran over to the door. I followed her and watched her draw a man on the brown door: a circle for his body, another smaller one for his head, with outstretched stick arms and legs. On his round head she drew two smaller sticks, his horns. Then we shouted "the devil, the devil" and ran away, scared by her drawing and hid behind Tusia.

"Help us, Tusia!" I screamed.

She turned toward the door and pointed her right hand at it.

"Go away devil, go away."

I peered out from behind Tusia's skirt and whispered: "It's still there, Tusia. Please, make it go away."

Then Tusia laughed and pushed us back to the kitchen table.

"If you don't eat and hurry on down to the *Nazaretanki*, he'll come and get you. The sisters don't like you late."

At noon, when school was finally out, we ran home, which wasn't far because our house was right by the schoolyard of the Sisters of the Holy Family of Nazareth. We ran, because we wanted to see what had happened with the stranger. Had he come while we were at school? Running up the stairs we passed a man groaning under the load of two buckets of coal.

My sister twisted the doorbell again and again until my mother opened the door.

"Is he here?" she shouted while running into the corridor. We threw our bookbags at the foot of the wardrobe and pulled off the berets of our school uniform. My mother drew the door shut after the man with the coal buckets had passed through. I looked at him but in the dim light of the corridor I didn't immediately recognize the stranger. He stopped in front of Mother and she nodded in the direction of the kitchen. Squeezing by me he smiled apologetically.

"It is so nice of Pan Najhudel to help Tusia," Mother said in a tone like the one she used in her prayers. "Pick up your bookbags and take them to your room."

I looked into the kitchen and watched him put down the coal buckets.

"Where is he going to stay?" my sister yelled and I saw Pan Najhudel's head turn in our direction. Mother grabbed my sister with her right and me with her left hand and pulled us through the open doors into the salon.

"Here, help me with the dusting," she picked up a yellow cloth and pressed it in my sister's hand. "Let's do the chairs first," she pointed to the ornately carved walnut chairbacks. I grudgingly picked up a cloth and traced the intricate arabesques with my index finger sheathed in a dust cloth. My sister wasn't as patient and she went over to my mother—who stood in the door—and asked her loudly:

"Why don't you tell the Jew to do it?"

At first Mother was silent and stood still, then she tried to pull my twin sister away from the door so that *he* could not overhear us, but Zofia bucked in the grip of Mother's hands, dug her heels into the corners between door and jamb, and when Mother didn't answer, she asked, looking directly into her white face:

"When is he going to leave?"

I am sure that Mother, had Pan Najhudel not been in the kitchen, would have slapped Zofia—and not just once—but since he looked over at us it stood to reason that he had heard my sister's remark. My mother bent down to Zofia and spoke to her, her voice hissing the way she always spoke when she admonished us in public:

"It is impolite to talk in front of a guest," and she stressed the word *guest*, "of his departure." She took a deep breath, hoping to regain her temper, but she just could not contain herself any longer.

"Go to your room!" With this she picked up my sister's school beret and flung it at Zofia, throwing it with such force that the pale blue enameled metal cross of the *Nazaretanki* hit her in the face. I still feel the thud of the impact as if my face had rocked back and not my sister's. Crying, she ran to our room.

I didn't follow my sister but instead looked into the kitchen and into Pan Najhudel's sweaty face. My mother gave up the family project of cleaning the salon at such an emotional time and I dropped my yellow dust cloth. Pan Najhudel smiled, whether at Mother, me or himself I don't know. My mother stayed close to me for a while in the salon, maybe she wanted to reward me with her company for not having been rude like my sister, or, as I think about it now, she might have needed me so that she could speak indirectly to our "guest."

"It is nice of Pan Najhudel to help us," Mother said turning her face toward the kitchen and speaking louder than she just had to me, "but what a sacrifice it is for this man to work on the Sabbath. And what a sacrilege for him to carry coal on his holy day. But he told me, 'I want to work on the Sabbath.' That's what he said. And all for his son. . ."

I began to feel guilty for being a child and her voice hanging in the stillness of the salon was like a lament over mine or my sister's transgressions.

I bravely walked into the kitchen. Tusia was there and she sighed when she asked Pan Najhudel to sit down and have some coffee and a sandwich. She asked me to sit down too—I was standing in the middle of the kitchen—"so that our guest will have company." He accepted humbly and remained standing until I had slid onto my chair.

"Such manners," Tusia often repeated when she talked about him later.

"In which grade are you?" he asked. All adults always ask children about school, I thought and wished—maybe for the first time—that it weren't so.

"I am . . . we are . . . my sister Zofia . . . we are twins. In the second grade of the *Nazaretanki*." I

111

blushed but was also proud and I sipped my milk as I had seen the ladies in our salon sip from crystal.

"So you know how to count?" He looked at me across the table, not paying any attention to his coffee or sandwich. I wished that he wouldn't just ask me about school as if I didn't know anything else.

"*Tak*, Pan Najhudel, I knew how to count before we ever went to school." What a silly question. I should tell him that my sister and I scored highest on the intelligence test given by a nun—who was a psychologist—to all *Nazaretanki* pupils. But already then I knew that this would be bragging and impolite, although Mother spoke often about the test to her friends.

"No . . . eh, what is your name?"

"Ala."

"No, Ala, I don't mean numbers, like one and one, I mean counting as one would who remembers things. Like a *mensch* who keeps lists of everything that happens. Writing records and lists, that is what it takes to make a human being." He took a gulp of coffee but looked as if he didn't know what he was drinking or if he was drinking.

"What do you mean?" I asked timidly.

"Lists of everything around you, such as the things in this room. Everything with life, including Tusia," he nodded at her and she blushed, turning quickly to stir a pot, "and the lifeless, the chairs, the table," and he knocked on it with the knuckle of his middle finger, "the spoons and pans, the calendar. . ."

"That's Christ," Tusia turned, happy to join the conversation again.

Pan Najhudel coughed sharply and turned away from us.

"Yes, I can count such things. But why?" I talked to him as if Tusia hadn't spoken at all.

"To record," he coughed once more, his face still red. "Nothing is forever."

I laughed loudly and spilled my milk. I laughed because it was so silly. We were born here in this house and we would always be here with Father and Mother and Tusia, well maybe not Tusia because servants changed from time to time, but the table and chairs, this kitchen where I sat with Pan Najhudel and all the things I saw from where I sat, had always been there, in exactly the same position, looking the same way and would always be there. I knew that.

He drank his coffee in silence and when he didn't touch his food I took it to my sister who hadn't left our room since Mother had banished her. But Zofia wouldn't eat the sandwich when she heard that it had been put in front of Pan Najhudel first.

When late in the afternoon my father came home from the *Krakowski*—the hotel he managed—he stopped in the doorway framed by the dark red drapes pulled back to the sides of the door, and watched Pan Najhudel scurry across the room, carrying bundles of freshly ironed laundry, muttering *pokuta, pokuta*, repentance, repentance. His eyes burned in his pale face and he didn't look at Father or any of us as he conscientiously carried his loads on that Saturday.

"Zofia," my father finally called out, sounding amused by what he saw, "you now have your own Golem just like Rabbi Löw?"

Mother didn't answer, although she had heard him.

From one of the kitchen cabinets hung a slate and from its wooden frame dangled a graver. It was an anachronism in our modern kitchen and it didn't reflect our social standing at all. Mother might have bought it for the same reason that she and her friends dressed in peasant costumes on country outings. The children of the poor had to write on slates when they went to the first grade of the public schools. We used to watch them from a window in our apartment when they ran home, laughing, hitting each other, and all the while red rubber sponges and cloth wipers bounced against their imitation leather school bags. At our school we wrote with pen and ink on paper, even in the first grade. But that was the *Nazaretanki*.

Itzek Najhudel took over the slate. Before his arrival Mother and Tusia had used it to order supplies and record deliveries, now *he* wrote on the slate and he wrote in straight lines—not like Tusia, whose lines wobbled like eggs rolling across the table—from one edge of the slate to the other, with a date in front of each entry. The letters weren't printed like Tusia's, who spat on her fingertips and wiped out her clumsy letters when, even to her, they looked illegible. His letters flowed across the slate, the capital "F" and "T" strong with horizontal slashes, big-bellied "D"s and pouter pigeon "R"s. Those letters I remember, because those characters scratched by his graver into the dark grey of that old-fashioned school slate became my model for writing and not what the Sisters of the Holy Family of Nazareth taught me at school. So when I write now—although in an entirely different language from the one I learned in Lvov—I write with the large masculine letters of Pan Najhudel and not in the dainty scroll-like script shared by the students of the *Nazaretanki* like badges of a sisterhood.

On Sunday Pan Najhudel rested from his labors because we did, and keeping a Christian Sabbath may have been yet another act of contrition for him, although it did not appear on our grocery slate.

During school on Monday I kept thinking about our "guest," kept wondering what he might be doing just now, and, as so often, I was reprimanded for my daydreaming. Tusia waited for us at the wrought-iron

114

gate, ready to take us home. When I saw Zofia daw-
dling with a group of girls in the schoolyard I asked
Tusia if I might not run ahead. She thought about it for
a moment, wondering if my mother would be angry,
but then decided to let me go on my own since she
could see the entrance to our house from where she
stood.

In the stairwell I almost passed Pan Najhudel who,
once again, was carrying two buckets of coal. He
stopped when he recognized me—putting the buckets down with a sigh—and smiled at me as sweat
dripped from his chin. He really wasn't dressed right
for this work, I thought, wearing the same *kaftan* he
had worn when he came to our door on Friday night.

I wondered what to say to him. What had I been
taught?

"May I help you, Pan Najhudel?" I said timidly
and curtseyed.

He looked at me, this time without a smile on his
sweaty face, and he was silent for a while.

"No, I have to do this alone." With this he lifted
the two zinc buckets from the landing, struggling to
stand straight. I picked up my school bag—tucking
it under my left arm—while with my right hand I
grabbed the handle of one of the buckets. I didn't
carry any weight at all—the bucket was too high up
for me—but my hand rested next to his on the
wooden handle and so we slowly climbed the stairs
together. Before we went in he stopped once
more—just in front of the door—and thanked me
for helping him, adding: "Now I must carry it alone,
because your mother wouldn't want you to haul
heavy buckets of coal."

I nodded because I knew that Mother would be
furious should she catch us, so I just opened the door
for him and then I followed him into the dark entrance

hall. Although I quickly dropped my beret and school bag at the wardrobe, by the time I came into the kitchen he was already at the slate and wrote "2 buckets of coal carried from the cellar." I watched him write and when he turned around to look at me he must have seen the intense expression on my face.

"Bring your school book and I'll teach you to write just like me."

On that day I learned how to write just like he did and what I wrote was the same as what he wrote: I copied his lists from the slate into my schoolbook, translating from graver to ink the two buckets of coal, the vacuuming—"on the Sabbath," he had added after the activity—and everything he had recorded since he had entered our lives. He pulled the slate off its hook and propped it up against a cookbook and I copied what he had written, line after line, labor after labor. Where flash and flourish had come naturally to his writing, I imitated as faithfully as I could the exaggerated bulges of certain letters as one would copy lines in a painting. I stayed at the kitchen table and kept writing that day, copying his list again and again. He found some time in the evening to praise me, while none of the others paid attention to me, until Tusia made me move away from the kitchen table so she could prepare dinner.

Everything I wrote down spoke of the most menial labor and having Pan Najhudel in the house was like having another servant—more cultured and civilized than the village girls from the Ukraine I remember seeing pass through our house—but a servant nevertheless. With one major difference: he invented his own labors and then asked my mother if he could do them, labors that were carefully calculated to demean and humble himself.

The next afternoon Itzek Najhudel and I were

alone at home. It hadn't been planned this way—
Mother would have never allowed this—but it happened. Father was at the *Krakowski*, Mother had gone
out and Tusia—who had been told to supervise us—
had gone to our downstairs neighbors to sit in the
kitchen with their maid, and Zofia had begged to be
taken along. And I, seeing myself as the hostess of our
home—as a new *pani domu* replacing my mother—
invited Pan Najhudel into the salon, forbidden to me. I
led the way through the double doors and he followed,
hesitating at first, then falling back into the sliding gait
of his. I stepped aside to let him enter.

Emerging out of the darkness of the corridor he
slid slowly into the brightness of the room toward the
window. By the time his eyes had become accustomed
to the light he had reached the window and turned his
head to me. In the midst of the turn, his gaze was
halted by something and he literally flew back as if he
had run into the wall. He threw up his hands and covered his face now turned fully toward me.

"Are you ill, Pan Najhudel?" I walked over to him.

"No, Ala," his voice was muffled by his hands
clasped over his face.

"But what happened to you?"

"That picture. . ."

"The picture? Oh, the Mother of God. Oh, that,
we've had that for a while." I talked about it as casually as if somebody had asked me about an overcoat or
the newly installed telephone. But I didn't think in
any special way about that old wooden panel, an icon,
which my parents had hung in their salon as a conversation piece, complete with the eternal light in a red
glass, the way icons might be found in orthodox
households and in churches. My parents had ac-
quired it as a work of art—and only Tusia nodded at it
when she passed.

Maybe it was the ruby red glow from the light that had startled him, rather than the subject matter of the painting. The icon was long and thin, like a board broken from a fence, with Maria on one side of the painting and everything else—whatever might have been on it—broken off. The paint was cracked in spiky vertical lines and it looked as if the painting was wrapped in barbed wire. Her left hand rested against her cheek and with her right she reached toward the unevenly broken edge. In a violet sky hovered an angel with one azure wing while the red eternal light flickered over her impassive face.

Pan Najhudel didn't speak when I tugged on his jacket and finally I pulled him away from the window and the Madonna. After a few steps he felt safe, dropping his hands with a sigh. He seemed in shock and both of us stood in the middle of the salon; he couldn't speak and I didn't know what to do or say. Finally, I asked him to sit at the same table where we had awaited his arrival. He opened his eyes and looked at the carpet on the wall, smiling in recognition.

"Woven by the mountain men, the Huzuls."

I was pleased to show him something he didn't fear, because by now I knew that the wooden picture had scared him, the same way Zofia and I had scared each other with the drawing of the devil on the door.

"I know the Huzuls. I came down from the mountains on one of their rafts. On logs lashed together I rode down the foaming mountain rivers from the Carpathians to . . . to. . ."

"How far did you ride?"

"To the Black Sea." He fell silent leaving me to think of a solitary man dressed in black facing the crashing waves of a sea as black as the ink stains on my fingers when I copied his words.

And then he began to hum a tune I did not recognize, humming, haltingly at first, as if he tried to remember something from long ago.

"What is the song's name?" I asked.

"It's a dance called the Kolomyjka, after a town in the Carpathian mountains name Kolomyja."

"That's where my mother was born," I said proudly.

He was silent.

"Were you ever there, Pan Najhudel?"

He did not answer and instead glanced at the floor in the corner where the Virgin Mary glowed and walked wordlessly from the salon.

When the others came I didn't tell them that I had sat with Pan Najhudel. When I was alone I thought about him and I remembered him as he sat in the salon, brooding silently. When I saw him I wanted to talk to him, but when I greeted him he didn't stop walking. I fell in step with him.

"How did you get to. . ." and here I hesitated because I wanted to say *Kolomyja*, but I didn't want to startle him the way I had yesterday and so I added "the Huzuls."

He didn't look at me.

"I sold things."

I didn't ask what he sold because I feared that he might have carried a suitcase through the mountains like the old men who came to our door with a case stuffed full of shoelaces, rubber bands, spools of thread, and needles in gaudy envelopes with palm trees and pyramids. I didn't want to think of him as a peddler among the mountain men.

He walked to the apartment door and I went to my room, sad that he didn't want to be with me.

Later, during the same afternoon, I saw him talking to Mother. I watched them through the kitchen door—barely open—but not even I could understand what was being said. Mother was very agitated, her

face was red and she moved back from Pan Najhudel.
He talked in whispers to Mother and advanced in her
direction moving his black arms and legs slowly, almost like my wind-up monkey. My mother raised her
right arm and held the flat of her hand toward him, as if
to push him back. And then he stood still, his head
bowed, waiting for Mother to speak.

Just then I heard steps in the corridor behind me
and I ran back to my room.

The next day he talked to Mother and Tusia in the
corridor while I listened and watched from the door to
my room as Pan Najhudel gave to Mother what
sounded like instructions.

"Tie me up," he implored her, holding up his hands.

"No," she shrank back and in turn raised both
hands against him. "No, I cannot do that." Tusia moved
closer to Mother.

"Yes," he took one more step toward Mother and
lowered his voice. "You must," he whispered. "Take
me into that room," and he pointed at the door to the
salon. "It is important for my son's soul . . . and for
mine." Then he stepped back into the shadows by the
dresser and I could not see nor hear him.

My mother, standing stiffly against the far wall,
whispered with Tusia and then walked resolutely across
the corridor and led Pan Najhudel into the salon.

Just as I had done, I thought angrily and sadly, just
like us. Then I followed the others carefully. Mother
and Pan Najhudel stood in the corner under the picture of the Virgin Mary and waited until Tusia had carried a kitchen chair over to them. The chair was placed
before the picture and when he sat down his knees
touched the walls joined in that corner. Mother and
Tusia tied him to the back of the chair using the clothes
line from the balcony and soon his chest and legs were
crisscrossed until the whole length of the rope had

been used up. He sat and could not move and both women stood framed by the drapes of the window and watched him. But now it looked as if he had changed his mind and his courage had left him. He tried to twist his head, but somehow his head must have also been tied to the chair, although I can't see how this could have been done. And so he struggled against the ropes and when this didn't help he blinked his eyes continuously as if the Madonna in the icon hurt his eyes. Or was it the red eternal light? When Mother saw his suffering she offered to untie him, but he whispered "no" and so Mother and Tusia left him in the devotional corner. When Mother saw me in the door she angrily waved me away, but I crept back and I sat under the round table unseen by the others. He didn't know I was there as I watched him during that long afternoon. His feet tapped a rhythm and now and then a shudder would run through his bound body and he sighed and later he hummed. I wasn't sure, but I thought then that it was the melody from Kolomyja he had hummed the day before.

When the door opened I hid behind the long fringes of the tablecloth so that Mother wouldn't see me, but it was Father who came back from work. He looked at Pan Najhudel tied to a kitchen chair facing the Madonna in the corner and he shook his head and called Mother. I don't remember how long I sat under the table, but nobody missed me. Life had become very different since Pan Najhudel lived with us. We had changed and so had my parents because they allowed us to do things we could never have done before *he* came.

Later the same week—my father had just come home from the hotel and was with Mother in the salon—Itzek Najhudel appeared in the room. He suddenly stood there as if he had materialized in a flash of lightning and asked if he could talk to Mother. Usually they spoke when Father was at work and I assume that they also talked when we were at school, but what he had to say must have oppressed him so strongly that it could not wait until they were alone.

"Madame Zielinski, may I ask you to intercede on my behalf?"

My father glanced up from the journal in his hand and my mother looked at him severely, the way she did at us when we misbehaved in public.

"I beseech you, Madame Zielinski, it is for my son's . . . my own soul."

"Yes?" Mother looked annoyed at the intruder.

"Could you take me to a priest?" He stared at her with eyes at once pleading and willing her to do as he said. "A Catholic priest," he added softly.

"You can go on your own, can't you?" Father dropped the journal on the table. My mother turned at the slap of the magazine on the table top.

"No, Albin, no! Leave this to me. This man isn't Catholic, not even a Christian. How would some of our less enlightened and possibly insensitive clergy understand?"

My father looked out through the window at the acacia tree.

"Madame Zielinski, would you accompany me on this journey?"

She may have nodded, I didn't see it, but by some sign she must have agreed. After a pause Pan Najhudel continued.

"We must go in a closed coach, with curtains drawn so that no one will see us. . ."

"Why, for Heaven's sake," Father interrupted him, "this sounds like something out of Flaubert. Nonsense."

"Albin," Mother said softly.

"If any of the other Jews from the community should see me visiting a priest, they would surely stone me." Pan Najhudel did not take his eyes off Mother during the whole conversation.

"Stone you?" My mother laughed. "This isn't Palestine, this is Lvov, a big modern city. They wouldn't stone you. Not here," and she laughed again, looking for approval at my father.

"Stone you?" My father interrupted Mother's laughter, "Maybe they would after all."

"Oh, Albin, how can you say something so silly," and she laughed again, louder and higher pitched than before, at the absurdity of my father's remark.

"Zofia, you remember Stanislava Stempién being stoned on the road to Zolkiev? For preaching in the market. . ."

"Oh, but that was different, I was there with . . . with, yes it was Tusia, and they just threw some rocks at the poor nun. . ."

"What do you think stoning is?" It wasn't like Father to contradict my mother, especially in religious matters. And she didn't answer him. After a moment's thought she looked up at Pan Najhudel who was still standing in the middle of the salon and silently she nodded. And so it was decided that they would go to see a priest. By coach.

In 1939 we certainly had automobile taxis in Lvov but he insisted on a coach. As Zofia and I were watching from the window of the salon—next to each other with our elbows on the windowsill and our chins cupped in our hands, like postcard amorettes—the coach drew up in front of our door. My father had gone to the *Krakowski* and Tusia had followed my mother down the stairs to see her off, like a lady-in-waiting accompanying her queen. The coachman dismounted slowly, his top hat rakishly tilted to one side, the whip clutched in his left hand.

The sidewalk was as empty as a stage in the uneven

123

light of dusk. The acacia tree still cast shadows, whether from the fading pale sun or from the street lamp already lit, I don't know, although I tried very hard to remember every detail of that scene. We watched as if we were at the puppet theatre: the coachman bobbed like a wooden-headed puppet by his toy coach, the coach oddly foreshortened, my mother dramatically dressed in hat and veil, turning and tilting her head to wave to us with a small white handkerchief drawn from the sleeve of her dark suit. Pan Najhudel followed on her heels, dressed as always in black, but this time also wearing a black hat with fur trim, walking straight and yet smaller, as if we had shrunk him in our service. He waited in front of the coach until Mother had been helped in and then he stepped up and disappeared quickly into the interior. The coachman pulled down the shutters before he mounted his bench high above the coach. His team pulled the carriage slowly from my sight. A tattered green ribbon tied to the coachman's top hat fluttered in the evening breeze as he raised the whip over the rumps of the horses. I tried to remember everything which took place on the few steps of sidewalk, between our door and the carriage, to register every movement, texture and color, even the angle at which I observed the happenings, because it was the last time I saw Pan Najhudel.

Tusia put us to bed before either of our parents returned, but she couldn't make me fall asleep as hard as she tried by telling stories from her village and from the lives of saints. Zofia had been asleep for hours when Tusia finally gave up and left me lying in my bed waiting for the return of the coach, for my mother or for Pan Najhudel. I wasn't sure for whom I lay awake that night.

When I didn't see him in the morning—he usu-

ally was already at work when we were preparing for
school—I went to his room. As always it was hot on the
landing in front of the maid's rooms. There were three
mansards—right next to one another—built into what
once had been the attic, and I knocked on the door
next to Tusia's. I knew Pan Najhudel lived there. Or
maybe I didn't knock, just as I didn't knock when I
went into any of the rooms in our apartment, although
my father had been angry with me for doing that on
more than one occasion.

The door swung open—a thin, cheap door as if
maids had no right to privacy or security—and in the
murky light from the dormer-window I saw no one in
the bare room. My heart pounded and I was scared as I
looked around. His suitcase was still on the floor, a
book, some papers, the dark shape of his black hat on a
hook in the wall and a long black overcoat thrown
across the narrow bed. I turned around and around
looking in every corner. Where had he gone? Had he
really left without saying good-bye to me? If he had
done this to me, I swore, I would stop writing forever.

I raced back down to our apartment, leaping two
steps at a time. In the kitchen Tusia was boiling water
and there was no one in the corridor or the salon. My
sister was in our bedroom cramming books and a pencil box into her school bag. Finally, I ran from my bedroom to the balcony, flinging the door open as soon as I
reached the handle. He hung from a beam of the
porch, dressed as I had seen him last night when he
climbed into the coach. His body did not twist or sway,
but hung still.

I wish that I could say that I hadn't yelled and had
quietly gone to my room, to remember forever how
every detail looked, but instead I screamed, stumbled
backward and fell over the wooden threshhold. I
screamed again because I couldn't get away from the

body hanging above me and yet I didn't close my eyes. Looking up at the soles of his boots I saw that they began to move as if the rope still twisted and untwisted itself. I continued to look at the body as if hypnotized, along the folds of his black *kaftan*—dusty in the morning light—and at his face, swollen and disfigured like the earthen mounds pushed up by moles in our garden. I would not have recognized him for who he was: Pan Itzek Najhudel, my friend.

Then my father was there. Boots and shoes thudded and scraped next to my face, skirts swished over me, fanning me with the scent of lavender. Or was lavender on the handkerchief held to my nose? And suddenly the chickens cackled in their cages as if only now they had awakened to the rising sun. My father bent down and picked me up and I heard my sister running and screaming the way I must have sounded, or maybe I was still screaming, I don't know.

We weren't sent to school and Tusia made hot chocolate while Mother pulled off my school uniform and soon I was sitting in bed—wrapped in my bathrobe—drinking hot chocolate. I heard much commotion in the apartment. Later in the day our doctor came and took my temperature. I am ashamed to say that I enjoyed the care my parents and Tusia gave me although *he* had died just a few hours ago. Maybe the doctor prescribed something and Mother put medication into all those lemonades she made for me. I remember the small Japanese lacquered tray—shaped like a cloverleaf—on which the glass of lemonade stood. I drifted into sleep, woke up and looked at my room as if it was a foreign place, but I was not in fear and I drifted away again. Maybe he had drifted just like me, I thought, and if I kept on drifting I would be with him.

People came and went and their voices droned far

away—maybe in the salon—and they were talking about *him. He was mad . . . an anarchist . . . an enemy . . . a lunatic . . . a Jew . . . a spy . . . a Jew . . . Najhudel . . . Neuhudel . . . Itzek Najhudel . . . Itzek. . . .*

And then it was quiet and dark and already Monday morning. And still I did not have to get up and go to school—my sister had to—and Mother talked to me more than before, but not about Pan Najhudel. When I was allowed to get up—later in the week—I walked through the apartment in my bathrobe but what I wanted to do most was talk to Tusia. I sat with her in the kitchen, but however much I begged her she didn't tell me anything, not anything that mattered. So I stopped asking her and Mother about Pan Najhudel. The less they told me, the more I kept thinking about him. Assuming that I was becoming stronger they didn't follow me around on my wanderings through the apartment.

I went to the door to the balcony, listening to the soft cackling of the chickens. In the dark corridor I looked at the light beading around the edges of the door and I kept listening. From the kitchen I heard the rhythmic tock-tock-tock of a wooden spoon in a bowl. Then the chickens fell silent.

I nudged the door open. It was the old familiar porch with the cages at the far end and some wicker armchairs with faded blue cotton pillows. I did not dare to look up, but I climbed into one of the wicker chairs and slid deep down into one of its corners. I pulled the bathrobe tight around me and looked out over the wooden railing of the balcony. The acacia tree wasn't too thick with leaves that year and I could look into the chapel of the Franciscan nuns, directly at their high altar. The church was on a higher level from our street, but we were connected by a series of stairs and plateaus. Zofia and I used to run and skip up there, but it seemed to me like that had been a long time ago. I watched the nuns as they walked back and forth and I could imagine some of the Latin words they were saying right now. Down below the church were greenhouses where they raised flowers for their services. Some of the nuns were taking off the reed mats that had covered the glass all summer, to open them for the weak light of the winter sun.

The floorboards creaked behind my back. I twisted in the chair and there was Mother. She stayed behind the backrest of the wicker chair looking in the same direction as I.

"First they run to put those mats up and before you know it they run to take them down again." The chickens, agitated by my mother's presence, flapped their wings. "That's how fast the year goes by," she added slowly.

She couldn't be right. It had been a very long year. Maybe she just said this because I was sick and I wanted to stay sick, just watching the nuns—little creche figures at their dollhouse altar—scurry with mats and flowers.

After my mother stroked my hair she left. I went to the kitchen and climbed on the counter so that I could reach the slate. As I unhooked it, I looked back at the door hoping that no one would come in. Then I hurried with it to the balcony. I propped up the slate on the table where the maids killed the chickens or squabs—they never let us watch when they did it but we had listened more than once, waiting in the darkness of the corridor for the *tchuck* of the cleaver—and I dragged over the chair. Once more I began to copy everything he had written on the slate down to the I N signifying the completion of his labors. While I wrote a sparrow flew onto the porch and began to peck at the wood of the railing. I didn't stop to watch the small bird but I began the next page in my book, listing everything I saw on the balcony. Then I filled page after page, copying again from the slate. I did not notice the cold nor that it was getting dark. My hand hurt. I didn't write very well yet and when I later looked at that book there were pages filled with scribbles, carefully written, almost drawn at times, but scribbles nevertheless.

Then the door was pushed open and my father stood by my side. Without a word he scooped me from the hollow of the wicker chair and I had just time enough to reach down from his arms to grab my book from the table, clutching it as he carried me into the kitchen. While Tusia made tea, Mother began to scold me, but Father pulled her away from the table where I sat. After that I was put to bed again.

When either one of us or both of us were sick—which happened frequently—we were allowed to keep the light on in our bedroom. My mother threw one of her scarves over the lamp on my nightstand to soften the light. On that night it was a dark green scarf, a print of medieval hunting scenes with stags, boars, and what seemed a herd of hares, and I lay quietly in the greenish glow until I was drowsy. Then my sister came in, already in her nightshirt. I looked over at her bed and I saw her as she raised herself on her elbow—a dark shape beyond the reach of my pale green light—and she asked: "When you were out on the balcony today, did the dead Jew scare you?"

I gasped and then I wanted to throw my pillow at her as I had done often when we fought, but I was too tired and I fell asleep.

At the breakfast table we quarreled again. My mother scolded me for having such a puffed and swollen face. I didn't remember having cried that night. Zofia grinned at me across the table and whispered:

"The dead Jew, the dead Jew." I cried again. Mother became so angry with Zofia and with me that she reached over the counter to the cabinet and yanked the slate from its hook. She pulled with such force that its wooden frame split and the slate slipped through her hands shattering on the tiles. I leapt up and flung myself on the floor trying to cover the pieces of slate with my body. I now know how hysterical I must have appeared, but then I sobbed and screamed and after gathering a pile of pieces I hovered on all fours over the shards. One sliver slid under the table and when I crawled over to the kitchen table I saw my sister's leg come down and the tip of her black patent leather shoe kick it to the far corner of the room. Then, still on all fours under the table, I heard my mother pull Zofia from her chair so that it toppled and fell next to me. Zofia screamed, the door opened and closed and there was silence in the kitchen.

I gathered all of the pieces—at least those with writing—and carried them to my room in my apron, and assembled them in the lid of a game box. When all the pieces were laid in their proper places, I put my school book on top of them and carried the box to the balcony. I walked quietly so as not to jar the contents of the box but also so that nobody would hear me. But when I reached up to pull the handle, the door wouldn't open and it was kept locked as long as we lived in this apartment. I quietly carried the pieces of slate and my school book back to my room and once again I began to copy what he had written. Sitting on the edge of my bed I wrote on the top of my nightstand, having moved my lamp to the floor to make room for the box with the pieces of slate. When I came to the last line—the line he had signed with his initials—I saw that someone had added to his I N the letters R and I. I thought that I had made a mistake and so I moved the lamp back on the nightstand and when I switched it on I saw that these letters were really there. I sat back, suddenly scared. I couldn't imagine who might have written this and since it was printed I couldn't tell whose handwriting it was. After I had looked at it for a long time I decided to add it to my school book. From that day on I kept my writing hidden from the others.

When I asked my mother where Pan Najhudel had been buried, she didn't tell me nor did she say anything about his funeral service. And when I asked her what INRI meant she said that I should talk to a priest.

Mother took us to the Franciscan church for a talk with Father Dzukowski. Walking along the street, Mother held us by our hands. I was too nervous to play games, like walking with one leg in the gutter or hopping over sewer gratings as if hell's fires were burning beneath. Obediently by my mother's side—my clammy hand tightly gripped by her gloved one—I squeezed my eyes shut, thinking what I would say to the priest, when I blindly walked into the post of a gaslight. Mother angrily pulled me along, but I didn't cry and didn't even feel the bump growing on my forehead.

We waited in the empty church, sitting in the first row of pews by the crosswalk. Sliding nervously back and forth on the wooden bench I happened to look over at a painting on the right wall. Two rows of brown robed monks carried the body of a dead man on their shoulders.

"What is it?" I asked Mother who kept glancing at a door by the side of the altar.

"They are burying a bishop." She whispered although we were all alone in the church.

The men were all painted in profile, their shoulders bent under the weight of the body. They looked

131

straight ahead except one young monk whose round face looked directly at me, open-mouthed in amazement.

"Why is he so strange?" I nudged my mother.

"He sees the ghost of the bishop," she whispered.

His foreign almond-shaped eyes looked directly at me. Why, I thought, what have I done?

I was interrupted by steps on the stone floor. Father Dzukowski, a heavy-set man, chatted smilingly with Mother, calling her "my dear Zofia." Then he talked to us twins, fancifully naming us "the alpha and omega"—as he always did, because our first names began with letters from each end of the alphabet—and, after he paused to wheeze, he added "the which is and which was and which is to come."

I couldn't wait any longer.

"What does INRI mean?" I was so eager to know that I clutched the edge of the prayer bench.

He looked Mother and she winked at him.

"Iesus Nazarenus Rex Iudaeorum."

I wanted to ask something but as soon as she stopped speaking Mother made us kiss his ring—a turquoise surrounded by diamonds—embedded in a flabby hand. When he patted us on our heads I looked up into his jovial face—jowly and crowned by a fringe of red hair—and I innocently sensed that he knew nothing of Itzek Najhudel just as Mother didn't understand about the strange young monk who stared at me from the painting.

I didn't speak on the way home. When we came into the kitchen Tusia saw the bump on my forehead and pressed the heavy cool blade of a butcher knife against it.

"So you won't look like a goat before its horns grow out," she said holding the knife down, "or like a little devil."

Since they did not speak about him when I was present, I withdrew. It was then, my mother said, that I became different from my sister. She surely must have guessed the reason for my changes. I sat in the kitchen or by the dining room table—only when there was no one there—and wrote in my school notebooks. I was bent over the open books, often in the twilight after school, my eyes close to the thin blue lines, my cheek almost touching the paper, writing carefully the tall "T"s and "F"s slashing like lightning, as I recorded everything I could feel and touch, but above all else, everything I could see, writing in a hand that was not mine.

My sister now quarreled even more with me and I became secretive. My face became different from hers, gaunter, its shape triangular instead of round. I know, because I still have a photo taken when we were vacationing and we were swimming in the river Prut. Big somber eyes in a thin face staring out over the surface of the muddy water. Children don't look like this anymore.

My mother worried about my cheerlessness, the drudgery of my writing and most of all about my frequent vomiting. She took me to our doctor who patted me on my page boy, pressed a spoon handle on my tongue—I retched and threw up at his feet—and then took my temperature. After that he whispered with Mother by a muslin screen hiding the window, but I heard what they whispered, just as I heard what was being said in our house ever since his death. But the doctor was wrong, it wasn't Itzek Najhudel who caused my illness, the others were making me sick.

I must have fainted at the doctor's office, because I was back again in the green glow of my lamp. My sister was temporarily moved out of our bedroom and I spent days and nights in silence. Mother and Tusia looked after me, but I was also left alone for what seemed to me long hours. Father came and brought me a small table and two chairs he had made for our doll house. He was kind and gentle and it was nice that he had made the furniture. But they didn't understand, I merely wanted to follow *his* hand, indeed, become *his* hand and write down what I saw and heard and they wouldn't let me do it. So I lay and listened and tried to remember.

One day I heard voices from the salon, all of them female. Mother and her friends, I thought. I heard the name "Najhudel" several times and then Mother spoke for a long time.

"But he didn't have a son," a voice shrilled. I couldn't imagine which of Mother's friends that could be. I sat up in my bed.

"He was not even married." It was the same voice, then others said, "Shh, shhh," and the first voice spoke again, "And it was *he* and not his nonexistent son who was involved with a Catholic woman."

I got close to the door and then crawled back into my bed. Which woman? I was confused. But it didn't very much matter to me what was being said in the salon. I felt jealous, angry that maybe this woman made him die, but I refused to want to know anything they were saying. I just wanted to write my lists. Lying awake that night I looked at the green scarf and I traced the lines of hares with my fingertips and I wished life were as orderly as the green hunt.

During those days in bed I didn't want anything to eat but one day as I was lying there I sniffed—Tusia was frying potatoes— and I called my mother and told her that I wanted to be in the kitchen and eat with the others. Zofia moved back into our room and brought some flowers Mother surely had given her for me. Later Mother let me have my school book to write my lists and when she sat on the edge of my bed she stroked my hair and called me for the first time *wyliczajko*, my little listmaker. I wasn't sure that I wanted her to stroke my hair and hug me, and yet I did.

They tried to make us a happy family again. On a Sunday Uncle Maniu came and brought his camera. We were dressed in our best and our hair had been brushed until it gleamed. When the flash powder exploded my sister and I embraced under the stern but loving gaze of Mother. When the plate was developed my mother hung the photo, now in a golden frame, on the Huzul wall carpet. Not above it or next to it; she pinned the hook directly to a strand of the fabric in the middle. And there we were upon the old jagged patterns from the mountains, pinned between the blood red jaws of the triangles jutting out from the left and right, a design as old as the mountains were. "They kill for love," as a popular song said, that we had learned from one of the maids.

It was a proper ceremony with coffee and cake and Uncle Maniu and Aunt Lola toasted us as if we were princesses. My parents acted as if all was well now, but I lived in the shadow of the hanging man and I did not forget.

There was something odd about the picture of us twins pinned to the Huzul carpet, because, once again, I look exactly like my sister.

Through all the events of the fall and winter of that year—the beginning of the war and the Soviet occupation of Lvov—I kept writing my lists. One late afternoon in the November of 1939—the darkness settled fast—I saw from our balcony overlooking the Kurkova Ulica how a line of trucks began to form at the intersection at the bottom of the hill. I was called inside because it was cold, but my mother checked on them from time to time. But the trucks stayed in a

135

mute drab line and through the silence of the night we heard their billowing tarpaulins snap in the wind. By the time I woke up, the trucks were gone.

When Father came home for lunch he told Mother that the deportations had begun, but nobody knew how the people on the trucks had been picked: Poles, Ukrainians, workers, intellectuals, richer people. It made no sense, he said.

"Where are they going?" Mother asked worriedly.

"Siberia. . ."

"Siberia, Siberia," she interrupted him impatiently, "everybody is always being exiled to Siberia, like Dostoievsky. At least he knew why he was being sent, but what have we done?"

"And Algeria," Father added softly.

"Algeria? But that's in Africa. Are you sure, Albin?"

"That is what I heard. Some are being sent to the west of Poland occupied by the Germans."

Mother didn't speak for some time, then she asked, not looking at my father nor at me standing in the doorway:

"What is best, what is worst for us?"

Father looked at me and came over and patted me on the cheek, but then he closed the door in my face.

That evening and the following nights we stood on the balcony and waited for the arrival of the trucks. Later in my room I wrote the lists: five trucks, two trucks—on a very quiet night—four trucks, seven trucks. Mother multiplied the number of trucks with the number of people she thought might fit into such a truck, but I was content just to note the number of trucks, because that was all I could see. I didn't worry about deportation like my parents did, because I didn't understand what it meant.

When our turn finally came—we were being repatriated to Warsaw—I knew that we would never come back to this apartment and I wanted to grieve and cry as best as I could. Uncle Maniu and Aunt Lola came to help us. Amid the packing and in the rush of carrying everything down to the truck on time, I forgot to cry. Riding on the truck as it climbed up the steep hill was a new excitement and by the time I remembered to glance over the tailgate our house looked already small and insignificant and not much different from the other houses on the street.

Although the Huzul mat was left behind on the wall of our apartment, to this day I can still see its geometric pattern before my eyes, severe and demanding, and I can hear Pan Najhudel's voice as he answered my questions about the people who had woven the mat.

"How did you learn about those people?"

"I wandered through their villages in the dark forest . . . and I hear the Huzuls singing in the night."

"Huzuls . . . what a funny name. I know Huzuls from my vacation, but what does the funny name mean?"

"Ala, they didn't call themselves Huzuls. Foreigners named them that to make fun of them. They call themselves *Chrystyjani*."

"What does that mean?"

"Christians."

And I still hear my father's voice—although I think less often of him than of my mother—singing as he marched us girls around and around the Christmas table, walking in front of us as if he were leading a procession, singing with his high voice:

Pójdzmi wszyscy do stajenki
do Jezusa, do panienki. . .

And I hear our small voices singing as we marched

137

after him through the flickering candlelight, marching
and singing "do Jezusa, do Jezusa," to Jesus, to Jesus.

✻   ✻   ✻

A bucket clatters at the door followed by a
small cough.

"I really need to do this room. How much longer
are you going to be?"

With my back to the woman in the door I rum-
mage for a handkerchief. I try, but can't answer and
after some hesitation she tells me in a resigned voice
that she'll be back later.

As I grope on the mattress for a handkerchief my
fingers touch the mahogany box. Should I open it?
What would I find? My mother had been the last one
alive who could have given an answer to the questions
of that night when *he* died. Did he confess at church?
Can you even confess when you are not Catholic? I
don't know, because I don't go to church anymore. But
if there was a confession and there was penance,
where was absolution? There he hung—I will always
see him—twisted into saintliness. For what? Whose
fault was it anyway? Who was guilty? Who killed him?
Maybe, like the Golem in the legend, he should not
have left the house? And what happened to us in those
years after his death, our lives blighted and cut short?
And it all began with his death, he left us first, then
Tusia fled to her village in the Ukraine, which was destroyed in the summer of 1941. My sister Zofia was
lost from us between the Warsaw Uprising in 1944 and
Vienna, where my father died, a week after we finally
had been allotted our own apartment, once again. And
now my mother is dead, here in America. And although my sister was found many years after the war,
she is dead to me.

Between my palms I hold the inlaid lid of the box,

inlaid with flower petals like a spiny star. The lock had been pried open, not by a thief but by my mother when she lost the key. A bundle of airmail letters from Poland fills almost the whole box. Most of them are written by Aunt Lola and I know all of them because my mother had read them so often to me. A photo is lodged among the letters, a picture taken of us twins some time before our first birthday. I wipe my eyes to see more clearly. Two pairs of eyes, set in faces wider than high, gaze solemnly at me. The two bodies, swathed in layers of baby clothes, look like one with our heavy heads balanced on ornate lace collars like exotic food on baroque platters. In the darkness behind us smiles Mother.

Lifting out the whole stack of letters I find beneath it a smaller bundle of papers, covered like a web from edge to edge with my mother's handwriting. Picking it up eagerly I see that these aren't papers at all, but the white cardboard nylon stockings are folded over. The first card is covered with a copy of a poem by Maryja Konopnicka—a woman writer—from Lvov like us. I often saw her grave at the cemetery, with her head in bronze on her tombstone. Although I liked another grave much better that had a monument of a man on it, but also of his dog, who had died faithfully on his master's grave. The poem, which she must have copied from memory, is about a young blond boy in court facing a stern judge. I turn to the next card and find the same poem again, and so on the next and the next after. Each stocking card is covered by the same poem, a diatribe against social injustice toward women and children, a special concern of this poet.

I drop the cards on the mattress and feel with my fingers for anything hidden in the box. In one corner nestle our *Nazaretanki* badges, the pale blue enameled crosses we had worn on the berets of our school uniforms. Weighing them in the hollow of my hand like coins to be spent, I slide the fingers of my other hand across the backs of the badges and feel that one of the pins is broken off. Putting my reading glasses on I can decipher our student numbers engraved on the back of each badge. The one with the lower number must be mine, because my name comes first in the alphabet, so the damaged one has to be my sister's. I drop the badges on the nightstand and once more I let my fingers slide over the smooth wood of the box, feeling in every corner, but there are no hidden compartments, there is nothing left. I don't know what I wanted Mother to leave me in her mahogany box. An incriminating letter, a confession, or at least a grey sliver of slate in one of its dusty corners?

Is that all that is left of us? I have done my part, I have written all those years. In writing it down I thought that I could save everything and if I saved it all, all would have meaning. But it did not.

Now I am piling the stocking cards, the letters and the photo back into my mother's mahogany box—closing the lid as best as I can over the tongue of the broken lock—and then I place the box on top of the pillows in the bag and tie it up. All that is left for me to do is the nightstand. I put the picture tree into another bag without looking at the photos of the family; that wouldn't help me now. The Christmas tree is a problem for me. The way I feel I can't strip the decorations off. At the best of times this is a melancholy task for me and in the last few years I have taken the tree down later and later. So I slip the whole tree with all of its bells, glass balls, handcarved soldiers, miners and shepherds, into a greenish plastic bag, the kind I use in the fall to hold raked leaves.

The badges. I pick them up and look at them once more—the light blue cross on the ornate golden

background—then I step over to the mirror and pin mine to the lapel of my suit. Then I carry the bags to the storage room down the hall. Christmas music comes from the dining room. I walk slowly back to her room and pause in the door to look for her wheelchair, the way I had stopped to look those nights I had visited. I hear the rustling of quick movements from behind the dividing curtain; walking softly to the curtain I pull it back and see Mrs. Teleshkin with her hand on my mother's nightstand.

"Mrs. Teleshkin, you know that this is not your room."

She looks up at me as if she doesn't understand the meaning of my words. Then she blinks and begins to mumble—in halting Russian—"The Heaven's angry face is scowling."

"Mrs. Teleshkin, this is not your room," I repeat, summoning all of my strength to sound stern. Why do I bother and what does it matter if she is here or there? My mother is gone. The Heaven's angry face is scowling. Then I say it aloud:

"The Heaven's angry face is scowling."

"High over the swiftly swirling snow," she smiles at me, glad that I finally understand her meaning. Now I, too, remember. Pushkin's "Winter Evening," dedicated to his old nurse. We had to learn it by heart in our Russian class, and Mrs. Teleshkin had to learn it, too, many years before me.

"Do you know the next line, Mrs. Teleshkin?"

She stands very still in front of me, her arms hanging quietly by her side as her lips silently search for words learned seventy years ago. She finally nods and begins to recite slowly at first and then finding the rhythm, happy to please me, like an obedient school girl.

141

The Summer House

> Here in our dwelling old and roomy,
> Dilapidated, sad and dark;
> Companion, nurse, old woman gloomy,
> Why sit you silent. . .

In the middle of the last line I reach for her hands and in clutching them I feel the shape of my sister's badge in the palm of her hand. Looking into her eyes—their blue almost faded away—I say the lines of the poem with her and I speak words I have not thought for many years, but now they flood back, welling up in me like tears, telling of a bluebird beyond the sea and mourning the maiden who fetched water in the mornings. When one of us falters she only has to listen to the other one and look at the lips speaking a language which has grown foreign to them. We say the lines in unison, stumbling only here and there, until we come to

> Come let us drink, before we slumber
> You kindest friend of early days

and now I cannot help myself and I cry as I look into her creased face, listening to her words whose meaning she might not understand anymore. *You kindest friend from early days.* I press her hands and when she recites the last line she sighs and smiles, relieved to have finished. I hug her stooped bony shoulders and cry and she reaches up to me and pats me on the back.

Slowly I walk her down the bright corridor to her room and I hold her arm. Yes, I will come to see you tomorrow night. She smiles slyly like an old peasant because she still clutches the badge in her hand.

II
The Winter House

A Death
In A Quiet Town ─────

The rain had stopped just outside of Salzburg, and
as I drove from the cool green woods near St. Wolfgang
and the Moon Lake to Linz, the landscape changed
into the gentle dullness of Upper Austria. I had been
sent here from Essen by our law firm to locate a grave
and arrange for its care. More than ten years had
passed since the war ended, yet many still hoped to
find survivors; when they failed they wanted graves.
There was nothing in the soft meadows, lowing cows,
and prosperous brick buildings around me to remind
of fire and death—yet here, outside Germany, I
thought more about the war than when I was home. I
had still been in school when the war ended, had cowered in the shelters with the women and the other children. Why did those memories return so strongly

when I crossed the border? I rolled the window down and breathed the fresh, rain-washed air.

Late in the afternoon I arrived in Payerbach, a small quiet town in the shadow of the Rax and checked into the Horn-Hof, whose facade, unlike the other buildings in town I had seen, was freshly painted. I decided to start my search for the grave while sunlight still slanted into the narrow valley. If I found it soon, maybe I could leave sometime tomorrow and spend a day in Vienna.

The graveyard clung to the flank of a steep hill, and the earth-filled steps, bulging and splitting their pineboards, were high and hard to climb. I imagined the pallbearers of a black funeral train struggling and swaying uphill under the weight of the dead. Unaccustomed to the altitude, I sat down on a narrow bench near a worn headstone and looked over the deep valley growing darker in the gathering twilight.

A man spoke behind me with the evenly droning voice of a museum guide. "Payerbach was a nice town . . . before the war, that is." He added, in the tradition of the Alps, "*Grüss Gott*." I stood up to bow and shake his hand, for he was old and it was only proper.

"Yes, quite a nice place before the war. Everyone who mattered came here from Vienna and the rich and the noble mingled, or that is at least what the rich thought." He chuckled wickedly at his observation. "They used to stay at Fischer's—do you know the town at all? No? Fischer's is a hotel on the road to Reichenau, near the viaduct." He gestured in the opposite direction from my hotel. "Quite naturally, many had their own grand houses here and there are still a few of those palaces left. And some of our summer guests stayed on. . ." He smiled and pointed to the faded headstones around him, stones bearing noble names and plumed crests.

"I come up here every day and if there is anything you want, young man, I will help you. Age brings love of youth and youth brings. . ." He stopped for a moment and he shrugged off the rest of the sentence. "Yes, I will help you." He nodded and his threadbare green lodencoat flapped against his thin body. Then he pulled off his black felt hat and his straggly white hair blew in the breeze.

After a time he said, "The townspeople climb up here reluctantly, just for the funeral ceremony, and afterwards they scurry down those steps, without greeting each other, without even a drink at the inn. The whole burial is indecently rushed. None of the old customs. The *pompes funèbres* . . . the horses swathed in black velvet caparisons and nodding plumes . . . prancing. . ." He laughed and his legs moved as if he heard the dirge. Then he leaned back against an alabaster angel poised for flight, but with one of its wings broken off.

"Are you looking for someone?"

I told him of my assignment, the request from the United States, a lady in Boston, who wanted to provide funds for the planting of flowers on the grave each season.

The old man nodded. "I know many of the dead and properly my stone should be among theirs. Over the years I have scratched the moss and lichen off some of the older headstones and I have traced their names with my fingertips. . ." His hands slid over the face of the stone supporting the one-winged angel. "Whose grave are you trying to unearth?" He laughed grimly at his pun.

"Golik," I said.

"Golik?"

"Charles-Louis Golik."

He laughed, "And Charles-Louis yet. Viennese

147

parvenu, no doubt." He shrugged. "Golik?" He shrugged again, apologetic. "One really got to know only the people of one's own class." He smiled. "I never knew a Golik." He pronounced this name with such distaste that deep lines fanned from the corners of his ancient mouth.

Not wishing to irritate him further I said I would come back in the morning and look at some of the stones. "My name is Heinsius," I said, "of the firm of Mollenhauer and Faber in Essen. . ."

"Essen? I was in Essen once, to visit the Krupp factory," and he smiled mildly at me.

"Will you be back here tomorrow?"

"Of course. Where else would an old man go?"

"May I ask you your name, Sir?"

"No name, young man. Since they took away our titles, after the war . . . the other war. . ." His voice drifted, then he looked back and smiled and whispered, ". . . the *other* war. For you in Germany, even now, a duke is still a duke and he has his crown. You know about the treaties of St. Germain and Rapallo—for you. . ." and he pointed vaguely to the north, "for you, it was Versailles, but for us here in Austro-Hungary it was Rapallo. Since then my name sounds rather bald and I don't like to use it."

I bowed with embarrassment. "Till tomorrow, then," I said, trying to sound cheerful. "Till tomorrow."

He nodded, smiled and shook my hand politely and firmly. His fingers were cold and quickly his hand disappeared behind his back. As if he were reciting a line from a play he added: "It was so nice. I enjoyed it so much." Black hat in hand, he walked off solemnly, his head bowed, until he disappeared down the steep steps into the valley of Payerbach.

I walked over to the rail at the head of the steps and looked down. Not a single light shone from the houses clustered like earthen mounds in the falling darkness.

The dining room of the hotel was empty. I ordered a *Pariser schnitzel* from the man who had carried my suitcases and who, I learned, was Herr Brack, owner of the Horn-Hof. He came to my table after I began to eat, bowed from his waist, clicked his heels lightly, and asked if he might join me. I spooned the sour milk of my cucumber salad and nodded. The waitress brought him wine and he began talking. I wondered if he thought that by telling me local stories he could persuade me to stay indefinitely in the most expensive room and take all my meals here.

What he said didn't interest me much— pleasantries about Germany and how wonderful the German officers had been who stayed in his hotel during the last war. I didn't order dessert and got up with an excuse, leaving the innkeeper standing behind the big round table, bowing slightly while I walked into the night.

Beside the river, channeled narrowly in concrete, I came upon a rambling old house. Barely visible letters on a crooked sign proclaimed this ruin to be "Fischer," and I recalled that the old man in the cemetery had mentioned this as the hotel where the rich Viennese had stayed. It sat back from the road in a black, overgrown garden, the building's bulk emphasized by the cottages pressing against its base. Stories of wooden balconies jutted over planked verandas and covered walks, and outside stairwells spilled from the dark shelter of the overhanging roof, flooding the weeds with rotten wood. Scabby window shutters, painted red and white, hung askew. Huge turrets loomed over the edifice.

I could hear Herr Faber's voice booming through our offices, with just a hint of Westphalian dialect to sustain the impression of his harmlessness: "We would have cleaned this up ten years ago. Slovenly brothers, the Austrians; could never rely on them in the war either."

I walked slowly back the way I had come. Not a single light shone anywhere, although it was only nine o'clock. I did not meet anyone in the streets. When I was almost at my hotel, I saw at last a lighted place. It was Buchta's *Konditorei*, a combined pastry-shop and coffeehouse with a gold-lettered glass door. The door creaked and jarred to a stop on the uneven floor as I opened it; the only sound heard inside was the echo of the rattling door pane. The room was so bright that my eyes took time to adjust and I saw the marble-topped tables and the chairs, shiny with black lacquer.

One table was occupied by two men so bent over a chessboard that their heads nearly touched over the black and white figures. From the other end of the room came a small man who looked at me like a mourner.

"*Grüss Gott*," he said and asked me what I wanted.

"Ice cream," I said. He barely opened his dry lips, "No ice, sorry." He spoke faintly, but the two chess players drew their heads back and looked over as if he had shouted. I stood and stared at them until their heads melted together again over their chessboard.

When I pulled the door shut I stood under the low branches of a big linden tree in bloom and its smell rose sweetly in my nose. I stopped under the tree and in a moment everything was back that had been lost: the window from my room facing the linden trees of our street back home in Silesia, before the fire, before the exodus. At night the smell drifted through my open window and I could hear the older boys outside talking to girls; I could hear their whispers, their laughter, the rustling of leaves. During the day boys scampered into the trees, gathering linden blossoms in pillow cases hung around their necks, to sell for herb tea. I took a few deep breaths, letting the air wheeze from my lungs and then I threw my arms up into the sweet smell and gulped the dusty fragrance of the yellow-winged linden blossoms until my chest hurt and I felt giddy.

The hotel was only a few more steps through the darkness. The innkeeper, sitting behind the same table where I had left him, waved and called me over to join him. Amber wine glasses stood in a neat row before him. I walked over to his table and he looked straight at me. Until then I had never looked directly into his face. When he had checked me in, taken my passport, made me fill out the police registration forms and waited on my table, he had never looked at me with his yellow hunting-dog eyes.

"Sit down, Herr Heinsius." He pointed to an ornately painted chair next to him, a chair done in peasant style with red and blue flowers. After a time he said, "Where did you go, Herr Heinsius?"

I told him I'd gone for a short walk and had found a derelict house with red and white shutters.

"Fischer's," he said. "We love to paint things red and white around here. Do you know how we got red-white-red as our national colors?"

When I said nothing, he hurried on, "It may be just some story. Maybe a legend. A knight rode into combat wearing his armor and over it his white battle shirt. Then he belted on his sword." He leaned back into his chair. "I don't know when all of this happened. After he was victorious the knight's battle dress had been drenched with the blood of his foes and the only part that had escaped the blood and had stayed white was the center portion of his battle shirt protected from the gushing blood by his broad sword belt." He

151

laughed and drank a slow sip. "So you see, blood was at the beginning of our history, our flag—"

I interrupted him. "From there I went to get a fruit-ice at the *Konditorei*, but he didn't have any."

"Do you want some dessert?" he offered. "Maybe a plate of *Salzburger nockerl*?"

Briefly, I considered ordering *nockerl*, puffed clouds of egg white and powdered sugar, but thought better of it. The too-sweet smell of the linden blossoms still lingered heavily in my throat.

"Thank you, no, but I'll have a wine and soda."

"Josefa!" he called to an anemic-looking girl polishing glasses at the bar. She poured wine and splashed soda from a seltzer bottle. She wore a poorly fitting black dress and took the row of empty wine glasses from our table, smiling at the innkeeper, and placing full glasses before us.

"So you were at Buchta's," he said.

"I guess that was the name of the place. It's hard to tell. Everything is so dark in your town."

"Did he say anything nasty?"

I looked away, "No. He just didn't have any ice."

He thought about my answer.

"Maybe you didn't talk enough so that he could hear. Hear you really speak, so that he knew you were from across the border." He made a derogatory sweep across the table. "He doesn't like Germans. They hanged his wife."

"The Germans?"

"The SS. You know all the nice German officers I told you had stayed at this hotel? That was a lie. No nice officers. No nice Germans. The whole place swarmed with the silver skull of the SS. They weren't the blacks, the political SS, but a group just back from fighting partisans in the Ukraine. They took over the whole house, from the cellar to the maids' rooms, your room, my room. That was in the spring of 1945. Josefa, bring two more!"

My impulse was to leave. His words and tone upset me. But I stayed. Nothing is gained by flinching.

"The SS found out that when the Russians came the Buchta woman was going to hoist a white flag. I watched her execution from the kitchen window. At that time I had just come back from the Russian front with a shoulder wound, shot straight through." He swiveled in his chair, pointing his once wounded shoulder at me. "It was an early morning, bright and pleasant. I was frying eggs on the stove near the window, frying eggs for *them*. I watched her being taken from the *Konditorei*. One put a rope over a low branch, another lifted her up, as if he was going to give her a ride on his shoulder. He lifted her up and just dropped her and they came back in, ate their eggs and complained because there was no meat on the table. That was all. Those were your nice Germans."

I said nothing.

"The reason I looked at all through the window was because she screamed. The fat sizzled on the stove and the window was closed, but I could still hear her screams. She screamed and did nothing but scream. She walked between these two soldiers in their grey-green uniforms and heaved those high-pitched screams."

He suddenly stood up and clutched the edge of the table, bunching up the tablecloth in his fists, so that the glasses swayed and clanked against each other, and he tilted his head back and screamed three times against the dark-beamed ceiling. I gripped the arms of my chair and glanced over at Josefa, who looked steadily at the screaming man. Her shining eyes were the only life in her sallow face and her dull black uniform absorbed the light like a sponge in the corner where she stood.

The innkeeper stood silently at the table now, and kept his head cocked as if he expected screams to echo from the dark corner. He lifted his glass and looked at the bubbles clinging to its curved amber belly.

"One of them bent down and put his silver-braided shoulder against the inside of her knee and wrapped his right arm around both of her legs, while another slipped the noose around her neck. The one who had lifted her stepped suddenly back and she dangled from the tree, trying to take the weight off her neck by kicking her legs as high as she could. Her skirts billowed as she kicked the tree. One soldier came back and, reaching up into the green branches, pulled sharply at her legs. And it's true, I swear it by the Virgin Mary, I heard the crack of her neck break-ing through all the bubbling and exploding grease in my frying pan and through the closed windows. Then she went limp and hung there among the leaves. And the soldiers had their eggs. That, my dear Herr Heinsius is why Buchta doesn't like Ger-mans and that is why nobody in Payerbach likes Germans. Josefa, another. . ."

I interrupted and said that I wanted to go up to my room. He nodded and bowed, I don't know whether from politeness, condescension or irony. From the stairs I looked down through the baroque banister posts and saw him standing alone at the table until Josefa walked over to him and put her face against his chest. If he was aware of her he gave no indication. I looked at them a while longer through the railing, past thick pillars painted over and over with red hearts and blue forget-me-nots.

The room was ice cold and I groped through the dark to close the window before I switched on the

lamp on my nightstand. Its small circle of light warmed
me, and fell on things I had laid out that afternoon: the
travel alarm clock, ticking almost noiselessly in its
leather case; a small leather-bound Bible which I
rarely read anymore, but carried on my trips; and a
paperback edition of Camus's *Plague*. Its shiny cover
of yellows, pale orange and hospital-green reflected a
smudge of light onto the ceiling. It was still chilly, but
this cold room was better than being downstairs with
the raving innkeeper, or out in the quiet town smoth-
ered by night.

I undressed and slid under the covers, but the
sheets were clammy and stiff and the bed was too
short. Pulling my knees up as high as I could I lay on
my side staring into the room. This is what Harker
must have felt like in *Nosferatu* when he entered the
land of the vampires. True, I had met some inhabitants: the disgruntled old aristocrat in the graveyard,
the innkeeper and Josefa, the sullen men in the
Konditorei. Others had to be somewhere, perhaps
hiding in their houses behind thick walls, peeking
out from small, deep-set windows shuttered against
the night.

Early morning filled the room with noise and an
impure grey light which made everything look tawdry.
Leaning out the narrow window, I saw no one in the
street and couldn't find what had awakened me. I
dressed and walked downstairs to the lobby. I heard
footsteps behind me. It was Brack, the innkeeper.

"*Grüss Gott*, Herr Heinsius. I'm sorry about last
night, I hope you took no offense . . . too much wine."
He performed his tightly executed ritual of bowing
stiffly, smiling and clicking his heels. "And if I insulted
you, forgive me, I beg you to forgive me . . . the wine,
you know." He smiled once more. "In vino veritas," he
said. "You know about the truth in wine. It may be as

bad for me as for you." He paused, laughed and showed me his gold-filled teeth. As an afterthought he added: "It was so nice. I enjoyed it so much." I said nothing and his mouth stayed open, the dim morning light gleaming from his metal fillings.

I walked in the same direction I had taken last night and stopped at the dirty window of the *Konditorei*. The door was propped ajar with a zinc bucket. I rapped the thin glass and Herr Buchta appeared, trying to tie the strings of his apron behind his back.

"What can I do for you, Sir?"

"I've had no breakfast. Perhaps you could. . ."

"Certainly, Sir. Some coffee, a boiled egg or two, some fresh rolls?"

"That sounds so nice, thank you."

He took two black lacquered chairs off the marble table near the window. "Here you are. I'll only be a minute."

The window was open and the smell of the linden tree drifted into the cold empty room. Everything outside was dusted with the tree's yellow pollen, blown by the wind into sulphur dunes against the tree and the wall of the *Konditorei*. I leaned back and sniffed the air. Mine had been a quiet street, but on Wednesdays the drum and fanfare corps of the Hitler-Jugend came and practiced on the greensward right by our house. My father hated the noise of the heavy lansquenet drums that boomed into our home. I used to watch the young men from the window of my room, but my father hated the noise. Maybe it had been more than the noise, but at that time he didn't dare tell me.

A small girl walked by the window, her red dress flashing in the pale rays of the early sun. Her shoes scraped the sidewalk and she wailed like a siren.

"Here is your coffee and egg. If there is anything

else I can do, let me know. Oh yes—I've sent out for fresh rolls. Mine are from yesterday."

And the whole time the little girl howled along the street. I remembered being shaken in the middle of the night and packed off to the shelter.

Herr Buchta left, then returned a few minutes later with crisp rolls on his plate. "She has always wailed like that," he said,"—at least since she could walk and talk. As you can see, she wasn't even born until the war was long over. She isn't quite right up here." He pointed his thin finger at the middle of his wrinkled forehead.

Before he could say anything else the little girl passed by again, filling the room with a siren's long wail. She circled the tree and disappeared down the street in clouds of yellow dust spreading the sweet pollen of the linden tree through the town.

"They throw rocks at her. Sometimes she's bleeding, cowering behind a bush, wailing."

"Somebody should do something."

"Nobody ever does anything."

I shook my head and decided to say to him what I had come to say. "Herr Buchta, I am very sorry about your wife's death. The innkeeper told me about it last night."

"Yes, it's sad, but years ago."

"The innkeeper said that everybody here, and you in particular, hates Germans."

"Oh, the innkeeper. . ." he paused as if to spit. "He should watch himself and not talk so much. It was the war, you know, the war." His voice grew louder to drown out the wailing of the child, who was returning to the tree. "It was a bright day. Not like now. I don't know what causes this weather. . ." He stopped and turned away, wiping the marble top of the table with his damp rag. "They took her right through the door you came in by. One of the soldiers walked first, then she, then the other soldier, leaving the door ajar." He wiped another table and came back. "And there she was. I could see everything from the upstairs window. I wasn't drafted because of my weak chest." He coughed a few times to convince me. "She was a small woman, no match for the men who took her out to the tree. She was so small she swayed in the breeze. The rope was a proper executioner's rope made from black and white strands. There was no trial, just the hanging . . . and the proper rope. It twisted and untwisted, turning her slowly, the way she used to turn to show me a new dress."

He took my dishes and wiped the table again, leaving the marble clammy beneath my hands. Tears filled every line of his face.

I walked all through Payerbach; the place was undistinguished and worn as a piece of driftwood. Shabby store signs shuddered in the grey air. A circular band pavilion hunched in a brown park like an empty shell left gaping on the sand, senseless in its carved splendor. No orchestra would ever play there again. The floor had been pulled up, probably used as firewood. Houses were piled around the park, with dusty displays and faded posters in the shops.

Near noon I stopped in a small *gasthaus* under the viaduct. I ordered and had every intention of eating, but I had to ask just one more person about the hanging. I can't remember what the waiter looked like, but he talked to me, at first reluctantly, then freely.

"Were you here when it happened?" I asked.

"Yes. I wasn't drafted. I worked as a foreman in the factory over the mountains in Hirschwang."

"I talked to Buchta at the *Konditorei*. About the hanging."

The man was silent.

"Did you see the hanging?"

"All of us did."

"The whole town?"

He nodded, then stood sullenly at my table. "All of us saw it, but some of us not on the first day."

I was stunned. "You mean she hung there longer than *one* day?"

"Just until dark, every day. When the vesper bells rang the soldiers marched up to the tree, like taking down the flag. They took her down, carried her over to the hotel's basement and hid her there through the night so nobody would sneak over in the dark and bury her. She was supposed to show us—in death, of course—what would happen to traitors and defeatists. Every morning they marched back and hung her in the tree."

"How long did it last?"

"Four weeks."

"How many marched and carried her?"

He looked away and didn't speak.

"How many carried her?"

"All of them."

The evening was dark and smoke heaved in brown bands over the valley. I went back to the cemetery. The pineboard steps seemed higher than last night.

The old man was here at the same grave as yesterday. "How was your day in Payerbach?" he asked. "You're late," he added curtly.

"You waited for me?"

"You're late. Did you find a trace of. . ."

"Golik," I said. "No. Last night and today I was told of an execution, a hanging during the war. I followed it up."

"Yes, the hanging at the pastry-shop." He smiled. "The Russians didn't come for another month, but the Buchta woman they hanged."

159

I sat down on the narrow bench and he stood leaning against the alabaster angel. "Why does everybody say, 'It was *so* nice. I enjoyed it *so* much'?" I asked. "You said it yourself and I've heard it from others."

"It was *sooo* nice. I enjoyed it *sooo* much." He smiled again, savoring the drawn out sounds. "Our emperor used to say it. Franz Josef used that phrase for many decades, with his hands folded behind his back."

"But why?" I asked impatiently.

The old man slowly shook his head, "Once in his life he spoke his mind, after the opera had been built on the Ringstrasse in Vienna. He criticized the building and the architect put a bullet through his brain. After that, our emperor confined his public utterances to 'It was *so* nice. I enjoyed it *so* much.' And he stood by for more than half a century with his hands behind his back while all Europe went up in flames." The old man fell silent. At last he said, "He once stayed at Fischer's. There are not many of us left. . ." He started to mumble, but suddenly he jerked his head back up and he looked out over the valley again.

"Look down there, to the left of the wooden cross. That is the Horn-Hof, your hotel. You can't see the trap door leading to the basement—that's where they brought the body out every morning. Through that door. By now you know who turned her in."

"The innkeeper?"

"Such men would have been impossible in my time. There was honor in the ranks. . ."

Fatigue made me less polite. "Where were *you* when she was hanged?"

"I was there. I was right there with everybody else." He was eager to admit that he was a witness. The old man closed and opened his eyes slowly.

I said, "It must have been a ghastly experience to have the town terrorized by a troop of the SS. . ."

160

"A troop?" He tilted his head until his right ear touched my mouth.

I said, "The innkeeper told me about it and so did Buchta himself. All the SS troops, the detachment in the hotel. . ."

The old man straightened up and laughed in a way I had never heard anyone laugh before. "A troop . . . a detachment! Did you know how many there were? Two! *Two!* And not even their uniforms with all the silver skulls, braids and medals could make them look bigger. Two men."

"That's not possible," I said. " Who carried her into the tree and guarded her corpse? Just two men? Did they never sleep?" I couldn't believe what he had just told me. "Couldn't someone have done something? At least buried her?"

"Two men, and not very big ones at that. A troop—*lächerlich!*" He laughed so hard that he had to grab the foot of the broken-winged angel. His laughter echoed through the tombstones.

I understood suddenly and yet I didn't really understand the emptiness of the town. "Where are they all?" I asked.

He did understand the meaning of my question. "They are dead. Their bodies still twitch, but they're as dead as their houses, buried under layers of dust." He spat on the ground at the angel's foot.

"The war," I argued.

"The war! The war!" he shouted impatiently. He had to catch his breath, then he sat down, as if his knees had failed him.

I tried to calm him, "What should they have done? You didn't have guns and the others did."

"They ought to have buried her. *I* should have buried her."

I sat down next to him and huddled in my

trenchcoat against the gravestone. The town below was half-submerged in the darkness of the valley.

He whispered in my ear. "Leave! Go home! You're young, you didn't have anything to do with it."

That same night I drove to Vienna. On my return to Essen, I filed a report on Charles-Louis Golik. Gravesite unknown.

III

A
House
In
Ruins

Miner's Tattoo _____

Dirk had decided to wear his burgundy red pin-striped suit, a hand-me-down—but its American label made up for that. He looked at his mother, who watched from the kitchen door as he finished dressing. She smiled with pride at her son, but frowned when he pointed to his dark red sweater, which puffed out between the lapels of his double-breasted jacket.

"Do you really need that heavy sweater?"

"It'll be cold riding the bike at night," Dirk answered, while he smoothed the two large stags roaring at each other across his chest. His sweater had been sent to Germany by the same relief organization which had supplied Dirk with his pin-striped suit. He sat on the edge of the lower bunk and hunched over to pull on a pair of bright yellow slip-ons. They didn't match

his suit nor were their crepe soles likely to slide on the
dance floor, but he had to wear them today. He had
bought them with his mother here in Herne, in a shoe
store on Bahnhofstrasse. They were his first pair of
new shoes after the war, and when the clerk's back was
turned, Dirk held the shoes up to his face. He smelled
America, although the shoes had been manufactured
in West Germany; he smelled the mixture of gasoline
fumes and oil, jeep tires and asphalt softening in the
early summer heat of 1945, when he had seen the
Americans first. He had crowded with other kids
against a fence and seen them, loose-jointed, with
laughing faces under the upturned bills of their fatigue caps, loudly at ease among their convoy of jeeps,
tanks and trucks.

He and his mother had saved up a long time to buy
that pair of yellow shoes. At first, they had decided to
buy a pair of dark brown ones in the store window, but
when his mother saw the slip-ons she said that they
were the color of real bee's honey. "You were too
young when the war started. You never tasted it." They
both knew the shoes were right for Dirk, even though
he had nothing else to wear with them. Whenever he
wore then now, he imagined people staring at them
and thinking of Dirk as an exotic visitor from overseas.

"I wish I could do something about those
pants." His mother walked over to the bunk and
took a closer look at his trousers. "I really can't let
them out anymore, with those false cuffs. Maybe
you'll stop growing on your seventeenth birthday.
You're tall enough as it is." She sighed. "In this
country they just don't make clothes for anyone
who's almost a two meter man."

Dirk laughed and thought that even if they made
suits in his size he couldn't afford to buy them. He
stretched out his legs and looked with satisfaction at

his shoes. "If my pants are too short, at least everybody will look at my shoes." His mother smiled for a moment, but grew serious again.

"Stand up!" She knelt down and tugged at the cuffs of his pants, trying to pull them down to the tops of his yellow shoes. "Make sure that you don't get any bicycle grease on your best suit."

Only suit, Dirk thought. He folded his cuffs over to put on his bicycle clips, to keep his pant legs from being pulled into the gear and chain. Now that he was dressed, he felt less intimidated by his first dance class. He had worried about his size, sure that he would look awkward and foolish.

"Stand straight when you dance." His mother had read his mind again and she was right, because he didn't stand up straight; he stooped so he would be more the size of the other boys.

"And I hope that they have nice girls at the dance," she added.

He hoped that too. As Dirk walked out, as erect as his mother demanded, he bumped into the door frame. Massaging his forehead angrily, he swung his leg over his bicycle. His mother laughed as she waved good-bye.

It wasn't far to the *Gasthaus* where the dance class was to be held, so Dirk had time to bicycle slowly and to avoid the slick streetcar tracks. Although he was apprehensive about it, Dirk knew he had to take this dance class if he was to fulfill his mother's wish that he become a gentleman. A gentleman—he let go of the handlebar as he thought of that foreign word. How could he become a gentleman, not having even finished school and now working as a pitman? Dirk remembered how his mother had told him that this is what he should be. She had sat on her bed in the corner of the kitchen, while the two of them shared a can of plum pudding Dirk had brought from the pit. The English military government had distributed army rations to the German miners and Dirk had received a can of plum pudding, which he gave his parents as a Christmas present. His mother had decided to save the can for a special occasion.

The small tin stood between them on the kitchen table. When the can opener sliced into the lid, the fragrance of the plum pudding permeated the kitchen and for the next hour visions of the wide world filled their one-room house. Sharing this delicacy with her son made Dirk's mother voluble and she leaned forward, spearing a moist crumb here and there off the chipped plate, while she talked of Dirk's future and America. She said, "Dirk, you have to become a gentleman." When he asked her what that might be—he didn't even ask why, for the spicy fragrance of the plum pudding had settled that—she answered, "A gentleman is a man of honor. He knows how to dance, drive an automobile and ride a horse."

Dirk sat straight in the kitchen chair as he listened to his mother's statement, which rang like a genuine revelation. Then she had washed and saved the empty olive-colored tin as a reminder to Dirk of their resolve to send him from this coal basin town into the universe of adventure and opportunity.

A car honked behind Dirk and he quickly grabbed the handlebar. If I don't pay attention I'm going to die right here and I won't have to worry about going to America.

Dirk's first step toward becoming a gentleman was the dance lesson. The other talents his mother mentioned would just have to wait. He couldn't afford automobile driving lessons and he didn't even know anybody who owned a car. To become a horse rider in Herne seemed even more absurd since there were no

168

horses. Dirk suspected that if any had been left over when the war ended, they would have been slaughtered in the bad winter of 1945. There was one horse in town, however, which pulled the junk dealer's cart. The old man bought scrap copper and anything else the miners ferreted past the guards at the company gate, but that horse was so gaunt it barely pulled the cart up the little incline to the canal bridge.

He chained his bicycle to the lamp post in front of the "Westfalenschenke" and scanned the passersby for others likely to take the dance class, but no one stepped with him into the dark entrance hall which smelled of beer. Dick took his bicycle clips off and then checked every door in the corridor so that he wouldn't have to go into the bar itself to ask.

"Heh, don't stand in my way!"

Dirk jumped aside to avoid being hit by a beer barrel being rolled down the passage to the bar. He didn't want to ask the surly man in the leather apron where the dance class was. If he could only find a sign announcing that the class had been canceled, then he would be free to run to his bicycle and be on his way home. Instead, Dirk found the right door—a small poster next to it proclaimed, "Dance and Etiquette Instruction." He opened the door carefully and peered into a large empty room.

"Come in, come in!" A man, the dance master, rushed from behind a dilapidated black piano and pulled Dirk through the door shaking his hand at the same time. "Everybody else will be here shortly," he added cheerfully and shook the boy's hand again. Dirk noticed that he had only one arm, but that was not unusual in the years after the war.

Dirk uneasily examined the big room and was intimidated by a row of straight-backed chairs lining

169

each of the walls. Uncertain what to do, he leaned on the piano and tried to look like Fred Astaire.

Soon the first boys came, in twos and threes, mostly from the pits, their eyes still rimmed with coal dust. Some were already scarred with miner's tattoos, which slashed their cheeks. They joked and scuffled with each other, looking from time to time at the door. Dirk looked at the door, too, waiting for the girls to come, but no girls came. He knew none of the boys and none talked to him. The dance master checked lists and seemed unaware of anything happening around him. He carefully placed a record player on one of the chairs and then told the boys to dance, in couples, he added, never once commenting on the absence of girls. Slowly walking around the circle he pointed at every second boy and said, "You are a man." He said nothing to the others. He explained to those who danced as males the proper way to hold their partners; but he was not satisfied with the way the boys kept each other at arm's length. He admonished them, then shook his head and switched on the record player.

"Listen to the rhythm and dance!" He shouted over the tinny din of the record. "Turn and dance! Turn and dance! All of you. Turn and dance!"

A few started to dance willingly and shoved each other clumsily around the floor, but they soon broke up with embarrassed laughter and stumbled to a stop. Dirk had not even tried. He was supposed to lead, but he didn't dare look at his partner, although he laid his right hand on the other boy's shoulder.

From the center of the circle the dance master shouted at him: "No! No! No! A gentleman places his hand just below the shoulder blades of the lady. Yes, that's right. Now draw the lady toward you."

The boys giggled and Dirk felt himself blush, wishing that he were smaller or not in this room at all.

The dance master stopped the music and the needle whined on the slowing record as he addressed Dirk again.

"The only time you don't put your hand in the middle of a woman's back—" He was interrupted by the throaty laughter of one of the boys. The dance master looked at him and the laughter stopped. He continued in mid-sentence, "is when she wears a gown cut low in back and then you place your hand on the nearest bit of fabric." He stopped for a moment and looked around the circle; there was no laughter. "But you never, never put your sweaty paws on the bare back of your inamorata."

Nobody dared ask what an inamorata was, and the boys danced closer to avoid a tongue-lashing. Then the dance master drew intricate lines on a blackboard propped up on the keyboard of the piano. For the next tune he changed from the military march he had played to "On a Slow Boat to China." As Dirk listened to this melody he missed the girls even more. To compensate for their absence, he danced vehemently, paying little attention to the languid tempo of the music.

The room grew hot and he wished that he had not worn his stag sweater. Could he simply stop dancing and take it off? He didn't know if this was proper etiquette and so he kept on dancing, perspiring like his partner, whose blond hair fell limply onto his forehead.

Round and round they danced, circling the room like black-blinkered whim horses, Dirk thought. Crack the whip and round we go. Dirk's partner counted his dance steps under his breath.

"Dance! You wicked Valentinos! Dance! Dance!" The master shouted, jumping from one leg to the other, stomping to the beat of the music.

Dirk, taller than anyone else in the room, tilted his

head while he danced, looking, as his uncle Paul once
observed, like a stork waiting for a frog. That had still
been in Silesia . . . back home. . . Over the scuffle of
heavy shoes on the wooden floor the words of the song
drifted tinnily from the phonograph. He was studying
English after work, particularly since the letter had
come from the American consulate in Bremen, in-
forming him that he was now registered for emigration. He tried hard to comprehend the words; most
were meaningless clumps of sound, though he understood the simple ones. To his delight he actually saw
before his eyes the second part of the line: "Out on the
briny with the moon big and shiny."

He danced gracefully to this song, or at least he
thought he did; he envisioned the Pacific Ocean and
soared over the bobbing heads of the other dancers to
seek the nameless ship heading for Hong Kong or
Shanghai. Maybe his flight lasted only a dozen beats,
but he traveled far and he heard the wind in the palm
trees, rustling like nothing he had ever heard before,
and he saw the moonlight on the calm tropical waters.
The warmth of the night felt like dew on his cheek; it
subdued miners' sweat and overpowered the scratches
in the record. "On a slow boat to China. . ." Instead of
the clumsy *Kumpel* in his arms he held a beautiful
woman, his hand positioned correctly below her
shoulder blades. She wore white silk, cool to his touch,
and she smiled. Then she leaned back against the railing of the ocean liner next to the white lifeboat and all
he now felt was the sweet warmth of the tropical night.

The circle of boys moved steadily as the dance
master waved his arm like a giant baton, whirling in the
center of the ring. Dirk heard the man count, but he
didn't want his flight to stop, he wanted to hold this
woman and dance with her. But suddenly she was gone
and all he could clutch was the whiteness of her dress.

Dirk fought against waking from his dream and he thought sadly that she wore white and that you can't wear white in Herne; everyone's dressed in black and if you wear any other color it turns black in the soot and grime. The boys, in their drab woolen jackets, looked to Dirk as if they had been blown in by a gritty wind, a North Sea gale, lashing across the mine yards, shunting tracks and cokeries, smelling foully of coal, steam and sulphur.

The song went on and Dirk still swayed on the mahogany deck of his dream liner, but he also heard how the record player was rewound repeatedly and now he only pretended to fly just as he pretended to sleep in the morning when his mother called him to go to work in the mine. He repeated a line to himself he had heard in the song: "Leave all your lovers weeping on faraway shores," but he didn't understand its meaning.

He was glad when the class was over and he knew, when the music stopped, that he wouldn't be back for the next lesson, even if he lost all the money he had paid in advance.

Next morning Dirk didn't wake up. His mother kept calling from the kitchen, but he stayed asleep, shrunk into his straw sack. Then she pushed a spoonful of cereal between his lips, and after swallowing, Dirk finally opened his eyes.

"It's almost five o'clock," she whispered, bending over him. "You have to go to work." She unlatched the shutters and pushed them open. It was still dark outside. Dirk sat up, banging his head against the slats of the upper bunk, where his father slept when he was in town, and then sank back down. He pressed the bowl against his chest and while he ate he slowly woke up, remembering suddenly that today was to be his first day underground. Until now it had been "above day"

173

for him: repairing broken coal cars in the mine shops or unloading timbering logs.

He quickly pulled on his corduroy pants and his shirt in the chill of the small dark room, glad that he didn't have to shave every morning. His mother came back into his room to make the bed.

"How was it last night?" Her voice didn't sound as if she was particularly curious.

"Terrible." Dirk didn't feel like explaining.

"What happened?"

"No girls came." Dirk was trying to remember where he left his workboots and he rummaged in the corner near the window.

"Shame." She was bent over his bunk, fluffing his pillow; her voice was muffled, but to Dirk it sounded relieved. "Did you at least learn how to dance?" She straightened up, rubbing her back.

"Yes." He had found his shoes and squeezed by his mother into the kitchen. "But I'm not going back," he said, standing by the stove and warming his hands. His mother didn't answer and he listened to her rummaging while he wedged his feet into his stiff workboots.

"That's fine, too. We'll find other ways for you to become a gentleman."

She had been upset when he told her that his assignment had been changed and that from now on he would be working below day. Hunched over to lace his boots he said those words again, "below day, below day." As the blood flowed to his head he feared that he would never see the sun again. And that was silly, he thought as he sat up and buttoned his shirt. His mother was worried because below day was more dangerous and she had also been unhappy because it was so final. They couldn't pretend anymore that he was going back to school, although he had done poor work there, and that he would stop working at the mine as soon as things were better. They needed the special rations for miners which he received, the extra bread, flour and meat. The free ton of coal, which every miner had delivered to his home, carried them through the winter. Above day he had been classified as an apprentice, but below day he was going to be just another miner.

As Dirk rode into the darkness, his mother stood in the lighted doorway and called after him: "Good luck! Good luck on your first day down." He switched on the bicycle light; he didn't think at all, but just listened to the humming of the generator against the front tire. All he could see was the small white band of light bouncing along the cobblestones in front of him. When he came closer to the mine, bicycle lights cut through the darkness from all directions. Dawn shone dimly and Dirk knew the sun would be too weak that day to burn through the haze.

Once through the *Shamrock* iron gates he moved in a long double line of patient and silent men to pick up his brass shift tags: one for his lamp and another for the timekeeper on the loading platform. He changed hurriedly in the steamy washroom, because he had already learned his first lesson of working underground: the earlier you went down, the earlier you saw daylight again. He hung his clean street clothes on hooks at the end of a chain which he hauled all the way to the ceiling and locked in place. Then he pulled on his work pants and shirt and crammed the stiff leather helmet on his head. Now, for all to see, he was the new boy in the mine, with his shiny helmet, a butt for all the old jokes. He could hear them now: "Heh, you long drink of water, get me a paper bag of compressed air from the machine shop and fetch me a bucket of rubber rivets. Hurry up, or I'll throw a hammer at your stupid head."

As he trudged to the lamp shop he followed an old

miner and matched his step. Dirk felt uneasy and he concentrated on the miner's worn-out boots, trying not to think at all. The man's boots were laced halfway up with red shooting wire used to detonate explosive charges in the rock face. Dirk knew about that, because he had found strands of the thin wire in the cars that came up filled with coal and debris to be sorted by the boys. The miner's ankles flashed white between the tops of his boots and his short, ragged pants.

The line stopped at the lamp shop. Dirk carefully put one of his brass tags down on the zinc counter and was handed a heavy grey cylinder topped by a dome of thick glass with a sharply pointed brass hook dangling down. Dirk thought that from now on this lamp would be charged every single day; no, he corrected himself silently, six days a week, just for him.

He carried his lamp by its spiked hook, just as he saw the old miner do, as he followed him up the steep stairs in a long line of men heading for the basket. The metal stairs trembled under his feet and the whole stairwell, actually only a sheet metal housing to keep the rain and the wind away, reverberated with the noise coming from the pithead of steel banging on steel.

The old miner stopped and spat black gobs on the steel steps, bowing his head in his helmet, whose leather had silvered with age and had been beaten by years of use into a glove's softness. He fought for breath to go on and Dirk knew that he had Black Lung; many others around town suffered from it. But Dirk was too impatient to wait for the coughing man, and he pushed by him. The old man looked up and muttered, gasping between words: "Take your time . . . take . . . your . . . time . . . there'll be another . . . basket." In passing Dirk glanced at the man's ashen face and saw that he couldn't be more than forty; his face was drawn and the dark blue scars of his miner's tattoos cross-hatched his cheeks and nose.

Dirk hurried the last steps up to the loading platform. Around him coal cars slammed into each other, then tumbled upside down dumping rock and coal onto shuddering grading screens. Empty cars clattered over a maze of track in apparent chaos; in reality the cars were merely obeying the law of gravity and a series of crude switches.

As the line of miners moved forward, Dirk thought that "basket" was really the wrong word for the huge four-storied cage which swallowed the miners. A white-suited inspector stopped some men at random and made them empty their pockets. If matches, cigarettes or a lighter were found, the miner was fired on the spot, but Dirk wasn't searched, maybe because he looked as innocent as he was, cleanly scrubbed under his brand-new shiny helmet. He was allowed into the basket without a second glance.

Dirk jammed with the other miners into the top level of the basket and was pressed by them against the steel grating of the side. Tilting his head back he looked directly at two monstrous steel claws, poised on each side of the basket to strike into the wooden guide beams which ran down the length of the shaft like rails. These claws had been explained to him as they were to all of the miners going down the first time: if the cable hoisting the basket should snap—and the instructor had laughed, assuring them that it never happens— then the safety dogs, the two steel claws weighing more than a ton, were released and they smashed into the oaken shaft guides, shredding them as the basket hurtled down, breaking its fall before it hit bottom.

The night after his instructor's introduction to the mine's safety features, Dirk stayed awake. Staring at the wooden slats of the upper bunk, he saw the basket, heavy with miners and equipment, screaming down the narrow shaft. Shoulder by shoulder, the men stood silent under their helmets, in a spray of sparks and splintered wood. Dirk had pushed open his shutters and smelled the sulphur of the night air. The sky over *Shamrock* was flame red from the cokery flares burning off gas, dyeing the steam which swirled from the cooling towers. The vague shapes of the cokery were illuminated like the superstructure of an ocean liner and Dirk thought of America.

The basket dropped suddenly with ear-popping speed and, close enough to touch, the rock face rushed by. The blackness of the shaft alternated with flashes of light from the levels where the basket didn't stop. The cable didn't break, although whenever the basket stopped to let work crews off it bounced as if the steel cable was nothing more than a rubber band. When Dirk stepped shakily from the basket onto the concrete floor, he was disappointed because the loading area looked just like the pithead above day: rails leading off into tunnels, cars heaped with dusty chunks of coal, and signal lights flashing while locomotives shunted noisily in the confusion. Supervisors shouted assignments to the miners scrambling from the basket into trains heading for the pushes in the coal face. The whole area was brightly lit and with its bricked-out vaulted ceiling it reminded Dirk of the air raid shelter where he hid during the war. You can't be scared here, Dirk thought, it's another freight yard, which just happens to be three thousand feet underground. He pretended not to mind.

He climbed onto one of the narrow gauge cars taking timber to the push and again he was penned in with many others. It occurred to him that it wasn't even six o'clock yet and that it was only now getting light above day. The train passed through a massive gate whose solid steel wings stood wide open into a lower and narrower tunnel. A pinch-faced miner, whose bony shoulder pressed against Dirk's, looked up at the boy's shiny helmet.

"First day?" he muttered, barely opening his mouth.

Dirk nodded. "Yeah." He hoped that he sounded right and he decided to take advantage of the other's friendliness.

"What about those big doors we just went through? Are they ever closed?" For a while he only heard the rattle of the train and the screech of its wheels in the turns as they rolled deeper into the mine.

"Fire doors." He didn't turn to Dirk; he looked instead at the walls moving by. "You don't want to be around when they are shut." He laughed—at least Dirk though that it was a laugh, though it sounded more like a bark. "When there's a fire up front," the miner continued, pointing with his right thumb in the train's direction, "they shut those doors in a hurry. Chokes off the fire. Cuts the air. Lets it burn itself out. That's how they think."

By "they" Dirk presumed that he meant the upstairs offices of *Shamrock* or maybe all of the *Hibernia* mining concern. Or maybe "they" think that way in all mines.

"What happens to the mates working up front?" he asked.

This time the miner twisted around to look at Dirk and there wasn't even a smile on his grey face. He spoke very slowly as if Dirk was a foreigner and needed to watch a speaker's lips to understand.

"They stay where they are," he whispered hoarsely and then turned back to face the rock wall. Dirk didn't say anything and he felt like a fool for having asked the question. He was scared. The train stopped and men jumped off, hunching over so that neither their heads nor the shouldered shovels would touch the bare powerline of the train overhead. At one stop Dirk looked up and saw a board directly over him, crossing the tunnel from wall to wall, heaped with grey powder.

"What's this?" He pointed up.

"That? Rock dust." The miner might have laughed; if he did it was so slight that it was swallowed by the noise of the train. "When the gas explodes . . . up front," he pointed again in the direction of the locomotive, "it knocks off this board and a whole lot of others like it in the tunnel. All the dust piled up there is supposed to fall down . . . like this. . .," and he waved his hands, wiggling his fingers the way a child shows that it's raining outside. "It comes down like a curtain and it's supposed to cool down the fire blowing through the tunnels, pounding off all those boards with rock dust on them."

He sounded doubtful that this safety mechanism worked at all. Dirk sensed that he shouldn't ask if anyone gets out alive once the blast comes roaring through and he didn't really want to know anyway.

The train stopped and Dirk got off. He followed three others as they filed into ever lower tunnels twisting away from the light and the cool draft of air. The tracks and a channel of water followed the contours of the tunnel; Dirk remembered the daily walks he had taken with his father, hand in hand when he was small, and later at his father's side, through the park and across the open fields, often right next to the railroad track, just like now.

Finally they turned into a short side tunnel bored into the coal seam.

"This is it. No more walking now. Hang up your lamp, here, like this." One of the miners, a muscular man with a pockmarked face, showed Dirk how to slam

the spiked handle of this lamp into the overhead timbering. Dirk took a deep breath of the air in the stuffy
chamber, and he noticed in addition to the attic
staleness, a faint forest smell from the pine logs.

"You shovel," was the last Dirk heard before the
compressed air hammers roared up. With the first coal
chunks broken off, dust filled the air, dimming their
four lamps. The miners working the hammers braced
their bare backs against the coal, their bodies jerking
and shuddering with the vibrations of the air hammers. It was hot and Dirk took his shirt off. His shovel
had such a large pan that he was barely able to lift each
load of coal to the rim of the car to dump it. Once the
car was full he pushed it to the main tunnel, but he
couldn't twist it on the steel plate which served as a
turnaround. He walked back to the push and asked,
but nobody heard him. Finally he grabbed a sweaty
shoulder and yelled into an ear sticking out under a
helmet rim. The miner turned. Dirk couldn't tell who
he was; he yelled: "Piss on it!"

Piss on it? Since Dirk had been warned about the
jokes they pulled on you on your first day down, he just
laughed and stayed where he was, waiting for the real
answer. The miner looked at him, shut down his hammer and pushed Dirk ahead of him, shoving him so
hard he nearly fell. He crowded past Dirk to get
quickly to the plate. He unbuttoned his fly and uri-
nated under the wheels of the car, carefully spraying
all parts of the steel plate. Without looking at Dirk he
rushed back to the push. Dirk twisted the car and slid
it onto the right track.

The hammers boomed through the chamber and
the hot air grew gritty with dust. Their lamps were
now only faint brown spots in the darkness, marking
each man's position rather than shining on the rock
face. The shovel had become part of Dirk's aching

arms and everytime he scraped coal and rock up, he had to hunch over the car, because he was too tall to stand up straight.

Suddenly the noise stopped. The miners left their air hammers jammed into the coal face and climbed down, stretching and bracing their arms against the roof of the tunnel. They didn't say a word as they squatted down, their backs against the timber uprights. One man carefully pried apart the two halves of a tin sandwich box, while another gulped water from his oversized canteen. The dust had slowly settled once the hammers stopped, but Dirk still couldn't tell them apart, for their faces had become black masks.

They didn't speak during the break, not like in the shops above day. In the silence Dirk became aware of the creaking of the timber as the mountain shifted overhead. The stiff helmet hurt his head and he took it off, wiping his forehead with the back of his hand. Then he put the helmet in the coal dust next to him.

"Put your helmet on!" shouted a miner. "You want to get your stupid head bashed in by a rock?"

"Excuse me," Dirk said, and he quickly put his helmet back on while the others laughed. Then he leaned back like they did and listened to the groaning of the wood.

"We got to do some timbering," one of the others said to Dirk, pointing at the roof. "You know how?"

Dirk nodded. They had taught him in the training workshop above day.

"Bring logs!"

Dirk went immediately and was glad to be able to walk where he could stand straight and stretch and breathe air that circulated. Trundling the logs back on a flat car he shivered and wished that he had put on his shirt. When he got back to the push he was shown where the toolbox was so that he could find an axe and also where to dig the shallow footing holes. Dirk knelt down to chop at the log, trying to cut a smooth point, when a rock thudded against the wall next to him.

"You idiot! We don't have all day." The man who must have thrown the rock pushed Dirk away from the log. "Here, don't sharpen it like a pencil. Just knock off the outer layer. You're as dumb as a box of rocks." He knelt next to Dirk and with a few swift blows he chopped a crude point on the log. "This here, it's pine, is soft inside." He threw the axe into the dirt. "When the mountain presses down, it squashes the point. If we put in oak, which is hard all the way through, the mountain snaps it, comes down and squashes you instead." Then he sawed out the notches for the joints at the top and rammed the log into the floor. "That's all the time we have. We get paid by the ton. Do it right and fast." He turned and climbed back to the coal face.

The hammers started up and the dust swirled again from the push. Dirk barely saw where he chopped, but he forced some timber against the roof, careful not to tangle his logs with the air hoses snaking up to the hammers. The coal started piling up between him and the face and he knew that he had to start loading again.

Suddenly, with three or four explosions, the supporting timbers behind Dirk cracked and the mountain fell. His way into the main tunnel was blocked and he stumbled backward against the seam. Rocks crashed into the chamber and blowing dust blacked out their lamps. Dirk couldn't see but he heard the whining, bending and breaking of logs. Slowly a timber upright gave way next to Dirk and forced him into the coal dust, pinning his legs to the floor.

The fall stopped and it was silent. Then Dirk cried out in fear.

"Where are you?" a voice asked. Muffled by the dust it seemed to come from far away.

"Here! Over here by the wall!" Dirk answered softly, worried that a shout might bring down another load of rock.

"Stay where you are . . . all of you." It sounded like the same voice.

"No! Let's get out while we still have air." That was a different voice, Dirk thought, but it sounded just as far away.

"No! Stay until we can see how bad it is."

"Damned dust. Got to wait till we can see."

Coughing came from the dark. Dirk tried to move, to twist his legs out from under the log until he screamed in pain.

"Stay where you are! Don't move! Wait!"

Dirk lay on his back and dust settled softly on his face. Like snowflakes, he thought, as he listened to the others breathe somewhere in the dark. Then he began to see the dim points of their lamps. One of the men crawled over to him, feeling for the boy's body in the debris of shattered logs and chunks of rock and coal. When Dirk felt the miner's hand, he grabbed it and held tightly, afraid the man might crawl back into the darkness.

"Are we going to die?" Dirk whispered as the other bent over him.

"I don't think so. Where are you hurt?"

"My legs . . . under the log." He was gasping, his face pressed against the other's shoulder. The miner straightened up and tried to heave the log off with a broken piece of timber.

"Over here! Give me a hand! His leg's caught!" The miner shouted in the direction of the lanterns. Pain squeezed Dirk's eyes shut and tears ran through the dust on his cheeks. The two other miners now

184

crawled over to Dirk, dragging their lamps through the dust. One of them examined the boy's face, sliding his hands slowly over Dirk's cheeks and forehead. Then he held his hands close to his lamp.

"Blood. You're cut," and he took off his own helmet and placed it carefully over Dirk's face.

"Hope you aren't scared of the dark, but this'll keep the rocks off your face."

"I can't breathe . . . Get me some air!" Dirk shouted into the helmet covering his face.

"Just wait! Let's see if we can pry this off your legs."

Dirk heard their grunting as they tried to lift the log from his legs, but he didn't feel the timber move.

"Go knock! We forgot to knock. Let 'em know we're alive!"

Dirk couldn't see anything but he heard the banging of metal on the compressed air pipe. Then he heard another voice in the dark.

"They'll have us out in a hurry. This isn't a bad fall."

Maybe they are saying that to make me feel better, Dirk thought, maybe we won't ever get out of this hole. Not even when we're dead will they pull us out, and he remembered the bricked-off entrance to a coal seam that had been burning for the last ten years. Maybe they left the mates before the push, waiting, just like us.

His back ached and he squeezed his eyes shut, whispering into the sweaty leather of the helmet: above day, above, above day. Then he wondered what was up there, straight up, beyond the helmet—rock, level five, four, three, tracks, timbering with the smell of pine trees and more rock. What's above day? A street, surely a street. Maybe Von der Heydt Strasse with the toy store. Dirk stopped his bicycle there to look into the window, ashamed that one of his friends might see him. He knew that he was too old to stare into a toy store window with hardly a thing in it, just those dogs. Wooden dogs on wheels, stained a runny purple, with string to pull them along. The string, like all string at the end of the war, was made from paper. That kid's going to lose his purple dog when it rains. He laughed and gasped for breath. Slow down, he thought, slow down. He breathed shallow sips of air smelling of sweat and coal dust. The others are so quiet. Maybe we're under the Bahnhofstrasse, Dirk thought, maybe directly under the "Westfalen-schenke."

The continuous tapping on the pipe had grown into a pounding inside the helmet on Dirk's face, as sweat steamed under the leather.

The air was getting hotter and hotter. Like a jungle.

"La Paloma. . ."

Dirk remembered the time when he was a kid and he had waited with his school friends for a commuter train that was already two hours late. They were happy, because they were on their way to school and the late train made them miss more and more classes. To pass the time they sang all the hit songs they could think of. When they howled the refrain "La Paloma, oheeee. . ." into the cold air of a winter morning, one of the other passengers called the station manager to quiet them down. La Paloma, oheeee . . . moon big and shiny . . . white silk and the wind in the palm trees. . .

"I can't breathe!" Dirk flung the helmet from his face. One of the miners propped Dirk's head up and held a lamp close, probing with his fingers for the cut on Dirk's face. When Dirk screamed, the man's hand stopped and rested over the wound.

"Not bad. Cut in the cheek. Feels all right."

It may feel all right to you, it doesn't to me, Dirk thought, happy, though, that the other man's hand remained on his face. Like being sent to bed and having

his father stroke his forehead. Sleep well, good night.
Please, leave the door open, I don't like to be in the
dark, but the door was closed.

The monotonous pounding on the pipe suddenly
stopped. In the silence Dirk heard the faint answering
knock from the other side of the fall.

"Hallelujah, they're coming for us," shouted the
miner who had his hand on Dirk's cheek. "You hear
that kid? They're coming to dig us out!"

"I hope they're coming before we all suffocate,"
one of the others complained. Dirk couldn't see
him—he must have crawled back to the push. Sweat
ran down Dirk's legs and he heard the others gasping
for air. Maybe that's how I sound. One of the men
climbed up into the fallen rock and broken timber, but
didn't get very far.

"It's sealed off. Not a breath of air coming
through." His voice came muffled from the top of
the fall.

They all squatted silently near Dirk, whose
back ached from rocks pushing against his spine.
But he didn't dare shift his body for fear of bringing
other rock down on him. The knocking on the pipe
had stopped.

Suddenly one of the miners near Dirk stumbled
up and shouted, "The air! The air! Why didn't we think
of that before?"

The others looked up at him without moving.

"The compressed air line! We can suck on that and
hang on forever!"

The other two got up slowly. "Can you breathe
that stuff?" one worried.

"Maybe the line is squashed so it won't work anyway," the other added. The one who had thought of it
was already at the pipe. He wrenched off the hose
coupling from one of the air hammers. When he slowly

eased the handle open, Dirk heard the hiss of escaping air.

"That's something. Listen to that . . . hissss. I'll open it just a little and we can take turns breathing."

The three hovered over the pipe and pressed their faces in turn against the coupling, gulping air like boys drinking from a faucet.

"What about him?" One looked over his shoulder at Dirk. "He can't get over here." Then he turned back to the pipe.

"What about me?" Dirk shouted at the coal-darkened backs hunched over the pipe. "I'm lying here and I'm going to die right here. You don't even know who I am. Dirk Burcgrave, remember that. When you get out, tell them that I'm Dirk. . ."

"We'll tell them. . . . Listen!"

Dirk heard it too, the scrabbling and scratching from the other side of the fall.

"They're getting us out! They're coming for us!" The three shouted and stumbled up from their pipe. One of them bent over Dirk.

"Is there anything?. . ."

"My back . . . it hurts. I'm lying on some hard rocks," Dirk whispered.

"There are no soft ones. Here," the other reached over and pushed his shirt under Dirk's back.

"Better?"

"Yes . . . but I can't breathe. . ."

"Air for you?" He jumped up. "Air! We can get air for him. . . . A hose . . . all we have to do is drag a hose over here."

Two of them pulled a hammer from the coal face and fumbled with the coupling.

"I'm getting sick." Dirk gasped.

"No, you aren't getting sick in here. Where is the axe? Chop it off, just chop it!"

They pulled the hose across the rubble and pushed its end in Dirk's mouth.

"Suck . . . just a little bit . . . here."

The stale air hissed in Dirk's mouth and he bit into the rubber hose caked with oil and coal dust. Clutching the hose, he inhaled deeply and closed his eyes in relief, but the hose was twisted from his hands. All four of them put their heads close together, passing the hose from mouth to waiting mouth. The lamps stood clustered between them, shining up into their faces and, for the first time, Dirk felt safe, like being back in the park, playing Indians around a camp fire. Indians from Karl May novels, Winnetou and Old Shatterhand. And he still needed to learn how to ride if he was going to America. Maybe, the way his legs felt, he wouldn't be able to ride anyway and his face might never be the face of a gentleman. He carefully felt his cheek, sticky with dust and blood.

They hadn't talked for a long time. Dirk listened to the sounds from the other side of the fall and he could tell that they were coming closer. He could tell the sound of hammers from the high-pitched pings of shovels hitting rock and he imagined that he already heard their voices. When Dirk moaned, a miner put his hand on the boy's shoulder.

"We'll come through fine." He left his hand on Dirk's shoulder until the rescue team broke through at the top of the fall.

A voice shouted: "Any dead?"

"Not in here. One pinned under the timber. Go easy and don't drop anything on him. Hear?"

"Right, mates. We'll do it by hand."

Two of the miners crouched over Dirk shielding his body with their backs. Soon, air blew in.

"They brought a fan. Good mates."

A head with a helmet lamp slid into view at the top of the fall.

"Need a stretcher?"

"No. We'll carry him out ourselves. Just pull the junk out of the way and we'll march right out."

The white-suited *Steiger* climbed over the debris into their chamber and he shone his helmet light on Dirk. Together with the three others he pushed the log away. Then he examined Dirk's legs.

"Nothing broken," he announced matter of factly. "His legs are bruised and sure will hurt a while. Anything else wrong?" Nobody said anything about the gash in Dirk's cheek and he didn't mention it either, reasoning that they must not worry about small wounds like this in a coal mine.

The digging was close by and noisy. The rescue team supervisor wanted Dirk Burcgrave carried out now, but one of the miners said that he wanted the boy left here for a couple of minutes and then they could have him. The *Steiger* announced that it might be another half hour before the debris was cleared and new shorings were in place. The miners decided to stay at their push until all of them could walk out together. Dirk thought that this might be a point of honor with them, not to leave him, even if they didn't know who he was. But he wasn't sure.

Dirk was still lying on the ground where he had fallen and the miner who had insisted that the boy not be carried out squatted next to him.

"This is going to hurt like a rock on the head, but you'll thank me later, later when you're back up there. Above day. You're not going to stay down here with us. I've watched you through the shift and you never do things right. . ."

"But it's only my first. . ." Dirk protested.

"Just listen! That doesn't make any difference.

You don't even look like one of us." He gently pushed Dirk back down. "You don't belong here." He must have felt Dirk's struggling to get up, for he kept his hand heavily on the boy's shoulder. "Look at me!"

Dirk looked up at the man, whose face was black, solid black, from the short visor of his helmet to his chin. A face more round than anything else. Dirk tried hard to look at this face and see anything extraordinary, but all he saw was black. He wasn't sure that he would recognize him in the washroom, should he turn around and ask him to soap his back. Dirk was going to speak, but the other put his hand over the boy's mouth.

"No, look at me. I'm a pitman and I look like one. If I get on a streetcar here in Herne and rattle fifty kilometers into the beet fields somewhere in Westphalia, people will say, 'There goes a *Kumpel*.' So I'm going to stay right here, make the money in the pit and take the extra food and booze and rations and live."

He spat in the dust and stopped speaking, rocking back on the heels of his boots. The sounds of digging and the voices of the rescue team were close by now. They were laughing and joking now that they knew none of their own had died. The other two miners in the chamber hadn't said anything for a long time— they might have dozed off against the coal face. Their lamps were still by Dirk's head. The miner leaned forward again.

"How can they tell that I'm a pitman? By the way I walk and by the way I never get the coal out from under my eyes and most of all by my tattoos." He pointed first to his cheeks, then to his nose and his forehead, where he knew that his dark blue scars ran, scars Dirk couldn't see, because they were hidden under a coat of coal dust.

"Your name isn't even right. Mine is Wischnewski. That's a miner's name. And you're too tall. What are you going to do when we have to work a thirty-inch seam? We have to crawl on all fours up into the coal, dragging the air hammers after us. It feels like you're carrying the mountain on your back. You couldn't take it and they would have to drag you out." He spat in the dust.

"I'll look after you, if you promise me that you'll get out of this damned hole. Go to work at something else." After a moment he added, "You aren't doing any good down here."

"Bring the boy out!" shouted the *Steiger* from the other side of the fall. "We have to get back into production."

"Another minute" shouted the miner, then he whispered to Dirk, "I've got to hurry. This hurts, but you won't look like a pitman. Girls don't like you all scarred up." He laughed and reached into his pants pocket pulling out a small object wrapped in a piece of cloth fastened with red shooting wire.

"I carry it every day, because you never know what's going to happen. I learned a little too late about it to do me any good." He carefully undid the shooting wire and unwrapped the cloth strip. Then he kneeled down behind the boy and clamped Dirk's head between his own knees. He took off his helmet and put it in Dirk's hands.

"Here, bite on the rim."

Dirk jerked his head and tried to get out from the vise grip of the other's knees.

"No, stay still and take my helmet. The leather's softer. Been knocked around more. Bite on it and don't scream." He moved his lamp closer to Dirk's head and then daubed with the cloth strip at the wound. He spat on the cloth and wiped the blood and dirt from the boy's cheek.

"Now bite!"

He forced the wound open with his left hand while with his right he plunged a toothbrush in and scrubbed. Dirk screamed and the helmet fell from his mouth and rolled in the dust.

"What's going on back there?" Someone yelled across the fall.

"The boy's in a little bit of pain. We'll have 'm ready in a moment," the miner shouted back. Then he whispered in Dirk's ear: "Keep your mouth shut. I'm fixing your face so you won't have any miner's tattoos. No one'll ever know that you've been a pitman."

Dirk's scream also roused the other two miners at the coal face.

"What're you doing to the kid?" One of them asked.

"Scrubbing out the coal dust."

"Why bother? If he doesn't get scarred today it'll be on tomorrow's shift. Why put him through the pain?"

The miner didn't answer and he scrubbed while blood ran into Dirk's mouth. Dirk choked and spat, his body twisting between the other man's legs as the brush tore into his wound.

"Hold still!"

Then Dirk stopped moving.

"Now he's passed out." The miner pulled his brush away.

Dirk heard them speaking, far away, just voices.

"Some water left?"

"My canteen was crushed."

"Here. It's warm though."

Dirk felt the tepid water dribbled on his forehead and cheek. He moaned and moved slowly. The other man dragged him to the wall and propped him up.

"Are you finished with your little nap? You feel better? Yes?" When Dirk nodded he yelled at the others, "Let's take him out!"

The three miners whose black faces Dirk couldn't tell apart hunched over the boy and carried him out—one on each of Dirk's arms and the other holding his legs.

"Heh, look at the size of this guy's shoes. Next size up: children's coffins." He laughed, but the other two didn't turn around. When they passed the rescue crew, the other miners cheered, while some laughed.

"Had a good rest, mates?"

The *Steiger* paced back and forth by a stack of oxygen tanks the rescue team had never used. He looked down on Dirk, who was still being carried by the three miners and he picked up the shiny helmet resting on Dirk's chest.

"First day?" He turned the helmet in his hand, looking at it from all sides and then shook his head.

"Here he is, *Steiger*, you can have him now." Wischnewski said. "I forgot to mention that he was cut in the face. Let the mine doctor look at it, if he isn't too busy."

The mine doctor told Dirk to stay home for three days, more out of consideration for having been trapped on his first day down, than out of medical necessity. He pronounced the gash in the boy's cheek to be very clean, although he didn't examine it very closely.

Dirk didn't tell his mother about the cave in. Instead he said he had stumbled and fallen. During his sick leave another letter came from the consulate in Bremen announcing that his quota number was moving up rapidly and that, very soon, he would be cleared for emigration to America. He carefully refolded the strong white paper, and, holding it by its edges slid it carefully back into its envelope. Longer than ours, Dirk thought, a country with envelopes like their cars, and he propped up the letter behind the empty plum pudding can.

But America
Is Far_____

You can't lie to your mother, Dirk thought as he
lifted his heavy jacket from a nail by the door. Not for
long anyway.

Turning his back to his mother, he struggled into
the stiff sleeves of the coat he wore on his way to the
pit. "It might rain."

"Where *are* you going?" she asked, reaching up
over his back to pull out his shirt collar as she always
did when she saw him off.

"To the hospital," Dirk admitted, his shoulders
sagging. Earlier in the week, when he came home from
the pit with both of his legs bandaged, he had told her
that he had stumbled at work, but even then she didn't
seem to believe him. He wasn't hiding anything
shameful, but since he had to keep on going down into

the pit, she shouldn't have to worry more than she already did.

"I'm going to have my legs examined." Turning around, he bumped into his mother who stood closely behind him in the narrow hallway. At first he couldn't say anything while he was looking down into her face, but when she hugged him, he haltingly began to tell her how it happened that he had been buried in a rock fall, halfway through his first shift underground. He tried to find bland words that wouldn't be hurtful to her when she remembered them later, waiting for him by the same door where they stood now, listening for his bicycle bell. At shift end she would remember every word he told her now.

Dirk was already so tall that he could look over the crown of his mother's head, which made it easier for him to tell his story. But caught up in his own adventure he soon forgot his concern for her as he laughingly told of the rescue team burrowing through the rock fall, searching for *him*, trapped "a thousand meters below day."

"Did it hurt you much," she asked gently, "when that log was lying across your legs?"

"Stemple," he corrected her, "in miners' language . . . we call a log a stemple."

She touched her fingertips to his lips.

"Instead of talking like a child, you should wonder what it means."

"It was just an accident," Dirk protested.

"Not *just an accident*," she insisted, "it means something."

"But what could an accident in a pit *mean*?" he asked defensively, as if he were to blame.

"An *accident*? What happens to you has deep meanings. All you need to do is listen." Her voice sounded matter of fact, as if she were giving instructions on finding a street address.

"Ah," was all Dirk could say before her fingers touched his lips again, silencing him. She stood with her head tilted while her blue eyes looked off to the side, at nothing in particular.

"We ought to hold still under the hand of God . . . hold still and hearken."

Maybe it was from an old hymn—out of her youth, before she was ever baptized into the Mormon Church—or a line from a pious calendar leaf with sayings by the Silesian mystics she liked so much: Jakob Boehme or Angelus Silesius, Dirk was never sure which one it was. It was hot and he wished that he could wriggle out of his jacket, but his mother had grasped his arm, holding it tightly.

Sweat trickled down his neck as he touched the door handle, not daring to press down on it. Instead he stared at the wall, so close in front of his eyes that he could see how the knots had risen from the warped boards. Like knobby elbows sticking out from thin arms. The green lumber must have shrunk. He could see sunlight flickering through the joints where tongue and groove had drawn apart. In the silence he heard the racing pigeons cooing from their neighbor's coop. It felt like being trapped in a crate hammered together from scrap slats. A burst of machine gun fire would tear this wall to splinters, ripping through us and then probably killing some of the pigeons outside, he thought. How often did the four of us hide from the machine guns of strafing planes? Guiltily turning toward his mother he knocked his elbow against the wall.

"Ouch," he said while his mother shook her head as if she were unwilling to think any longer about whatever had occupied her mind.

"Do they know how young you are?" Her voice sounded normal again.

He nodded.

"I don't mean the people in the office. They know how old you are, they have your records, but the man down below, the *Steiger*, does he know?"

Crowded into the corner by the door, Dirk looked through its small glass pane at the stretch of land overgrown with weeds. This will be our garden, whenever I spade it.

"Dirk?"

Would it make her happy if I told her that the other boys hauling coal with me are the same age I am?

"You look older and you always have, because you're so tall, but however big you are, you're just a sixteen-year-old boy . . . and barely that." She reached up to touch his face, but her fingertips stopped short, floating shyly over the cut running from his cheekbone down to the corner of his mouth, as if the wound had turned her son into a stranger.

"You had such smooth skin—not like the boys your age—without a blemish. You were so handsome with your dark hair and with gooseberry green eyes. And now this." She pointed at his cheek as her voice drifted off. "What will they think of you when you go to the consulate in Bremen? That you fight and brawl in the street? And what will you look like by the time you finally arrive in America?" She shook her head.

"But I'm fine." Dirk beamed as if he suddenly remembered long forgotten good news. "The doctor at *Shamrock* said that my face wouldn't scar." I'm lying again, but just a little. The doctor didn't say anything at all about my face, it was the pitman who brushed the coal dust out of my wound who promised that it wouldn't leave a blue scar. "The doctor examined my legs and said—and these are his exact and true words—*After three days of celebrating sick have your legs checked at a miners' hospital. The one closest to you is Bergmannsheil in Bochum—"*

"*Celebrating* sick?" Mother interrupted Dirk. "Is he accusing you of being a malingerer, who signed on in the mine for the extra food rations but who then decides to shirk the hard work?" She grabbed his sleeve.

"No, after three days of . . . of . . . everyone who has been in a . . . mishap has to report to a miners' hospital for an examination." Dirk tried to sound like a book of regulations.

"But *celebrating* sick? What kind of a doctor would say something so frivolous?"

"No, everybody calls it *celebrating sick*, even the management on the bulletin board . . . it's official."

"If you were to lose your job. . ." She turned and walked the few steps into the kitchen.

What would happen if I did? We would lose the hard labor ration card, but we are also living on company land, in a house we bought from the pit. The table in the kitchen, my bunk, Mother's cot, the locker, everything we own came from the pit. Even permission to move into this town, they only gave that after I had found work at the pit.

"It's official," Dirk repeated.

"Maybe I should go with you?"

"To the hospital?" Dirk imagined the waiting room filled with rows of miners smirking at the sight of a boy brought in by his mommy.

"No, not the hospital," his mother said with a tired voice. "I might have looked into some of the stores in Bochum."

With or without ration cards there is almost nothing for her to buy in any of these stores; besides, she doesn't even have money enough to buy what little there is. It would help if I were to get full miner's wages instead of the few marks an apprentice earns.

He hurriedly kissed his mother on the cheek.

"I'm late for the hospital," he lied, because he didn't have an appointment.

"When you come back, we'll talk," she called after Dirk, who was already halfway across the piece of broken field they hoped to turn into a garden.

✿ ✿ ✿

From the streetcar Dirk watched a column of miners—one pedaling directly behind the other—threading its way around the potholes of the bicycle path. The mates are rushing to catch the early baskets for the two o'clock shift, Dirk thought, as he happily leaned back against the wooden bench, feeling only now that he really was on a holiday from the pit. With a groan he stretched out his aching legs.

"On your way to *Bergmannsheil*?" mumbled a man who sat across from Dirk.

"Three-day check." Dirk tried to be as grudging with words as the other man, whose face was crosshatched by blue scars.

"What pit?" he sucked on a short dead pipe, scarcely moving his thin lips when he pushed out his words around the pipe stem.

"*Shamrock*."

"Worked there myself. Funny foreign name for a German pit."

"*Shamrock*? I know that it means *Kleeblatt* in German," Dirk answered eagerly, catching himself in time before blurting out *I learned that in school*. Soon after going to work at the pit, he had learned the hard way that you don't talk about your schooling to those who had none. True, everybody had to go to elementary school, but his family had sent him to a *Gymnasium* where he had learned English at nine and Latin at twelve.

"I remember hearing that Irish engineers put down *Shamrock*'s first shaft. Same's put down *Erin* in Castrop-Rauxel. Mates from Dublin and Portland. . ."

"Portland, but Portland is in America," Dirk impulsively interrupted the miner, before falling silent. Keep your mouth shut about what you learned and what you're reading. Just shut up.

The other man contentedly rubbed his shoulders against the slats of the bench. He didn't seem to mind Dirk. "I don't know if the Yankees have one, too," he took the pipe out to yawn with a wide open mouth. "It wouldn't surprise me, they took everything else from us here in the old country. This Portland though is supposed to be in Ireland. You see, that's why the Tommies didn't bomb the city of Herne much during the war. Oh, here and there they did, but nothing like what had happened in the other coal basin towns like Essen . . . Bochum." Leaning forward, he lowered his voice, "They didn't dare to bomb *Shamrock* with all of those shentlaymun shareholders back home." He chuckled and Dirk grinned at his mispronunciation of *gentlemen*, but he knew better than to correct him.

As the streetcar rattled and lurched across the switches, Dirk felt as proud as if he, too, were a gentleman shareholder of *Shamrock* and not merely one of its injured apprentice miners. What really made him happy was that a grown-up pitman talked to him as if they were equals, while down below day the men only grunted or yelled at the boys shoveling coal.

Wanting to act like a grown miner, he decided it would look best if he scowled, but instead he felt a blush spread across his face. Since he couldn't think of anything else he could do while sitting down, he leaned back and rubbed his shoulder blades against the wood of the bench, as he had seen the miner do, until his back ached.

❁   ❁   ❁

"Burcgrave! Dirk Burcgrave next!"

Walking into the doctor's office Dirk groaned with every step.

"Your name?" called a woman's voice, sounding like Dirk's heel taps on the white floor tiles of the office. Then he saw her, seated behind a small desk, not looking up at him as she continued to write.

"Burc-gra-ve." He carefully pronounced his family name so that she could hear that it had three syllables. He had learned to do this since they had come to Westphalia. To the people here it seemed a funny name, but back home in Brockau everyone had pronounced the name right and when he walked with his father, they had said "Good day, Herr Burcgrave" and the men had tipped their hats.

"A foreign name?" For the first time she looked up at him, her pale blond eyebrows raised.

"Not foreign," Dirk said quietly, "but not common either." He remembered how the corners of his mother's mouth used to drop when she declared something to be common. "We are from Silesia."

"Refugees. Are you Polish? Ethnic German?" Her fountain pen was suspended over the paper, where Dirk did not believe a question had been printed that asked *are you Polish*? Don't get angry, he told himself, she might get you fired from the pit.

"No, we are Germans like everyone else around here." This is funny, he thought, half of the men in the pit call out Polish names at the timekeeper's window. *Kwiatkowski*, and then the rattle of the brass shift tags in the tin trough under the window, *Schimanski*, and rattle, rattle, rattle.

203

She stepped around her desk and didn't ask any more questions about Dirk's name. You can't blame her, though, he thought, a lot of people feel this way about refugees showing up in their town, with nothing except what they're wearing, wanting food and shelter when there isn't much of either.

Silently the doctor nodded in the direction of Dirk's pants. He turned halfway from her, but she grabbed his shoulders, twisting him back toward her.

"We don't have all afternoon," she said briskly without raising her voice. "You undress everyday in the washroom with the other pitmen, so what is so different here?" Dirk blushed and didn't answer. Again she touched his thin bony shoulders—gentler this time—probing them with her fingers.

"Where do you live? In the camp at *Shamrock*?"

"No, no," Dirk answered hastily, as if it were a shame to live in a mining camp. " I moved out from there because we now have a house of our own." He didn't tell her that it was only a one-room shed with a board partition between the corner of the room where his mother cooked and slept and where his own bunk stood. They had been very happy when Dirk was able to move away from the camp at the pit and, once again, the three of them could live together, until Father had been called on a mission for the church.

"How old are you?" Her voice sounded more gentle.

Dirk told her while she examined his chest, slipping one cool hand under his shirt, while the other knocked hollowly on the back of her hand on his chest.

"So you were fifteen years old when you went to live in the camp?" She listened a long time to his lungs.

I hope that she doesn't find out how weak my lungs are.

"There really isn't anything wrong with my chest." Dirk drew back from the touch of her cool

hands following his movements softly and surely,
which might lose him his job. "I am healthy," he said
quickly, "except for my legs. I was in a rock fall."

Her ear had been close to her hand cupped on
his chest and now she looked up at him without saying a word.

"I have to keep on working," he said quietly, looking down into her eyes. "I am the only one in my family
who can work."

She motioned for him to sit down and while she
peeled off the old bandages—hurting him no more
than she had to—she didn't look once into his face.
Then she rebandaged him, silently and efficiently.

Dirk was already at the door before he glanced at
the slip in his hand, noticing that it granted him six
extra days of sick leave before he had to go back down
into the pit. He said thank you, but she didn't say good-
bye, already reading another man's file.

The sky sat like a gray dripping lid on the sooty
walls of the houses. He turned up his collar and walked
as fast as he could, but he was soaked by the time he
reached the stop. The streetcar was crowded and he
had to stand on the platform of the second car, squeezing in among a group of mechanics. Over the peaks of
their black caps he watched the railroad sidings swing
away into the rain, past loading docks gaping by the
side of the tracks.

He closed his eyes while the shoulders of the men
pressed against him like heavy wet logs. Stand still and
hearken. I couldn't move even if I wanted to fall down.
The sour smell of wet sweaty wool rose into his nostrils. Hearken under God's hand. Mother seemed
smaller than usual, holding a hand cupped behind her
ear as if she were hard of hearing. How silly, he
thought, but it occurred to him that Mother was in real
danger, because the heavy hand could fall at any time

and crush her. Hearken, but all he heard were the windows rattling in their wooden frames—some still painted blackout blue from the time of the air raids—as the wheels squealed and ground to a halt.

When he clumsily climbed down to the street his legs were hurting again and so he took a shortcut through the beet fields to the line of low houses he could barely recognize through the streaming rain. Limping along the muddy path he thought how much like him all of this was: I go down a single day and they send me back up an invalid—true, not quite—while Mother hopes that, by learning how to dance, ride horses and drive, I'll turn into a gentleman who is going to live in America. She dreams and I go sloshing through a beet field with my shoes filled with mud.

After Dirk had pulled open the door, he stood still in the entrance, catching his breath in the warmth coming from the coal fire. He didn't see the water running in threads from the bill of his cap, as he felt for a moment or two, as if he had stepped again into Hagmann's bakery. He stood and snuffled like a dog on a scent, searching for the fragrance of baked bread, just pulled from the oven, cooling in shiny brown rows on a trestle table in the corridor of the bakery.

"You're sniffling as if you've already caught cold. Come in or by tomorrow you'll be in bed with pneumonia," Mother said, tugging at the sleeves of his jacket. "Everything on you is wet. Sit by the stove and take off your shoes and I'll make you a foot-bath."

"The doctor gave me another week," Dirk said, while he scraped the mud from his shoes, not telling his mother that the doctor was a woman.

While she was heating water in her big pot, he put on a dry shirt. Sitting by the stove made him feel better. One good thing about working in the pit, he thought, they give you enough coal to stay warm all year. The baker used to slide those long-handled peels out of the oven, with shiny brown loaves on the blade. He sniffed again, but all he smelled was the steam curling out under the lid.

"Lift your feet," she said, pouring hot water slowly down the side of the bowl.

He had helped in the bakery, scrubbing the trestle table, cleaning the mixing bowls and running the mill that ground up rolls that hadn't been sold the day before. It had been a while, two years, no, two and a half years, in the spring of 1945 when they hoped that everything would be better soon.

"Are you hands dry?" she asked Dirk, wiping her own hands on her apron. "Uncle Karl has written a letter and he even sent a picture." She handed him a photo, making sure that it did not pass over the water bowl. "I'll read you the letter."

Dirk didn't listen, but scrutinized instead the two figures standing in front of a white house: an older, balding man, who was obviously European—Dirk took him to be Uncle Karl—while the other was a seventeen- or eighteen-year-old boy, definitely an American. He was thickset and muscular—Dirk could not even see an indentation at his waist—and low on his hips rode his sharply creased slacks, held up by a thin belt. The cuffs of his long-sleeved shirt were carelessly rolled back from his thick wrists, and, from the collar on down, three buttons were left undone. His grinning face was framed by short curly black hair with a sheen like the broad back of the butcher's dog back home.

Dirk was most surprised that his uncle apparently hadn't objected to the broad grin nor to the boy's hand so casually thrust into the pocket of his slacks. Dirk's mother would have found the grin insolent and Father—without explanation or debate—would have told him to take his hand out. But this man didn't seem to mind what his son was doing, because his arm was proudly draped around the boy's shoulder.

As Dirk examined every detail of the picture, he couldn't understand how this drum-shaped, square-jawed American boy could have been fathered by a slight, oval-faced European man. His uncle had been less than twenty years in America, did *it* work so fast?

"Dirk, you aren't listening!"

"Pardon me." He glanced once more at the photo before sliding it onto the edge of the table.

"You shouldn't envy those people." She put her hand on Dirk's shoulder, who silently looked down at his feet in the bowl of water. "They live under palm trees and eat beefsteak all the time and so they look different from us." Reaching over Dirk's back she pushed the picture to the middle of the table.

Dirk wondered what beefsteak tasted like.

"Let me tell you what's in the letter, so you don't have to read it yourself. His handwriting isn't easy to decipher and he's forgetting his mother tongue. This time, listen. They've just returned from their vacation. Karl is tired, because he drove—in his own automobile—though. . ." She had to pick up the letter to recall the foreign names, "Idaho, Montana, California. Then he mentions national parks . . . Yellowstone and Yosemite. He drove more than 3,800 miles."

Dirk tried to convert miles into kilometers without having to ask his mother for paper and pencil. What kind of car does he have and why didn't he send a picture of his car?

"Isn't this nice?" She folded up Karl's letter.

"Yes, yes," Dirk answered without knowing what his mother meant.

"If you had paid attention, you would have jumped up, shouting with joy. They are going to send a food package."

"When?" asked Dirk quickly.

"You see," his mother's voice sounded as it did when she was not telling him the whole truth or when she found an excuse for someone else. "It's not easy for Emilie. You have to wait in line at the American post office and she can't be on her legs for very long . . . she's taking the cure."

Dirk nodded as if he were really interested in the sickness of a woman he had never met, not even seen on a picture.

"She's taking the cure for obesity," she said evenly, possibly hoping that Dirk might not pay attention to what she was saying and yet making sure that he had been told everything in the letter.

"*Entfettungskur?*" Dirk pronounced the word carefully, a word he had never used and hadn't heard since he had been a small boy. "You mean to say that she's fat?" he laughed. "No wonder she's not in the photo."

"You shouldn't laugh at that poor woman," she said. Seeing that he still smiled, she added, "It wasn't easy for her and Karl. They went to America as the Depression was about to begin and then Karl was without work for six years."

Dirk hadn't thought about America like that. As far back as he could remember, everybody old enough to work had worked or was drafted into the war and had come home on furloughs. Nobody had to look for a job. He had been told that in America you started by doing lowly jobs. He was willing to do that, after all, what kind of work was he doing here? But not to find work when you were looking for a job, what then?

"If Emilie hadn't done sewing. . ."

"How did *she* find work? They were both tailors."

"They were paying women tailors less than men tailors." She dragged the pot from the fire ring. "Lift

209

your feet." Dirk didn't say anything while his mother poured more hot water into his basin. "I'll be right back, I just want to see if we have a potato or two left in the shed."

Dirk wondered how hard it would be to say good-bye when he went to America. Maybe it wouldn't be so hard, because they had said it so often during the war, but he knew that this time it would be different, like it had been for the man in the picture. He had been told Karl's story, although his uncle had left Breslau before Dirk was even born. He had gone to America because his parents hadn't liked his girl, Emilie, so both had taken a ship for America. Karl never saw his parents again; they died—one after the other—during the war.

He remembered Sundays at Karl's parents. Dirk wasn't taken there every Sunday, but whenever they went—half a dozen times a year—it was always on a Sunday. He liked the meals Aunt Paula cooked, roasts with lots of gravy and dumplings—as many as he wanted to eat—but after the meal the adults talked to each other and Dirk, as the only child at these dinners, was left to himself. He usually went over to the black upright piano, which seemed to beckon him with two jutting brass arms, each holding an ornate candle. Since he wasn't allowed to make noise while the adults talked, he played instead with the hinged brass arms, until one Sunday he broke one of the candles. Since such a fancy candle couldn't be replaced during the war, it was left as it was and whenever he walked into Aunt Paula's living room during the next few years, the first thing he saw was the broken candle. But, just as before, he would sit on the stool before the keyboard, looking at two pictures on top of the piano of Karl as a young man. Somehow he had thought that Karl was dead, maybe because his pictures were displayed in black laquered frames on top of the black piano, with candles below, the broken one dangling from its wick. Now the piano had burned, along with the house on Steinstrasse, Karl's parents were dead and buried in Breslau, while Karl was alive with an American son.

Dirk dried his feet and went to his bunk to lie down, taking along the photo from the kitchen table.

✣   ✣   ✣

In the morning Dirk looked once more at the picture of the gleaming white house and he knew that he had to do something important today. When he had gone to ask about the price of a ticket to Bremen, he had seen the sign of a driving school across the square from the railroad station. If he learned how to drive, that would surely make Mother happy, because then he would be closer to what she wanted him to be. Gentlemen knew how to drive.

In front of the driving school Dirk chained his bicycle to a scrawny tree growing from the sidewalk, and rehearsed under his breath what he was going to say. Then he took time to study the gold letters raised in an arc across the old-fashioned glass door, which reminded him of a bank entrance—although he had never been in a bank—which made him wonder how they could have protected such a glass door throughout the war. Finally, after finding nothing else to admire, he slowly opened the door.

The large room seemed like a dark empty cave, until—far in back—he saw a tall girl stretching to reach the top of a blackboard. Coming closer he had to stare at the confusing jumble of red, blue and yellow chalk lines indicating complex turn maneuvers. He was sure that this was too difficult for him to learn.

"Can I help you?" Holding a piece of red chalk in her hand she half-turned toward him, smiling brightly.

She can't be much older than I am, he thought, as the heat of a blush spread across his face.

"I . . . want to learn . . . how . . . how to drive," he stammered. If Mother were here, she'd assure me that God was with me and after that she would tell me to stand straight and speak clearly. I shouldn't have come at all. Why do I listen to her and her dreams of me becoming a gentleman? "I want to enroll in your driving school," he added, now speaking very fast, to make up for having hesitated at first.

"What make of automobile do you own?" It was all very businesslike: her head was bowed over a stack of forms while her fountain pen was held at the ready over the first line of an application. Dirk really wanted to answer her, telling her anything she wanted to know, but instead he stared at the white line of skin where her brown hair was parted. Silently he reached up and put his cupped hand over the gash in his cheek.

She looked up at him, waiting patiently.

"I don't . . . that is, we don't own a car right now." His face felt even hotter and he was sure that by now his whole head had turned red.

"Is it a motorcycle license you want?"

"No, I don't own a motorcycle either," he had to admit. She must be as disappointed in me as Mother used to be when I was doing poorly in school. Maybe this girl will lose interest in me and send me away, politely, I hope.

She examined Dirk with cool blue eyes.

"Then you must use a truck driver's license at work."

Now she's making a fool of me. I'm not old enough to drive a truck. Anyone can see that. Even she. How can I explain to her that I'm supposed to become a gentleman and that such a gentleman dances well, drives an automobile and is a good horseman? And lives in America? Maybe I should carry a banner, the

212

way knights carried their guerdons on a lance or was it a shield? Perhaps I should explain?

"I am traveling to America . . . soon." It was true, the quota was moving up, maybe it would be *soon*. "My uncle has a car." That, too, was true, even if he hadn't seen a picture.

"What kind of a vehicle?" She sounded less bored after he had mentioned America.

Dirk looked through the window at a streetcar rattling by, to Recklinghausen on the other side of the canal. As he was watching, he felt as if he were standing on the sidewalk outside, freed from all these questions and the girl who kept asking them.

"A Buick or . . . a . . . Packard, something big," he said finally.

"Now I know what you need," she beamed, "an international driver's license. Do you have access to a car so that you can practice?" She had become enthusiastic. "Somebody could bring you here in this car and then you could practice with us in the driving school. This way you would be very familiar with this vehicle by the time you take your test."

"No, nobody can bring me." He tried to think of a plausible excuse. "Everybody is busy." *Everybody is poor* is what I should have said.

She briskly outlined his progress through the entire driving school program: first, the study of the traffic laws followed by the workings of the engine. Only then would he have to worry about the cost of the driving lessons. Scrutinizing Dirk again, she said, "You can pay for each lesson when you take it." She then quoted a sum which seemed very high to Dirk.

"Is this for the course *and* the cost of the driver's license?"

"No," she hesitated, "This is for each of the required driving lessons." When she saw the disappointment on Dirk's face, she added that an hour of class-room instruction would cost much less than a driving lesson.

As he swung his leg over his bicycle, he wondered what had happened to him behind the gold-lettered door. He had met a girl—whose name he didn't know—and had promised to pay a large sum of money, larger than anything the family had owned since they had become refugees. However crazy this sounded, he was convinced that he had acted in the interest of his whole family. As he rode into the wind blowing hard across town from the mine, he began to whistle, but stopped again when he tasted sulphur on his lips.

❀   ❀   ❀

Coming home, Dirk saw no light from any house on their street. He carefully opened the door and bumped into his mother in the dark.

"Strait is the gate and narrow is the way," she said and although Dirk couldn't see it, he imagined that she was smiling. "The light has been out all evening. They've cut the power again."

They stood by the door to his room, three steps from the front door, the window behind her back red with the glow from the cokery.

"What did you do today?"

"Oh, I rode around town, talking to the boys." He wouldn't tell her for a while about the driving school and maybe not at all about the girl. He wasn't sure that he would ever talk to his mother about any girl, it somehow didn't seem right. As far as he knew, gentlemen didn't talk about girls and so he was safe.

"Your friend Sperk isn't going to America, is he?"

"No, he's happy here. And none of the boys at church are on the waiting list in Bremen either." So

214

often, in good or in bad happenings alike, he felt singled out.

"They aren't refugees like us," she reminded him.

True, none of them were. All were born here and the fathers of some of them had already been pitmen.

"And even if they wanted to go to America they aren't as blessed as we in having a relative who might act as sponsor."

Dirk was silent.

"You haven't forgotten about the letter from the consulate?"

"No, I know that I have to go to Bremen. The medical examination worries me. They might reject me because of my lungs."

"You *do* want to go to America?"

"Yes . . . but I'm worried."

"So it isn't just the examination?"

"No. Sometimes I think that I would like to stay here with you and Papa, when he's back."

"If you want to, you can. We love you, but God has led us so far, he'll lead us to Zion."

Zion. It made him shiver. He remembered standing on the podium at church while his father was sliding song numbers into the hymn board and Sunday school was about to begin. He asked his father why they weren't singing a certain song anymore. His father whispered that this song was now forbidden. When Dirk asked why, his father whispered: "Any song with the word 'Zion' is forbidden and has been crossed out in the hymnal." While the harmonium was playing softly he thought that now he would never hear "Zion Stands with Hills Surrounded," a song he liked because behind the words he could see pictures of mountains and he had always wanted to live in a city with mountains instead of the flat place home had been.

"Yes?"

"Yes, yes, he has led us," Dirk admitted, "we always did go in the right direction. No, not always. When we went back into the Russian zone, that wasn't going in the right—"

"God had led us *far*," Mother said, again emphatically.

"Yes, he led the four of us, but what about those from Silesia who were killed when they were driven out?"

"I don't know. All I try to know are things that have to do with us four."

Us four. Father, Mother, Grandmother and me. But I, the youngest, I am the one who has to go away.

"Maybe we should open the Bible?" she asked.

He listened to the groping of her hand on the kitchen shelf before he heard the rustle as she crouched down in front of the stove. Then he heard her fumbling with the latch of the cast iron stove door and suddenly her face and the book in her hands were illuminated. Bent over the Bible with her eyes closed, she let the book fall open while her index finger hovered over the pages. Then her finger dropped onto the open book and she remained this way while the firelight flickered across the pages and up into her face. Leaning still closer to the stove, she tilted the open book toward the fire so that she could see better.

"It's Jeremiah," she said.

Oh, no, not Jeremiah, Dirk thought, this will be bad for me.

"*Gather up your stuff out of the country* . . . out of the country, are you listening, Dirk? *You who live in the fortress* . . . the fortress . . . this clearly is us again, when we had to leave Breslau after it was declared a fortress. See how this answers your question? But let me read on, *behold I will hurl out the inhabitants of the land* . . . this happened to us . . . and . . . no, this here does not agree with us anymore."

Bent over the open book she might have been praying before the fire, which, to the eyes of Dirk, had turned her face the color of piano keys or was it the wax of that broken candle?

"You can be like young Joseph, going into Egypt," she said, stoking the fire.

Dirk stood in the shadows by the door and he saw the finger of God pointing bright and demanding from the sparks of the fire. He had to say—and did say—clearly and too loud for the small room, "I will go to America."

The door to the stove clanked shut and in the sudden darkness he heard his mother get up.

"There is something from Jeremiah I know by heart: 'Am I only a God nearby and not a God faraway?' He'll be with you. It will be hard for you."

She didn't say *us*, Dirk thought, as his mother kissed him on his gashed cheek, and he fleetingly remembered the rock fall that had trapped him in darkness a thousand meters below day. Then his mother pushed him gently but surely into his room and when he said good night, it was to a door already closed.

Butcher's
Beguine_____

Bam, bam, bam.

The banging on the door sounded as if a plane were strafing the house. Ack, ack, ack, Dirk tapped his knuckles against the wooden wall behind his bunk, pretending a flak battery was returning the fire.

Bam, bam. "Begin de Beguine," a voice wailed in front of their house.

"Oh, it's Sperk, thought Dirk Burcgrave, swinging his legs slowly over the edge of his bunk. Will he never learn to pronounce "the"?

Bam, bam, bam.

"Get the door, Dirk," called his mother from the kitchen.

"Brings back de sound of music so ten-dah. . ."

"And tell Sperk to stop his serenade. His howling

218

is scaring the neighbor's pigeons. He's racing them this afternoon."

"Yes, Mother." Dirk knew how anxiously their neighbor waited for his pigeons with his clock at hand, ready to strip off the band from the racer's foot. Dirk didn't like the neighbor and wasn't too worried about his pigeons.

"Oh, oh, oh."

Dirk pushed open the front door—the only door of their temporary shelter—leading onto a patch of land they had been digging up for a future garden.

"You want to go to a soccer game?"

"Sure. It's a fast Sunday and I don't have to go to church tonight."

"You fast? How long did you fast?"

"Supper last night and breakfast this morning, but I didn't mind, there wasn't much to eat in the house anyway." Sometimes Dirk wondered if his friend went to any church at all; he doubted it.

Sperk grunted and shook his head as he walked toward the street. He was eighteen, two years older than Dirk and worked as an electrician's apprentice. Now and then Dirk wondered why Sperk—who smoked, drank and always talked about the girls he met playing in a jazz band on Saturday nights—bothered to be friends with a boy as awkward and naive as he. Sperk was gaunt, curly-haired and had a thin pointed nose; Dirk thought of him as Woody Woodpecker, except without color.

Germania's stadium—between the railyard and the canal—wasn't much: to watch the game they had to stand on slag banked down toward the muddy playing field. The game was dull and Dirk had a chance to tell his friend about the rock fall which had trapped him in the mine. Sperk laughed so hard about Dirk's misadventure that a tough-looking miner in an old navy coat told them to shut up. Dirk did, but Sperk just shoved the other man, asking him mockingly, "Are you losing any money on this flea circus here?" Then he gave the miner another good-natured push. The miner shrugged with a grunt, not taking his eyes off the game.

This is what I admire, Dirk thought. He gets along with almost anybody and doesn't blush, stammer or hunch over the way I do to make myself invisible. I definitely have to learn to act more like Sperk before I set foot on a steamer bound for America.

Without interest they watched the players fumbling and slipping on the bare patch in front of the goal. Their jerseys were now so muddy that Dirk couldn't distinguish the red and white of the home team. When the visiting team scored—or maybe it was an own goal of the home team—the Germania fan in the navy jacket belched and spat.

"Heh, this is dumb." Sperk grabbed Dirk's shoulders, pushing him in the direction of the exit.

On the path to the canal they leaned into the wind, their backs 'bent like fiddle bows,' an expression Dirk's father used whenever he reminded him to stand straight. Dirk could still hear his voice saying those words, although his father had left some months ago on a mission for the church. Walking ahead Sperk whistled "La Paloma," his fists thrust straight-armed into his trouser pockets, imitating the wide gait of a bargeman. The wind rattled and banged through a row of rusty sheds left over from the war. Dirk lagged behind, wanting to go in and explore for treasure— maybe some forgotten ammunition that they could pry open for the powder—but if he were to ask, Sperk might say that they were too old for scavenging. So he hurried after his friend, toward the dust-grey clouds scudding low across the canal.

Walking side by side along the tow path they looked for a spot to sit down on the embankment. Finally they found shelter from the wind in the lee of a barge which rode high at her mooring. It looked as if the crew had gone ashore, leaving a small black and white dog to patrol the deck.

Sperk spread a handkerchief under his navy-blue bell-bottoms, while Dirk lowered himself with a groan into the scraggly grass, not bothering to protect the seat of his worn brown pants.

"Still hurting?" Sperk asked, leaning against the incline.

Dirk pulled up one of his pants legs to show the bandages.

"The woman doctor at *Bergmannsheil* gave me another week off."

"You, a virgin, were pawed by a woman doctor?" Sperk laughed. "Some guys have all the luck."

From the other side of the harbor a pit siren shrieked shift change, from *Friedrich der Grosse*, whose smokestacks stabbed into the low clouds. In the sudden silence chickens cackled from a cage on the aft deck of the barge.

"Let me tell you what happened yesterday," said Dirk eagerly.

"What happened yesterday?"

"I signed up at a driving school, the one near the railroad station. . ."

"What for? Your people don't own a car."

"America."

"Oh . . . yes."

However much Sperk ruled over their conversations, when it came to America, he accepted Dirk's word. Sperk liked it where he was, but he admitted that his friend had to go to America, because Dirk was different.

"And I met this girl . . . class . . . world champion class."

Sperk pulled out a pack of cigarettes and lit one.

"Is she built?" He blew a puff of smoke into the grey sky.

"Slim." Dirk began to blush, though not as violently as he had at the driving school. The blush definitely has to be fixed before I go to America, Dirk thought, as if he were checking a list of what to pack in his suitcase.

"Slender . . . sort of."

"Oh," Sperk nodded politely.

"Splendid hair . . . really strong shiny hair." Dirk tried to describe her as best as he could, wanting to impress his friend, without even mentioning certain parts of the body that he didn't and wouldn't talk about.

"A helmet of strong beautiful hair . . . coming down like a waterfall."

Half-listening, Sperk tried to blow a smoke ring, but the wind flattened it out, driving the smear down to the water.

"Deep blue eyes."

Sperk threw a pebble at the oily water.

"She's tall."

"Oh, good." Sperk was not tall.

On any other day Dirk would have stopped talking about someone who didn't interest his friend, but for once it was *he* who had a girl to talk about and he was not going to be put off by Sperk's obvious boredom.

Sperk looked over at Dirk.

"All right, tell me again how she is built."

"I don't know . . . shiny brown. . ." Dirk was too shy to describe anything else but her face and hair. "Shiny brown," he said once more, knowing that in

order to excite Sperk he would have to lie and say "per-
oxide blonde."

"Piercing blue—"

"What? What?" Sperk was now impatient.

"The eyes . . . the eyes. Piercing blue . . . no, that
isn't right, grave, yes . . . almost severe, I should say."
As an afterthought he added, "And she has dark circles
under her eyes."

Sperk stopped throwing pebbles and suddenly
sat up.

"Dark circles? You know what that means? It
means that she's doing it." Sperk jumped up. "She
must be doing it all the time." Stabbing with his fingers
at his hair, he plucked at his curls until they stood up
like spikes. "That's how you get dark circles under
your eyes . . . by doing it all the time." Sperk looked in
awe at his friend as if he had found a treasure.

Dirk, impressed as always by Sperk's knowledge
of the world, was appalled by what he had been told
about this girl, his goddess, but he also felt attracted by
what he definitely knew to be sin. He didn't doubt
what his friend had told him, because Sperk knew
about women just as he knew about America.

"*Ach so,*" was all Dirk could say in his confusion.

"Have you . . . have you asked her out yet?" Sperk
was lying down again, grinning at Dirk while he pulled
out another cigarette.

"Long legs," Dirk added to his description of the
driving school girl, realizing too late that this was not
keeping the conversation as harmless as he had meant
it to be. He hastily found another subject.

"In America I have to know how to drive. They all
drive autos."

"How are you going to get to America without
money and without a . . . a. . . ."

"You need a visa to get to America. . ." Looking out at the canal, Dirk sighed, "If I had a boat. . ."

"A boat? Do you even know which direction you would have to take?"

Silently Dirk pointed to his left. "I would *not* sail through the lock and the harbor. That would take me to Dortmund and I don't want to go there. No, first Wanne-Eickel, then past Gelsenkirchen and on toward Oberhausen. . . ."

"And then Neu York. . ."

"No, *Nyew* York."

"You and your schooling. . . heh, look over *there!*" Sperk whispered.

On the other side of the canal, Dirk saw a brownhaired girl climbing down the embankment to the edge of the water. Glancing over at the boys—did she smile? Dirk couldn't tell—she slowly began to take off her clothes.

"Look at her!" Sperk whispered triumphantly. "She's going swimming, naked, she's going to be swimming naked!"

Dirk became aware of the hum of the traffic on the bridge, but he was sure that the drivers at that distance could not watch the girl undressing. Besides, why should I care, he thought, she doesn't. She has seen us over here and she doesn't mind that we are watching.

Kicking off her sandals, she tested the water with her toes, and turned her back to the boys. Then she draped a small brown blanket across her shoulders, tugging at it until it covered her down to her knees. In the shelter of her blanket she worked until her skirt dropped in a heap at her ankles. When she tried to wriggle out of her blouse, the blanket billowed out in a gust of wind, flapped against her back and then slid to the ground. She stood still as if she were thinking about what should be done next.

Sperk stared at the girl. Dirk, who thought that he might have turned away from the girl had he been alone, looked, too.

She didn't bend down to pick up her blanket, having pulled off bra and panties, she folded them, weighing her clothes down with a stone against the wind. They only saw her back, as she groped for her bathing suit lying on a rock behind her. When her hand failed to find the suit, she turned impatiently and faced the boys. Dirk, thinking about it later that night, was sure that she had stood there for a long time facing them— while the traffic hummed far away and the chickens cackled softly in their cage—before she unhurriedly pulled on a black bathing suit.

Once covered up again, she lost all interest in the boys. Climbing over several boulders, she dived from the last one into the canal, slicing smoothly without a splash into the murky water.

"Did you see that?" Sperk pointed at the girl who slowly swam away from them, with measured strokes, as if the boys were not there and had never been there. "Did you see *that*?" he repeated, gripping his friend's arm so tightly that Dirk thought that this must be the first naked woman that Sperk had ever seen. But that couldn't be, unless his friend had lied to him about his Saturday night adventures on the other side of the canal.

"You want to listen to some music?" Sperk asked.

"Where?" Dirk plucked a thistle bud from the cuff of this pants and threw it at his friend.

"I know a boy who has stacks of American records." Sperk pulled the burr from his sweater and threw it back.

When they walked past the barge, the black and white dog followed them silently the whole length of the deck.

"Tell me more about the girl you met at driving school . . . heh, let's go!" He pulled Dirk into the street, barely avoiding a streetcar whose driver stomped angrily on his bell-button.

Sperk laughed, "But don't tell me that she's tall," he yelled, wobbling a few steps on the toes of this brown shoes, mocking Dirk's admiration for this girl's size. "And don't tell me about her deep blue eyes." He grinned, batting his eyelashes like a pockmarked Cary Grant in a film whose title Dirk had forgotten. What he remembered was Cary Grant's breathy "Ohhh, Walter" and the quick twist of his hips. Dirk wasn't sure if Sperk was making fun of him or the girl at the driving school, but he had to laugh as his friend danced along the empty Sunday afternoon street—always a few steps ahead of Dirk—pulling faces and talking in a shrill voice.

"Here," Dirk stopped a gold-lettered glass door, "here is the driving school. . ."

"Where . . . she . . . works," Sperk walked on, pulling Dirk down the incline of the street into the railroad underpass, "but she isn't there now."

"We could have looked."

Sperk was running down into the underpass still pulling Dirk.

"Wait!" Dirk drew his arm out of his friend's grip and bent forward, putting his hands on his knees. When he straightened up and leaned his head against the wall—encrusted thickly with layers of posters and bills—he felt so dizzy that he had to close his eyes.

"What are you doing?" Sperk peered into his friend's face. "Are you praying?"

A streetcar rattled past them, filling the underpass with clanking and screeching that bounced back from the tiled walls. Dirk opened his eyes, taking deep breaths.

"Are you hungry?" Sperk asked quietly.

"Mother calls them growing pains."

"Growing pains?"

"She says that I grew too fast and not everything inside of me grew along with my outside."

"Could be. Are you hungry?"

Dirk didn't answer.

"Let's walk out the other side, away from the fumes and out into the fresh air." He took Dirk's shoulder, pushing him gently up the incline onto Bahnhofstrasse.

"Wait." Dirk stopped to wipe his pale forehead.

Sperk looked at his friend, not knowing what to do or say. Leaning against the wall, he pulled out a cigarette, but—after some hesitation—slipped it back into its pack.

"We're a little better off than your family for food. You're refugees, but as locals we at least have some things to trade for food, like tools, furniture and linens. I've seen your house; you don't seem to have anything to trade at all."

Dirk walked unsteadily ahead.

"Wait, we need to go through Post Strasse." Sperk pointed across the street. After they had crossed Bahnhofstrasse, they slowed down again. "Would it be easier for you if your father were living with you?"

"I don't know. He was always handicapped with his injuries from the other war and so he couldn't do a lot of things. Now he'll be gone a couple of years on that mission for the church."

"To America?"

"No."

"Oh." Sperk bought two bottles of lemonade at a roadside stand and they sat down on a bench nearby. Drinking the warm sweet liquid from the sticky bottle soon made Dirk feel better.

"So how is it working in the coal mountain?"

227

Sperk asked, pulling out his cigarettes again, but merely holding the pack in his hand.

"Since I've been below only one day when the roof fell on me, I don't really know what it'll be like going down all the time." Dirk closed his eyes and leaned against the back of the bench. "You know what I miss most, besides the sunlight and standing up straight? The bowl of sour cabbage soup we used to get for lunch when I still worked above day at the apprentice workshop. At first, I thought that I would never like it, but I miss it now. Besides that, while I'm celebrating sick, I don't even get to pick up the sandwiches at the check-in at six in the morning."

Bells began to ring from the Kreuz-Kirche.

"Are you all right now?" Sperk asked. "We should go."

"I am O.K.," Dirk said in English. As he got up, he took a small leap in the air, as if he were dunking a basketball, while Sperk took the empty bottles back to the stand whose owner was just putting down the shutters.

"I was worried about you. I've never seen anyone faint from. . ."

"Growing pains," Dirk added quickly.

Sperk laughed out loud and Dirk looked at him with surprise.

"Makes me think of that one movie we saw together about this man in Alaska who's going loony from hunger and who's chasing the little guy all over the cabin in the snow. . ."

"*Gold Rausch.*"

"And this miner—as big as a bear—takes off after Chaplin wanting to chop off his head because he's thinking that Charlie's a rooster." Sperk was standing on his toes—his shoulders hunched up so that he looked as tall as he could—staring up at Dirk from under a wrinkled brow. "I'm crazed with hunger and I'm going to get that rooster."

Dirk clicked his head to the right and then to the left, clutching his arms to his chest. Fleeing down Mulvany Strasse, he flapped his arms like stubby wings, darting with short steps to the left and then quickly to the right again, while shaking his head the way roosters did or the way Chaplin had done, he couldn't remember.

Sperk—chopping at the air as if he was wielding a hatchet—lumbered after him, while Dirk dodged his friend, clucking softly the way chickens do when they are scared. Am I afraid? Dirk wondered. He stopped running and turned back to face Sperk. Then he crowed *kikeriki* as loud as he could. He had learned that back home where they had kept chickens during the war. *Kikeriki,* he crowed once more, making Sperk stop.

"That wasn't in the movie," Sperk complained, dropping his arm with the make-believe hatchet.

"No, that wasn't in the movie," Dirk agreed, sounding more decisive than usual, and then he, too, let his arms drop. He wished that he could always win over others like that, by turning around and . . . and, he wasn't even sure what he had done. But he knew that he didn't want to be the boy anymore who was chased by the others, not even in fun.

"Heh, we're here." They stood in front of a butcher shop and Sperk pointed up at a sign— HAGEN UND SOHN—whose letters seemed to be cast in solid brass. While they were standing on the narrow sidewalk outside the door, Dirk noticed the smell that butcher shops always had and that he imagined was the smell of blood, but he wasn't sure if it was so.

Sperk led the way up the steep stairs to a door di-

229

rectly above the store. In the musty dark stairwell Dirk heard music. Sperk did a quick dance step on the landing to "Pardon me, boy," knocking on the door in time to the beat.

"We're here," yelled Sperk over the music. "This is Dirk Burcgrave. He's going to America." Then he pointed at a fat boy sprawling on the sofa. "And this is David Hagen, the *son* in the sign over the shop."

"It is and it isn't," David said in a booming voice. "There's always been a Hagen and a son in the shop. Right now it's my father and me."

"Hagen?" Dirk wondered, but he wasn't sure that he should ask a person about his name. "Like the Nibelung Hagen who . . . who. . ."

"Stabbed Siegfried in the back?" David laughed as he reached down from the sofa to flip back the tone arm of the record player. "Nothing so grand. No, we're from Hagen. You must not be from around here. Hagen is a town maybe fifty or sixty kilometers through the hills. Our family has butchered there forever."

They sat down, Sperk in an old leather armchair and Dirk—not finding anything else—on the floor, with his back against the leg of the oak table. David stayed on the sofa as if he were one of its big pillows.

"What do you want to hear?" He nodded in Sperk's direction and a second time at a stack of records by the side of the sofa.

"Saturday night I'm playing at a dance across the bridge. I'm trying to learn the words to *Begin de Beguine*. . ."

"*The* . . . *the* Beguine," Dirk corrected him impatiently.

"*The* Beguine. I can pronounce it." He laughed, posing with his head thrown back as if he had a baton in hand. "I want to learn the words by Saturday. David,

230

you're the only one I know who has a gramophone and a good collection of American records."

"You're going to sing in English at the dance?" David grinned.

"Sure."

"But you don't know English."

"Don't worry, I'm a musician." Sperk threw his head back again, as if he had already sung and was now waiting for the applause. "I know you have a *Beguine* disc somewhere in your mess, but what I really need are the words. So why don't you play the record a few times?"

"In a moment." David looked questioningly over at Dirk. "Do you want a cigarette?"

"No, he doesn't smoke," answered Sperk. "He belongs to an American church and they don't let you smoke and drink."

The fat boy rolled to the edge of the sofa, facing Dirk with some interest. "You do it with girls?"

Dirk blushed and again Sperk answered for him as if his friend couldn't speak their language. "He has a girfriend, they're going together. A really beautiful woman."

Thank you, Sperk, for lying for me, Dirk thought. No, they don't want you doing it with girls, either. He smiled at no one in particular.

"Oh," David said, running his fingers through his blond hair.

"Don't worry about Dirk, he's O.K., he's going to the U.S.A."

David, head, shoulders and arms hanging over the sofa's edge, rummaged among his records until his face turned red. Sitting up with a grunt, he leaned back to let the blood drain from his head.

"I can easily look through the stacks, I'm sitting down here on the floor anyway," Dirk volunteered.

David nodded and Dirk bent over the pile, picking up each record with great care because it had come, after all, from America. The glossy cardboard jackets felt so different from the local products—coarse brownish paper sleeves that looked like wrapping paper with a whole cut in the middle. He examined fifty or more records and while he was reading labels he wondered how these stacks of American records had found their way to a shop in Herne, Westphalia, in the English-occupied zone of Germany, two years after the war had ended.

Finally he found the record he had been looking for. Holding it carefully between curved hands, he read aloud "Begin the Beguine, music and lyrics by Cole Porter . . . Bluebird." Looking at the stylized bird on the label, he wondered how blue an American blue-bird might be. As blue as the sky? The only birds that he had seen that were blue were blue-black feathered crows or ravens. Maybe they were black.

Sperk looked over Dirk's shoulder and read slowly: "Artie Schaf."

"Shaw, Artie Shaw," Dirk corrected him, handing the disc to David.

"There's no vocal, but somewhere I should have a sheet with the lyrics."

"What's on the flip side?" Sperk asked.

David turned it over. "Artie Shaw's 'Indian Love Call'. Now that one does have a vocal, but that isn't a song you want."

Indian Love Call. Dirk thought that he could imagine what that song was like without ever having heard it.

"It's just a novelty tune." David said, looking for the sheet between the records. "Begin the Beguine? I've heard some woman sing that. It must be a wom-an's song."

"I'm going to sing it Saturday night, woman's song or not."

"Here are the lyrics." David tossed sheets of stiff paper into Sperk's lap, before he sank back into the pillows of the sofa.

Dirk heard a soft knock on the door and being closest, he went to open it. An immense woman faced him dressed in a red and black *dirndl* peasant dress. To him she looked as if she were playing a part in an old film comedy set in a Bavarian village. In silence he stared at the woman whose flesh filled the doorway as if it were merely an outer layer of clothing from which she struggled joyfully and rosily, her arms from the short sleeves of her white blouse and much of her breasts from its square-cut neckline. Finally—with a friendly and encouraging smile for the timid boy—she held out an oblong pewter plate heaped high with sandwiches.

"I thought that you young gentlemen might be hungry." She spoke as softly as a little girl, as if apologizing for being there. With a blush Dirk stepped aside, and as he let her pass by it seemed to him—although it could scarcely be—that this woman curtseyed hesitantly as she entered the room.

"My mother," David said from the sofa, blowing smoke rings.

Sperk rushed to push the scattered records to one side of the table, so that Frau Hagen could put down her serving plate, and he offered her his chair.

"No, I mustn't," she said while sitting down, "We—Herr Hagen and I—are so happy when David has friends who come and visit him." She smoothed her small white apron across her lap. "He's such a sensitive boy."

David looked at her without a smile or even a sign

233

of recognition on his face, as if he had never seen his mother before.

"I usually don't come up to his room," she blushingly looked from one to the other, "except to straighten up in the mornings."

Dirk felt sorry for her because she was blushing.

"We want David to have his privacy, especially when he has visitors." She looked at Sperk who perched on the armrest of the sofa. Dirk had not been introduced to Frau Hagen and he felt like an intruder.

"So David lives up here like the king of the earth."

It would be nice to have a room like this, a room of my own with such furniture and a record player. I could have my friends in—maybe even a girl—and have some tea. Tea and biscuits. Ladies and gentlemen take afternoon tea, although our church doesn't want us to drink black tea. I brought some black tea home from the pit, part of an allotment for miners, but Mother traded it away for bread coupons. I hope that *she* never calls me King of the Earth, making a fool of herself.

Dirk didn't dare to look at the plate that stood so close to him on the edge of the table. He could smell smoked meat and a fragrance, at once faintly sour, but also like moss in the woods, which must be the bread.

"Maybe the stairs are getting too steep for Mother." David looked straight at her. Dirk thought that she might be in her late thirties, like his own mother. How could he say that and be so disrespectful? He didn't even seem to be joking.

"I'm not *that* old, David." Frau Hagen blushed, offering the plate in turn to each of the boys. Dirk had never seen such sandwiches: slabs of smoked meat—ham? he wasn't sure—jutted out over the crusty edges of thick slices of black Westphalian bread. Holding one of the sandwiches in his hand, he tried to guess how much the buttered bread and meat might weigh. He did it instinctively, thinking of the ration card at home, where meat—whenever available—was figured in fifty-gram coupons. What he held in his hand was surely twice or three times more than fifty grams, maybe even half a pound. Should he try to carry part of it home to share?

Since David didn't take a sandwich from the plate that his mother kept offering him, Dirk at first didn't eat either, thinking it impolite to eat before his host. But when Frau Hagen nodded encouragingly, he began, taking very small bites and chewing slowly, the way his father had instructed him so often. But he didn't bless his food silently, as he was used to doing when he was with others. At home, of course, they folded their hands and prayed aloud.

"Heh, look at Burcgrave sweating," David pointed laughingly at Dirk. "Hard work, that eating, eh? Like bein' inna mountain." He had lapsed into a broad mixture of *Platt* and what passed here as a Polish accent, while mimicking a miner swinging a pick.

Sperk stopped chewing and looked up as if he was going to say something, but instead he took another bite from his sandwich.

Dirk was embarrassed and was thinking of a reply, when suddenly thuds boomed from the wooden floor, as if someone downstairs was knocking with a broomstick.

"Mine wants me back," Frau Hagen said, hastily leaving her son's room.

In the silence after the closing of the door, Dirk imagined one-eyed Hagen sitting down below, among gleaming meat hooks, knives and the chopping block, knocking angrily with the shaft of his spear.

David squashed out his cigarette, pressing down so hard that it split, spilling its tobacco into the ashtray.

All the smokers Dirk had ever seen gently tapped out their cigarettes so that they could be relit or the butt could be peeled and the crumbs rolled into another cigarette.

Then David rose slowly from the sofa. Bending over the table he made himself a sandwich by taking parts he liked from the other sandwiches his mother had prepared. With his stubby index finger he poked at the meat and bread, pushing the rejected slices to the edge of the plate. He ate standing up—chewing open-mouthed—burped and then clamped a new needle into the tone arm. Winding up the gramophone with exaggerated swings of his arm, he looked like the hurdy-gurdy man begging in the street.

"Now let's have some music."

When the disc began to turn, Sperk's right hand conducted an orchestra while his mouth tried to form words foreign to him. Dirk had to laugh at his friend's attempt at singing in English.

"How can I sing that? Nobody can sing that." In exasperation Sperk dropped the sheets to the floor.

"What's wrong with it?" asked Dirk.

"It's too long. I'll be out of breath before the song's over, sounding like a mate with black lung." He coughed while clutching his chest, his breath wheezing in and out.

"If you knew English. . ."

"Idiot! How can *you* fit this in?" He picked up the sheets and pushed them into Dirk's face, pointing at one line that Dirk began to read aloud: "Till clouds came along to disperse the joys we had tasted."

"All of this is one line," complained Sperk.

Dirk read it again, now faster, running the words together to shorten the line for his friend.

"Hagen, I don't believe you," Sperk said, "this

can't be American lyrics; it had to be written for another language first. The words just don't fit."

"It's O.K. I'll just play it until you know how to
sing it. I like to listen to it anyway. That brass sounds
like sex. Heh, listen to it bumping along." David
sounded phlegmatic even when talking about sex, and
Dirk wondered how much David knew. "By Saturday
night you'll be O.K."

The evening became an endless repetition of the
same record. The music flowed together for Dirk into
one long melodious stream, almost as if he had been
hypnotized by it. Sitting on the floor, he pressed his
spine against the table leg and felt the vibrations of the
music. Sperk had jumped from his chair and was dancing, his English sounding better and better.

"Oh, yes, let them begin the Beguine." His blue
and red-ringed bop socks flashed above his crepe-
soled shoes. "Oh, yes. . ." He threw back his shoulders
while he thrust chest, Adam's apple and chin forward;
his jacket threatened to slide off his bony shoulders.
David—a cigarette bouncing between his lips—
drummed on the cardboard jacket of the record, using
knife and fork from the serving plate at his sticks.

"And even the palms seem to be swaying." Sperk
had happened onto a patch of linoleum and his crepe
soles squeaked with every swing step.

Dirk wished that he could dance like Sperk. He
had gone to one dance class and he remembered shuf-
fling around with a circle of pitmen to "On a Slow
Boat to China." The palms are always swaying in
songs, he thought, but I like that. I want to be there.
Looking up into the smoke drifting past the table
lamp, he imagined that it could just as easily be coming from the smokestack of the ocean liner carrying
him to New York.

"To live it again," crooned Sperk while David followed softly with a bam bam bam of knife and fork on his cardboard drum, "is past all endeavor . . . except when that tune clutches my heart."

Did he love the girl in the driving school or even the unknown girl at the canal, who, with the flaring-out of the towel had revealed to him, for the first time ever, a woman's body? Would he, for that, stay here and not go to America?

"Let the love that was once afire remain an ember." Sperk sounded hoarse, but his English was much better, even Dirk had to admit that. Except when he came to the line "till the stars that were there," which he delivered with a trumpet-like blare. The "th" broke him up and with a giggle he collapsed into the leather chair.

Now it was just the incessant tropical beat trembling in his spine—no more Sperk singing or Hagen drumming—and now he wanted to be on the other side of the canal and be with the swimmer or with the blue-eyed girl whose name he didn't know either. Dirk didn't want the music to end, but it did. When he looked up, he saw that Sperk had fallen asleep in his chair, with his head angled back and his mouth half open, as if—at any moment—he would sing again.

When Dirk stood up he felt dizzy. Maybe it's from the smoke, he thought, but his stomach also hurt. David got up and stretched, throwing out his chest and belly as if he were in a gym class. Then he glanced down at the plate and saw the leftovers.

"You still hungry? If you're doing it with this girl of yours," he thrust his right index finger into the hollow of his cupped left hand, "heh, you have to keep up your strength." With a chuckle he slapped several chunks of meat between two buttered pieces of bread, forcing the bulky sandwich into Dirk's hand.

Dirk didn't know what to say, but he felt that he had to make a compliment to repay his host.

"This is a very find gramophone you have."

"You like it?" David beamed, bending down to stroke the leather-covered lid. "I traded meat for it. My old man," he pointed down at the butcher shop beneath the floorboards, "my old man thought that it took too much meat, but my old lady convinced him. Got that stack of records in the same trade. Those people must have liked meat more than Benny Goodman." He chuckled again.

"That looks like a fine collection of jazz," Dirk said, weighing the sandwich in his hand.

"I slaughtered it myself."

"Slaughtered what?"

"The calf. Really, I killed it myself."

Dirk felt the butter of his sandwich ooze between his fingers. He sat down on the armrest of the chair, next to Sperk still asleep in the same position.

"Sometimes my old man lets me do some of the butchering. I'm still learning and he keeps an eye on me . . . so that an animal can't get away from me." David stepped in front of Dirk, straddling his knees. "You want to see how it's done?" With his legs spread and his feet firmly planted, he looked to Dirk like the blacksmith waiting by his anvil in the mine repair shop, waiting for a boy to carry the hot iron from the furnace.

"Bam, bam," David tapped Dirk's forehead with his right fist, "and then . . . krrr." He swiftly drew his index finger across Dirk's throat grooving his skin with his fingernail. "Then you jump back," David did just that, "or blood spurts all over you." He smiled at Dirk. "Here, heh, you can't carry your sandwich like that. Let me get some paper for you." He glanced around the room but didn't find anything that suited him.

"Sperk, wake up." David lifted the sleeping boy's head from the chair. "You know the words to the song now?"

"Promising never never," he murmured without opening his eyes.

"He knows the words," David dropped Sperk's head back onto the armrest. Then he picked up the lyrics from Sperk's lap and placed the sandwich precisely on the fold of the double sheet, wrapping it quickly, the way he had learned to do in the butcher shop.

Holding it up toward the light, Dirk checked to see if butter was seeping through.

"It'll keep, it's American paper," David said, "I'm glad that you like the gramophone. *Wiedersehn.*"

"Don't let him be late for work," Dirk said quickly, but he wasn't sure that David was listening.

When the door had closed, Dirk sat down on the landing, placing his package next to him. The stairwell was dark and he felt dizzy, as if he would be sick. The meat and bread he had eaten lay heavily in his stomach and bile was burning his throat. Through a small window he could see the lighted span of the canal bridge reaching across into the deeper darkness of the far side. Where is the swimmer now, he wondered.

Then the music began again. As he listened once more to the Beguine, he now heard in its ending what he had not heard before. The clarinet danced lightly through the ranks of the lumbering brass, which, all night long, had pounded its beat into his spine. At times the clarinet peeped like a lost chick, then trilled as a bird might in a tropical forest, and finally, it rose higher and higher—above the trumpets, trombones and saxophones that were thumping below—until at last it crowed its victorious *kikeriki.*

He had walked more than halfway home before he realized that he had forgotten the sandwich on the stairs, but he decided against going back.

Copyedited by Rachel Hockett.
Designed by Frank Lamacchia.
Production by H. Dean Ragland,
Cobb/Dunlop Publishers Services, Inc.
Set in Caledonia by Compositors.
Printed by the Maple-Vail Company on acid-free
paper, and manufactured with sewn bindings.